WHEN OLD FIRES IGNITE

AILEEN & CALLAN MURDER MYSTERIES
BOOK FIVE

SHANA FROST

Copyright © 2022 by Shanaya Wagh

All rights reserved. No part of this publication may be reproduced, distributed, or transmitted in any form or by any means, including photocopying, recording, or other electronic or mechanical methods, without the prior written permission of the author, except in the case of brief quotations embodied in critical reviews and certain other non-commercial uses permitted by copyright law. For permission requests, write to author@shanafrost.com

This is a work of fiction. Similarities to real people, places, businesses, or events are entirely coincidental.

Website: https://shanafrost.com

WHEN OLD FIRES IGNITE

First Edition.

ISBN: 9789356073562

Written By: Shanaya Wagh as Shana Frost

Copyedited by Laura Kincaid

Proofread by Charlotte Kane

Cover design by GermanCreative

For Jean and Leonise

Thank you for being the best beta readers I could ask for:)

BOOKS BY SHANA

You can find an entire (latest) catalogue on the website: www.shanafrost.com/books

But here's what you can read next…

Aileen and Callan Murder Mysteries

When Murder Comes Home

When Eyes Don't Lie

When Birds Fall Silent

When Red Mist Rises

When Old Fires Ignite

When Distilled From Rage

Banerjee and Muller Mystery Series

Smokes of Death Beer

SCOTTISH GLOSSARY

Banlaoch- Female Warrior
Bairn- Child/Toddler
Bampot- Crazy
Ceilidh- A traditional Scottish/Irish social event
Feartie- Coward
Eejit- Idiot
Yer bum's oot the window- You're talking nonsense
Wee- Little

This book is written in English (UK)

PROLOGUE

Did they say goodbye without a hello?

He gazed into warm brown eyes. 'Thank you. Bye.'

She smiled. 'See you again.'

If life unfurled like he'd planned, there wouldn't be another time. He shook her hand. 'Goodbye.'

A farewell without a greeting.

The whitewashed home, treasuring his happy memories, fizzled away, and the road, turbulent as his life, jostled him in his seat.

He pulled into the lay-by and studied the car behind him. 'This is it.'

The seats of the black SUV were warm, a beckoning away from the ice the wind carried outside. 'Hello.' A greeting and a farewell…

'I told you to stay away.'

He smirked. 'I have no family. I have nothing to lose.'

'And you have no proof.'

'Who says? Every lie comes with a crack. Liquid seeps

through cracks, and the reek inside alerts the world of misdeeds.'

'Shut up!'

He chuckled. 'I don't think it'll be necessary. You'll shut me up, won't you?'

The blow came out of nowhere; he was waiting for it though. His nerves fired, and he shivered. 'She'll catch you. I swear to you. You can't hide any longer.'

And then darkness swallowed him whole.

Goodbye.

CHAPTER ONE

The mist hung low, a lost soul dragging its feet to hell. Rust-coloured tendrils of dead flora fluttered.

Fire, annihilation, ashes...

Crackle and *pop*! The fire thrust dark smoke into the mist; ash twirled towards the heath.

Sirens echoed like loud cries, racing towards the scene to cordon the billowing fires from burning down the entire snow-clad landscape.

Death's presence never looked beautiful, never pleasant, never serene.

'Over here!'

Water hosed down on the burning metal, the smell assaulting the nostrils of everyone in reach.

Detective Inspector Callan Cameron watched it before him like a movie, hands shoved into his black woollen jacket, cropped hair unmoving in the breeze. The firefighters fought the icy wind, struggling to hold the hose and battle the fire.

When he'd shrugged into his jacket just half an hour

ago, he hadn't expected fire – definitely not the life-ending sort.

'Detective!' A woman dressed in the firefighter garb hiked over, her headgear cradled in her arms. 'We'll no' get anyone alive out of that – they'll have been dead before we got here.'

An eejit would see the flames reaching for the sky and the mushrooming smoke and come to the same conclusion.

'Do we ken how many passengers?'

Her sharp eyes cut to the black ruins, so in tune with Callan's clothing. 'No, we'll get to it once we deem it safe.'

Callan sighed. Bloody procedures. 'Do we have a registration? A partial, at least?'

She shook her head. 'We're lucky the heath isn't dry. That would've been a catastrophe. Who'll be transporting the wreckage?'

'Wreckage?' Callan crossed his arms. 'Tell me, what's missing?'

When the firefighter blinked at him, Callan cursed. 'Don't move it until I say so. No one goes near it.'

Some people never truly *saw*.

His phone rang in tune with his thoughts. The caller was someone who always noticed what others missed.

'Aileen.'

'Where are you?'

Callan studied the burned vehicle. An arson investigator is what they needed. But they also needed him.

'What's that?' Her sharp intake of breath paid testament to his previous thought. 'Are you at a crime scene?'

He'd promised, so he opened his mouth. 'Came across a car fire at the lay-by.'

'Here?'

He heard her thoughts. 'Don't come over—'

The call cut off. Bloody hell! Who lost the plot when he hung up? And now she'd done the same thing to him.

If he'd had longer hair, he'd have pulled it out by the roots. Why date a woman who'd kill him off with worry?

Self-flagellation.

Callan stalked to his car. No time like the present to log in his statement and get to work. He always kept his badge on him.

'Robert.' His voice cut off any smart retort the not-so-green-anymore officer might have offered. 'The lay-by on the service road leading to the dual carriageway. A car's caught fire here – I found it, called it in. Get yer arse here.'

'Er, I'm not a firefighter.'

'How does a random car, one without a driver, sitting next to a layer of snow catch fire in a lay-by, eejit?'

A long pause echoed down the line. 'Er—'

'Get here. Now.' Callan's growl left no room for jokes. And this time, he hung up.

As if in mocking response to his command, a sedan rolled down the road. Of course, she'd respond faster than Police Constable Robert Davis.

Both were a pain in his arse.

The brunette parked the car right behind his, as if she thought he might run, then elbowed the door open.

Callan's heart flipped, as it often did, when those fierce brown eyes caught his in the side mirror.

Long, dark brown locks fluttered in the wind as her eyes lasered in on the scene and registered shock before meeting his again. And then she was making herself comfortable in his car.

The perfume she'd spritzed smacked him first as he slid into the driver's seat, followed by the dress that hugged her form and accentuated her figure. She turned to face him, and he swore.

Callan reached out with his thumb and swiped the lipstick from her lips. 'You don't need this.'

Aileen rolled her eyes. 'It's what women wear on dates.'

'I don't like it.'

'So?'

'Don't you want to impress me?'

'Excuse me?' Aileen curled her lip. 'I can do whatever the hell I want.'

She'd sat in his car, uninvited, after making her way here, to a crime scene, when he'd asked her not to.

'We have to cancel tonight.'

Aileen tucked her hair behind her ears. 'How could the car have caught fire? And where's the owner? Can it be linked to any robberies? This could be an attempt to ditch their ride.'

Sharp as a tack.

Callan shrugged. 'None of yer business—'

'Don't. We've had enough of that now, haven't we? And after last time…'

She reminded him of his blasted sprained leg and how she'd saved the day every time they argued, which was every day.

Callan sighed. 'Robert will tag the SOCO team, and they'll document the scene. We'll have to call in an arson investigator.'

Aileen tipped her head. 'It's a common make and model, too. From what I can see from here, anyway.'

'Aye.' He flashed his teeth as an animal did before they attacked. 'Here comes the bloody eejit.' He rolled his window down.

His eyes devoid of humour, PC Robert Davis hurried over. 'Ye weren't joking then.' He blinked at Aileen. 'Hey!'

'Did ye check if anyone's reported a car missing?'

Robert pursed his lips. 'Ms Harris did, but it was her son who'd taken it out for a joyride. He's only fifteen.'

And he'd be reprimanded for that.

This early on, the owner might not have reported the car missing. 'Look into any crimes in Loch Fuar and around involving a car. Let's see if they ditched it here. Get the SOCO team to document the scene. We need pictures.'

Robert saluted him and went off to do the digging.

Callan pushed his car door open. 'Let me see if they're done here.'

Aileen grunted, shoulders drooping. 'Off you go, leaving your date alone.'

'I asked ye not to come.'

'You need me.'

When she followed him, Callan let it go. He needed to cordon the area with police tape, so people like her kept their sleuthing eyes at bay.

The firefighter he'd spoken to earlier, the chief, nodded at him. 'There's not much we can do here now.'

'Any sign of the driver? Passengers?'

She eyed Aileen. Callan waved his hands and muttered, 'She'll sniff it out eventually.'

Aileen elbowed his side.

'The fire seems to have burned through the seats. Couldn't make anything out from the rubble.'

They'd need crime scene technicians and the arson investigator as soon as possible.

When the SOCO team arrived, Callan pulled Aileen aside. 'We need to cordon the area. Ye should head back.'

'It smells of burning rubber and fuel.' Aileen assessed the scene. 'And something else – it's foul, strange. The car's body is intact – well, except for all that molten plastic. You know, I was investigating this case once where the man's car caught fire.'

Callan laid a hand on her arm. 'Darling, there's nothing ye can do here.'

'He was trying to burn the handwritten ledgers that incriminated him.'

What did she mean?

Aileen shoved her hair behind her shoulders. 'It's not always about the crime; fire can also point towards the criminal.'

'An arson investigation will lead us to it.'

She turned to leave and stopped. 'Callan? Whenever you're done, come over. I'll put something together for dinner.'

He opened his mouth to argue, but she cut him off.

'I'm starving, and Dachaigh's just over those trees. If I'd've been paying attention, I would've noticed the fire.'

She could've and headed out to investigate before calling him. Not such a secluded spot was it, considering they were in the north-western part of Scotland where you could wander for miles and never see another human?

He nodded. 'I'll be over.' And he'd pick her brains, enjoy her company while eating a home-cooked meal good enough for an emperor.

She'd humour him too, even if he knocked on her door after midnight. That was just who Aileen Mackinnon was.

No wonder he enjoyed spending time with her.

Callan swivelled towards the crime scene where the police tape now fluttered and technicians wearing white scrubs worked the scene.

He had to suit up too and address that smell.

The added garb over his woollen jacket came as a welcome respite, especially as the temperature was dropping rapidly.

He ducked under the tape and made his way to the burned car.

The fire had eaten through the front seats and left just the metal bones. Burned plastic mixed with something that pierced Callan's nostrils and set his gut churning. The naked steering wheel hung on a destroyed dashboard. Newer makes had more plastic than the older ones and burned faster.

Behind the mask he wore, Callan braced himself. Time for the truth.

Something crunched underneath his boot. The intensity of the heat – though the metal was cooling now – smouldered against his exposed forehead and then he saw it – the reddened pink in the black.

Callan exhaled and stepped away. No wonder it stank of burned flesh – someone had died in there.

Motioning for a technician, Callan headed for his car. 'Human remains here. Get the photographs, document the evidence, and let's find an arson investigator. Figure out how many people were in the car. Get the evidence to the lab and run tests for DNA. We need to identify the victims.'

He moved away, letting the technicians do their jobs. They needed to find the owner of the car and figure out if they were the victim.

Callan found Robert, phone clutched to his ear and scribbling down a phone number in his notepad.

He hung up when Callan approached. 'Number plate in the back survived.'

'Whose car is it?'

'Amy's Rental and Taxi Services.'

'A rental company? Who—'

'They're looking into the data. At first, they said they'd sent the car to the garage for servicing. Now they're not so sure.'

Someone had stolen a rental and set it on fire with a human in it? Was this murder? Or a means to incite panic?

'Keep at it. If they dinnae ken, we'll pay them a visit. What are bloody surveillance cameras for?'

Robert crossed his arms. 'Most rental cars will have a GPS tracker built in, right?'

Callan bunched his shoulders. He'd learned basic technology, but the intricacies of GPS were beyond him. 'Find the name of the person who rented that car. We need to inform next of kin before the grapevine gets a wind of it. I'm heading to Dachaigh until then.'

THE TEMPERATURE HAD DROPPED BELOW FREEZING BY THE time Aileen shut the back door behind her. Driving around the cluster of trees and seeing the whitewashed inn with its pastel-blue windows and door had brought a smile to her face.

Sitting here on a wee mound, in the secluded part of Loch Fuar, its tranquillity and adventure hugged her every time she approached.

And she stood to lose it all.

Her muscles bunched up at that thought, destroying her sense of contentment.

'Aileen?' The voice snapped her attention to the clock on the wall.

She hitched her thick jacket onto the hook and shook out her hair before striding into the dining room.

The walnut furniture gave the place a homey feel. She'd dimmed most of the lights when she'd left and piled wood on the drawing-room fire so the room was cosy for the guest reading there.

'Hey, Bonnie!'

Dachaigh's teenaged part-time housekeeper leaned on the mop and huffed a strand of hair off her face. She'd agreed to stay on for an extra hour or two so Aileen could go on a date. 'How come ye're back so early?' she asked.

Aileen leaned her elbows on the table. Bonnie might not be a keen participant in the local rumour mill, but she loved social media. 'Callan's caught a case.'

A brow went up. 'A case? And he, like, ditched ye for it?'

'He'll come back here after. Anyone come in while I was away?'

She'd been gone just over half an hour, but there was no harm in hoping for a shower of customers, was there?

Bonnie shook her head. 'And I wasn't wearing headphones, like ye asked. Oh! Er, the postman dropped that off for ye earlier – I forgot to tell ye.'

Aileen frowned at the thin, book-shaped parcel on the dining table. Almost palm size, if she stretched her fingers a bit – A5 or so. She pulled the package to her and scrunched her nose as she studied the writing on it. 'Who the heck's written this? This handwriting is worse than Callan's!'

Seeing as a duck could write better than Callan, the address was practically unreadable.

She made out the 'A' and 'M', her initials, and 'D' for Dachaigh. Aileen stuffed it in a drawer. 'Must be a promotional booklet or something. I'll get to it soon enough.' She faced Bonnie again. 'I'm making dinner. Interested?'

'Can't.' Bonnie pushed the mop. 'I've got to call a friend ASAP. Boyfriend trouble.'

Aileen rolled her eyes. Wasn't it always?

She headed for the kitchen. 'Shout if you need anything.'

Bonnie suited Aileen well. She charged little – so Aileen could save precious pounds – and respected others' boundaries more than most Loch Fuar citizens... Though the fact that most of your life in the small town could get published in the local newspaper said little about Bonnie's discretionary skills.

Aileen brought out her pans and set to work. She didn't feel like anything meaty, so she stuck to soup. It was perfect for the brutal temperatures; Callan would need the warmth.

'Damn!' Bonnie's shout echoed down the corridor.

'Bonnie?' Aileen turned at the sound of rushing footsteps.

'I'm sorry. I'm sorry. I-I, like, legit forgot.'

Aileen tilted her head. 'What did you do?'

'Honestly, I-I...' She plucked a brown wallet from her pocket and clattered it onto the table. 'I didn't look inside, but it was in that nice man's room when I was cleaning it.'

'Is he still staying with us? Why did you take the wallet out of the room?'

'He checked out today, didn't he?'

Realisation struck. 'Oh, you mean Mr Macalister?'

Aileen squinted at the wallet. Its brown leather contrasted starkly with the marble countertop.

'Strange, isn't it? Strange he never realised it's missing.' Bonnie plopped onto the bar stool. 'I think it's loaded. It's heavy for sure.'

Aileen shook her head. 'Doesn't matter. I'll call him.'

'Open it!'

'Ever heard of privacy, Bonnie?'

'Aw, come on!'

The leather moulded to her hand, soft like a child's cheek. Aileen licked her lips. 'Let me see if I have his contact details.'

She lowered the heat on the soup so it could simmer away and headed to the reception desk to check her records. Mr Macalister, it turned out, had booked his stay a day in advance.

'Ten days starting on Hogmanay. Ah, I have his number and email.'

'Oh my goodness.' Bonnie smacked the desk, making Aileen jump. 'All that cash... Phew, that's a lot.'

'Bonnie! I just said you weren't supposed to—'

Bonnie leaned in. 'Who carries this sort of cash?'

Aileen's gaze, full of curiosity and mortification, fell on the wallet to find it was indeed stuffed with cash.

'Some sort of doomsday prepper, maybe?' Bonnie continued. 'Look here, it's only cash. There's no licence or any cards.' Bonnie's eyes shone.

Aileen snapped the wallet closed and shoved it into her apron pocket. 'Did you rake through it, then?'

The crimson in Bonnie's cheeks gave her away. Aileen continued to glare. 'Bonnie?'

Bonnie made her way towards the door. 'I just remembered about my chemistry homework. I'll see you tomorrow!'

Through the window, Aileen watched Bonnie dash away on her bike, puffing out clouds of dust behind her.

That girl was a hot mess.

Aileen had her own messes to clear up.

The wallet.

She punched in his number and listened while the phone rang and rang. Her fingers tapped along to the beat, then froze.

Mr Macalister didn't answer.

Crap!

Aileen tried again, only to reach his voicemail.

She opened the wallet and glanced at it. 'Who keeps £2,000 in their wallet and nothing else?' she murmured.

She dialled a third time.

Voicemail again.

Hell!

How could she get in touch with Macalister now? Was this his secondary wallet? That would explain why he hadn't missed it.

Email! She had his email.

Mr Macalister...

Aileen chewed her lip. She didn't want to sound like a thief. And... and though Bonnie had found this wallet in his room, what's saying it was actually his?

Of course it was his! Didn't she check the guest rooms to ensure none of her guests left anything behind? And if he'd stolen it from someone, surely he'd have taken better care of it.

Aileen got back to it. Wrote the words, deleted them, wrote them again and...

Mr Macalister,

Thank you for your stay at Dachaigh Inn. Our housekeeping staff found a wallet in your room. I've attached the pictures for you to confirm if it is indeed yours. Please let me know so we can have it delivered to you.

Best wishes,

Aileen Mackinnon

She hit send before she overthought it.

Aileen swivelled when headlights flashed through the windows, casting long lines before lighting up the car park.

She left the wallet on the reception desk and opened the back door for her visitor.

Not an hour since she'd last seen him and his stubble seemed to have further darkened that chiselled jaw. Not an hour since she'd last seen him and her heart still skidded to a halt before dancing away at the speed of a train.

God help her with DI Callan Cameron. The man was difficult, stubborn, and crude, but…

He stepped up to her, dipped his head, and pressed his lips to hers. Strong arms wrapped her in a warm cocoon.

Handsome, smart, warm, sometimes romantic…

She grabbed his coat's lapels and pulled him in. The light caught the rough beard and the weariness in his eyes.

Aileen stopped cold. 'What is it?'

Callan shook his head. 'Come here.'

He made a grab for her, but she placed a hand on his chest. 'You found a dead body in that fire. That's why it stank.'

He scrubbed his face. 'Can we just unwind like we'd planned to?'

'Don't you have to get down to the station?'

'There's nothing for me to do at the moment. We dinnae ken who it is. Robert's on it. He'll call me as soon as he gets an ID.'

Aileen wrapped her arms around his hard torso. 'I made soup.'

Callan took off his coat and rubbed his hands. 'Perfect.'

She did as he asked. They set the table, then Aileen lit a few candles and ushered him to a chair.

'Smells heavenly.' Callan took a spoonful. 'Gosh, ye sure ye didn't study catering instead of accounting?'

'I didn't, otherwise I'd've cooked books.'

Callan snorted.

Aileen grinned.

Cutlery clattered, and the soup quickly vanished. When Callan pushed up from the table and stood, announcing, 'I'll do the dishes,' Aileen replied, 'I'll dry them up,' and followed with the plates. Her curiosity was eating her alive.

They worked in silence, Aileen's mind puzzling out how to extract information. He'd never tell her if she just asked. But could she cajole him?

An idea formed in her mind. 'So, there's ice cream.'

Callan set the dish on the drying rack and faced her, cold eyes sharp. 'I'm not telling ye.'

'It's your favourite kind. Now, it's good manners to share. Surely—'

'Aileen, it's a police matter.'

'And I can keep secrets.'

Callan didn't react, so Aileen dabbed the water off the bowl she was holding. 'And I can help. I always—'

'Get into trouble.' The last dish clattered onto the pile. 'This time, I *will* lock ye up.'

Aileen scoffed. 'You wouldn't dare! And be careful with my plates!'

He descended then, a vulture diving for its prey. Callan's kiss bruised her lips, and his hands smouldered against her waist.

'Try it and ye'll see.'

Aileen shrieked into his mouth when her feet left the ground. 'Put me down! I have guests!'

'Ye should've thought of that before.'

When pounding on his back didn't work, Aileen bit him.

'Aye, aren't we eager? Did ye lock up?'

'Don't distract me!'

He lifted her like a sack of potatoes. 'I'm just being a caring boyfriend.'

Her attacks, from her upside-down position, had little effect on him. 'Callan!'

She'd be damned if his stupid threats scared her. Aileen pushed up, wrapped her hands around his head, and attacked him so his mind would explode. She took what she wanted; investigated what she wanted.

But she certainly never wanted to be set back on her feet, head swirling. 'What? Come back here!'

Callan's eyes zeroed in on something behind her.

'What…?' She gazed over her shoulder. 'Oh, it's a wallet a guest left behind.'

His wave dismissed her comment. 'The fire. Ye could've seen it from here.'

'But I was upstairs, getting ready.'

Callan's eyes lit up. 'Aye, but you're here, away from the centre of town. So why would a local use this road? Why would they rent a car? Unless they were staying here.'

Her mind screeched to a halt. 'No, no way. My guests are fine!'

'Yer surveillance cameras—'

'Won't show a black car like the one at your crime scene because I don't have a guest using such a car.' There'd only just been enough of the car left to see its colour when she'd arrived at the crime scene.

Callan drew her face in-between his hands. '*Banlaoch*, I'm not saying it was yer guest in that car. I just think they might've driven from hereabouts.'

'If—'

Callan rested his forehead against hers. 'Otherwise, I'll have to consider the possibility that whoever it was wanted ye to come look for the fire. That somehow a killer would've wanted to include ye. I wouldn't have that.'

'Killer? You mean someone's been *murdered* in that car?'

He drew her closer still. 'I dinnae ken. But I want ye to be safe. I want to ken who that person was. And why someone set fire to a car so close to the heath?'

Fear clouded her heart. 'If you hadn't driven down that road sooner, the heath could've... The way the wind's blowing...'

'The rain we've had saved Dachaigh, not me.'

Aileen followed when he tugged her towards the stairs.

She didn't have to be a genius to know fire loved heathland. Loved it because it would let the fire travel far and wide. Far enough to reach Dachaigh and burn her beloved inn to the ground.

Except it was January.

Crap. Did someone want her inn gone?

CHAPTER TWO

Callan frowned at the occupied parking spot. Bloody hell!

He pulled the handbrake harder than necessary then got out of his car and strode over to the police station.

Detective Chief Inspector Rory Macdonald looked up from his steaming cup as he entered. 'Ah, ye've finally chosen to join us?'

'I'm ten minutes early.'

'As opposed to thirty. I trust ye enjoyed a fun date.' Rory's grin confirmed his colleagues had had a field day gossiping at Callan's expense.

Callan's hands itched to wrap around Robert's neck. 'Is the arson investigator here?'

Rory slurped his coffee. 'Robert took him to the site. And the crime scene technicians say they found the remains of one human body. They can't say at the moment if the car had any more passengers.'

Callan ran a hand through his hair. 'I'll follow—'

'I suggest ye work on finding the identity of the person

first.' Rory set his mug aside. 'Nothing's worse than finding out someone ye love is dead on the news.'

'The forensic lab needs to get back to me, but... It can't be a local, I think.'

'We need to be sure.' Rory clomped to his office, muttering, 'Ye smell like women's shampoo.'

They'd never let him hear the end of this.

Callan headed to his own office and reached for the phone.

'Detective,' the lab technician answered. 'I'm sorry, but we haven't been able to process much.'

'I need to find the identity. Do we know what started the fire?'

The technician harrumphed. 'I've been here all night, Detective. That's how busy it is. So, *ta ta.*'

Callan smacked a fist onto the stacks of papers littering his desk. 'Crap!' Why did people think they could hang up on him?

His fine mood soured, Callan grabbed a stack of unwanted files and shoved them to the other end of his desk. Like a set of dominos, the files hanging on the edge tumbled to the floor with a thud.

The papers in his office would bury him soon or play a part in a major accident.

He reached for the blank board and the marker at the same time. No matter how many times he cleared the papers, they just kept popping up.

In his head, he wound his way back to the scene of the fire, played it out in his mind like a movie. What had he seen?

Smoke, mist and the wind trying to blow the raging fire over onto the heathland.

'The road's just wide enough for two cars,' he

muttered. 'That lay-by is the only one for about three quarters of a mile.'

Thrusting his arms wide, he pointed to one side. 'The car faced the front, headed for the dual carriageway, not the town. Why would someone from town take the longer route to get there from here?'

He'd checked Dachaigh's surveillance cameras and, as Aileen had said, none of her guests had a black SUV.

Where had the car come from? Loch Fuar? Or had the perp driven it off the dual carriageway and parked it in the opposite direction to mislead?

Callan uncapped the marker and scrawled. 'How long did the car burn?'

That would help build a timeline.

A knock at the door cut off his thoughts.

'Shit! What is it?' He swivelled to find a man with broad shoulders, a wrinkled forehead and dirty blond hair.

The arson investigator.

His boots clicked on the floor and almost crushed the files that had nosedived from the desk earlier. 'Er…'

Callan dismissed them with a wave. 'Detective Cameron.'

A labyrinth of scars traced the hand that pumped Callan's. 'Detective MacNeill. Detective Walsh from Loch Heaven sends his regards. He also told me to be careful about your girlfriend.'

'It's just us. I appreciate ye coming down here with haste. We need to identify the passengers.'

Rory plodded in, glanced at the papers on the floor, and rolled his eyes. 'What can ye tell us, MacNeill?'

After a couple of minutes of jostling, Callan managed to push the papers behind his chair and empty the visitor chairs.

MacNeill folded his arms. 'You've done a good job. The evidence collection is thorough, so even though I've yet to write a report, I *can* say someone deliberately set the fire.'

Words Callan didn't want to hear.

'From what I've seen, the yellow can found at the scene was used to pour petrol onto the tarmac. Someone emptied the can all around the car and set fire to it from the front, perhaps using a cloth.'

Callan ran a hand over his face. 'Part of the victim's clothes, maybe?'

'Maybe.'

Rory sat back. 'How long did the car burn?'

'Fifteen minutes. You're lucky you drove past it and got the fire brigade out so swiftly. I'd have had almost nothing left to study otherwise.'

Two possibilities stared them in the face. Either someone had set the car on fire with the intention of erasing the traces of the person inside or they'd hoped the fire would spread and burn Dachaigh down.

Rory's eyes met Callan's. The man understood.

MacNeill stood. 'I'm off to the garage to study the car a bit more. See if I can find anything else for you.'

Rory walked the man out. Callan lasered his attention back on the board.

'There's always a possibility the perp's an eejit,' Rory said when he returned.

'One thing I don't do, Rory, is assume the best-case scenario. It's too hard to ignore.' He pointed to the image of the car. 'That sort of fire's easily visible from the reception area at Dachaigh. If Aileen hadn't been finished for the day, she'd have seen it.'

'Seen it and gone to check it out.' Rory nodded. 'And if the perp was still around…'

'They wanted someone to see the fire but…' Callan

faced Rory. 'Aileen's always busy, not someone to have one eye out the window. If she hadn't seen it just after it started, she'd have seen it far too late. Too late to save the inn.' To save herself. 'With a patch of heathland and then a wall of trees between the lay-by and Dachaigh, the inn's hardly a few hundred metres from the crime scene.'

Rory laid a hand on Callan's shoulder. 'Why would someone want to harm Dachaigh? Aileen and her guests could've escaped out the back door. And the heath wasn't dry.'

'Lucky, wasn't she?' Callan knew it wasn't his story to share, but he had no choice. 'She's having financial trouble. She's been applying for loans but keeps being rejected.'

'Is the inn insured?'

Callan ran a hand through his hair. 'Aileen would never…'

'Aye, but remember how Langdon threatened her? Ask Aileen if someone made a bid for that property.'

Bloody hell! Ask her and let her know he knew? She'd skewer him before packing up and heading back to the city, where she'd get a job, eventually.

'Ye need to talk to her, Callan. Even when it's hard – especially then.' After almost forty years of marriage, three children and four grandchildren – or was it five? – the man knew his way through every possible 'couple fiasco'.

Not for the first time in the last twenty-four hours, Callan wanted to pull his hair out. 'Alright, but first I'm heading to the rental company. Let's see who rented out that car and why they don't have any documentation for it.'

SHOVING THE INEVITABLE ENCOUNTER WITH AILEEN UNDER the carpet, Callan made his way to Loch Heaven. He'd programmed the address for Amy's Rental and Taxi Services into the GPS, smacking his phone only once while doing so, which had changed the instructions to Swedish.

He followed the blue line now.

The road twisted around a river, curved over the bend, flew past a small fortress and entered the busy bustle of Loch Heaven.

A horn blared to his right, someone shouted a curse and when Callan stopped at a red light, a teenager ran smack into an old woman, sending her and her groceries flying.

Amy's Rental and Taxi Services took him well into the heart of town, past the police station and the café Walsh's wife ran, into a cluttered area. Judging by the smells of grease and engine oil mixed with the acrid stench of garbage, he was in the right place.

Another car door slammed behind him. Callan nodded at the trench-coat wearing detective who'd emerged from the car.

Walsh ambled over. 'Sure Tim needs to be pulled into this?'

When Callan had called Walsh, he'd learned the other detective kept tabs on this place and had befriended the owner. But friend or not, something about their story wasn't adding up, so that left Callan little choice. He said as much to Walsh, who nodded and followed him inside.

SOMEWHERE METAL CLANKED, FOLLOWED BY A CURSE. A mechanic wearing an overcoat bent over an engine while another lad washed a car.

Walsh nodded his greetings to a few men when a shout rose from the back. 'Tim! Walsh's here to see you.'

A second later, a door closed, and heavy footsteps pounded towards them.

The man with a thick ginger beard and bald head didn't fit the image Callan had of 'Tim'. He barely reached Callan's waist. The eyes lasering into his spoke of unsheltered monsoons. And the hand shaking Callan's gripped hard.

'Detective Cameron.'

'Tim Downie. Is this about your enquiry?'

'Aye, I wanted to ken who hired the car from ye.'

Tim gestured for them to follow him. They wound around cars and made their way towards a wooden door on the back wall.

'Amy, my sister, runs the rental and taxi part of the business.' He pushed the door open. 'It's on the back side.'

Amy stood taller than her brother, with blond hair, blue eyes and soft hands. 'You the bobby who called yesterday?'

Callan introduced himself after flashing his badge. 'I'd like to ken who rented out the vehicle.'

Lips smacking as she chewed her gum, she assessed him. 'Why do you want to know?'

Irritation flashed through him like a flame to petrol. 'We'd appreciate it if ye'd help the police.'

'And I'd appreciate it if you'd feature on one of those.' She pointed to a calendar fluttering against the dark peeling paint. 'But we don't always get what we want.'

His fingers fisted of their own accord.

Walsh cut through the tension. 'Amy, please. Someone's dead. You could help us find out who.'

Amy raised a sharp eyebrow. 'Why didn't you say so? I have no business leaving dead people hanging.'

Her bright pink nails clattered over the keyboard, grating on Callan's thinning control. *Get on with it!*

Her thick lashes batted. 'The black car. It was with Tim.'

Tim crossed his beefy arms. 'What business would I have had with your shit?'

Amy rolled her eyes. 'You said it needed the oil changing.' She pointed to the screen. 'Here it says out of commission.'

Callan leaned over the table – he stopped breathing when Amy's perfume began acting like chloroform – and studied the screen. 'Anyone else here who could've issued it? Maybe trying to earn a bit of money on the side?'

Tim huffed. 'I'd have to ask around. I wasn't here yesterday. The lads've a mind of their own.'

Amy's laugh whipped through the air. 'Mind in the wrong part of the body, that's what their problem is. Ask the lads – they'll know.'

Callan thanked her, even if it irked him, and followed Tim out.

'Hey, blue-eyed babe.'

He froze. What the hell?

'Aye, you with the badge. If you're ever interested in modelling, let me know, 'kay?'

When the sun melted.

He didn't reply, just strode away.

Walsh looked back at Callan. 'Why don't we start with that starry-eyed lad there? Maybe your blue eyes will work on him, too.'

Callan shot Walsh a glare, but judging by that stupid grin on his face, he was too late. He'd be butchered soon.

Walsh's starry-eyed prey, Carl, had a date with a girl who'd brought her car in for some washing.

'Black car. Seen the day before yesterday parked right here in the garage. Ring any bells?'

Carl frowned, trying to remember.

Another head peeked out behind the hood of the car. 'Ever seen how many black cars are out there?'

Callan flashed them a photograph of a similar model and rattled off the registration.

'Ah.' Carl's eyes lit up. 'Aye, I remember now – I worked on her some. Needed an oil change and a new spare tyre. Good as new otherwise. About 25,000 miles on her.'

Walsh stabbed a finger on the hood of a car they stood next to. 'Any ideas who took her out?'

Carl shrugged. 'Difficult to say. We got done with her yesterday morning. I parked her on the side when we had too much traffic. Amy usually drives them to the back later. Tim wasn't around yesterday, so it was tight.'

Bloody hell. Someone had lifted the car in broad daylight in a busy garage?

They needed something – a clue.

'Don't ye have cameras here?'

'Sure do. Ask Tim.'

They did.

Callan shuffled his feet, waiting for Tim to roll the footage. The monitor flashed and showed Carl reversing the car out of the garage. The cameras out front caught him disappearing to the side, off the camera's range.

Damn it!

Tim huffed. 'That's the way to the side. Carl's making room for another car. We don't have any cams looking over the side walls.'

Walsh twirled his finger. 'Keep playing it. If you've got no exit to the back, the perp had to have driven the car out of the garage from here.'

'Aye. It's grating when a car's lifted from under our bloody noses.'

Callan would've sympathised with the man, but the

hard truth was, if not this car, the perp would've lifted another.

They kept staring as the video rolled. Several customers came and went. Some for servicing and others for picking up their vehicles.

'There. Pause it.' Callan pointed to the screen. 'There's the car again – 9 a.m.'

Walsh leaned in. 'Whoever the driver is, they'd have had to walk in from the front door to pick it up.'

'Nah, I'm afraid not. We have a walkway leading up to the back. Ye can enter the rental shop on foot but drive out through here. And sorry, haven't got any cams back there. The assets are all here.'

Hell! They were back to where they'd started.

Callan took a step back. 'Can ye print an image for us? Let me see if IT can clean the image and find a face.'

It was his last hope.

AILEEN'S HAND TREMBLED. THE PHONE CHIMED, beckoning to her. If she didn't pick up, they'd come round and knock on her door. And if the guests heard them...

'Hello?' she squeezed out.

'Ms Mackinnon? This is Mr Russell from—'

Aileen swallowed. She knew too well where he worked and why he'd called.

A clammy palm settled on the paper. The words 'Loan Application Rejected' glared back in red. How had things come to this?

She'd used up her bank balance, dipped into an overdraft and still had a payment she'd yet to scramble together. Aileen had begged the bank manager to hold on for a fortnight, and now he wanted to know when she'd pay up.

Given her nosediving credit rating, the bank had rejected her loan application.

Aileen bit her lip to distract from the tension in her eyes. They stung, and so did her heart.

'I'll find a way,' she heard herself say to the man. 'Give me another fifteen days.'

A sigh came down the line. 'I have to speak with my boss. But I can extend only a day or two. That's all I can afford to stall. I'm sorry.'

The call came to an abrupt end – just like her dream life was about to.

No inn, no small-town living, no friends, no boyfriend. She needed a sensible job, the sort that paid bills. The sort she'd only get in the city as a forensic accountant.

She flipped the offensive letter over, not wanting those words to glare back at her.

'Ah!'

An eye, a very realistic one, peered from the paper. Aileen's mind flashed to the evil eye, the case that had led them to Loch Heaven and danger...

Someone had sketched it using a pencil. Sure strokes, artistic curves, impeccable shading so it looked like light was glinting off the pupil. And an emotion. The eye held an emotion – something forlorn, as if it were calling to her.

What in the world? A sense of melancholy settled about her – not fear of the evil eye, but a sense of longing.

Who'd done this? She'd left the paper here, or was it on her desk?

Aileen couldn't remember. Could it be Bonnie?

Yes, it must've been her. Hopefully, it wasn't a guest.

She remembered Callan wondering why someone would set fire to a car so close to the heath.

Fear dripped into her heart. Was this a warning? Had someone got her loan application rejected and tried to set Dachaigh on fire to destroy her business?

Her mouth went dry.

She needed a distraction! *Think of something to do*!

Aileen clicked away on the keyboard – anything to avoid her spiralling imagination.

The laptop pinged with an incoming email. Aileen's hands trembled at the name.

Ken Macalister.

He had replied.

Some tension leaked from her shoulders. She'd been worried about him, worried he'd been the one in the car.

The email loaded, and Aileen peered at the screen.

Please come meet me at 21 Garden Row, Loch Fuar.

No salutations, no greetings, no nothing.

Aileen scratched her forehead, curiosity tickling her. 'Why can't people be straightforward?' she muttered.

She read the response again. No fuss, to the point, yet *evasive*. Her intuition tickled a warning. 'Hell! I'll just get this done with.' Having a heavy wallet staring at her, especially when she had little herself, tortured her soul.

And it also gave her reason to step out of her misery, even if only for half an hour, and drive past the crime scene.

If Callan found her snooping, she'd be an imprisoned cat with unanswered questions.

Her sedan roared to life and quickly seeped some warmth into her freezing bones.

Thank goodness for a functioning car. It hobbled down the stone bridge, toasty and comfortable.

Aileen slowed down to a crawl when she neared the lay-by. No one worked the scene at the moment. A window of opportunity.

Leave it be, Aileen. Leave it be. Leave it— Crap! Crap! She parked her car on the deserted Highland road and hopped out.

'Oh!' Her hand clasped the hat on her head, battling with the wind to keep it affixed on her head. Her nose numbed to an icicle and watered. Damn it!

Aileen put one foot in front of the other, headed for the police tape.

She peered at the rubble skirting the heathland. Debris – rubber, metal, glass – littered the tarmac.

Aileen's hair blew into her face, getting in her eyes. One hand holding her hat and the other clutching her stray hair, Aileen tried to remember what she'd seen before.

Tilting her nose up and standing on tiptoes, she studied the scene until—

Splat!

Something landed on the top of her nose. A second later, it dripped down to her mouth. Another drop splattered her coat.

'Not now!'

The wind ate her growl, carrying it along as raindrops spat on the ground.

Aileen rushed towards her car. Trust the damned Scottish weather to spill water on all her sneaky plans!

Wipers on at full speed, Aileen drove past the market square. Isla's Bakery overflowed with customers wanting warm bread and a respite. Maybe if she shared her problems with her best friend, Isla's business genius might rub off on her.

Not now though – not when Isla and her husband, Daniel, were dealing with their own problems.

Garden Row faced a patch of dead grass and shrivelled trees. Gardens didn't look their best when the wind from the Arctic roared.

When she found an empty parking spot outside number twenty-one, Aileen grinned. At least she wouldn't turn into a block of ice hiking to this place.

Aileen blew warm air into her cupped palms for insurance and frowned. Why had Ken Macalister summoned her here? He'd stayed in the inn as a guest. He wouldn't have done that if he lived in Loch Fuar, would he?

Perhaps this was his friend's place. Perhaps…

Knock and you'll know, Aileen.

She hurried through the cold and jogged up the stone steps to the Georgian building. A warm glow emanated from the ground floor. This structure leaned into another on both sides, so they formed a row.

The knocker struck the door with a bang loud enough for Macalister to hear it over the cry of the wind.

Aileen's ears had frozen blue, the shade of her hat.

The glistening door remained shut. How long did it take to open the door? He'd called her here.

She was just reaching for the knocker again when the door swung open.

The man wore black trousers and a coat over a white shirt. His bushy eyebrows fell over beady eyes that held such sorrow, it grabbed at Aileen's throat.

'He's dead then.'

Aileen blinked. 'Er, I'm Aileen Mackinnon. I wrote to Mr Macalister about his, er, his belongings?'

Extending a frail, well-manicured hand, the man said, 'Elias Schneider.'

When he gestured her in and shut the door, Aileen blew out a breath. Her gaze travelled to the foyer with its curving staircase and a table in the centre topped with an empty vase. Then she saw the golden letters glistening under the bright golden light.

Schneider and Associates: Solicitors.

'I'm sorry. There has been a mistake—'

'I'm afraid not, Ms Mackinnon.' He held out his card. His name, in simple lettering, glistened on the crisp thick cream card. 'If you could just come this way to my office.'

Pocketing his card, Aileen followed the man.

Mr Schneider's office held a mahogany desk littered with a computer and heaps of books: *Case Laws*, the glittering covers read.

Books decorated the walls. Bookshelves ran from ceiling to floor filled with yet more case-law books.

Aileen sank into the velvety chair in a curious daze. Why was she here? Where was Ken Macalister? How was he connected to this man?

Schneider ran a finger over one bushy eyebrow before settling down into his leather chair. He let out a sigh. 'He told me a woman would email him – email him when it was all done.'

Aileen twiddled her fingers, unsure how to break it to him. 'I'm sorry, Mr Schneider. You don't seem to be making much sense.'

Those beady eyes flashed; an eyebrow twitched. 'The matter at hand is absurd.'

Why couldn't lawyers speak straight? Aileen shuddered, remembering her last encounter with a lawyer.

'Ms Mackinnon, is it?' The man's voice cut through to her.

Aileen nodded. 'I own the inn – Dachaigh.' At least for the next few days...

'Very well. How did you meet Ken Macalister?'

Aileen contemplated making a run for it. This strange man had misled her. What if he attacked her?

She knew self-defence, and Aileen had learned never to trust a stranger at first sight.

What choice did she have? What would she do with the wallet?

She fished around in her bag for it, then set it on the table. 'Ken Macalister lodged at my inn this past week. He's left his wallet behind.'

The lawyer frowned, running a finger over the leather. 'Strange indeed.'

Aileen cleared her throat. 'How do you know him?'

Mr Schneider leaned over and plucked out a thin, sealed envelope. 'I make wills, Ms Mackinnon. Ken Macalister visited last week to make this.' He shook the thin envelope.

'He changed his will?' Aileen raised an eyebrow. 'Why am I here then?'

He laid the envelope on the table and smoothed its unruffled edges. 'That's the strange part.' Interlocking his fingers, the solicitor continued. 'Ken Macalister and I have known each other for decades now. He made a will thirty-five years ago when he got married. And then he changed it last week. And here you are with his wallet.

'Last week, he came in here with a pre-typed will. We formalised it and he said the person for whom I should read this' – Schneider stabbed the envelope – 'would write him an email. All I had to do was tell this woman to come over so I could read the will.'

Aileen shook her head. 'Is this some sort of prank?'

Attend a will reading for a man she didn't know? 'How do you know he's dead?'

'Because he said you wouldn't write to me unless he is.'

What the bollocks?

Aileen pulled off her hat and ran a hand through her hair. 'I'm not sure I follow, sir. This is really… strange. I barely know him.'

'I must do as he told me.' And then the man began the proceedings.

Aileen held up a hand. 'Hold on! Didn't he have any relatives? Shouldn't we call them?'

Schneider glanced at the envelope. 'The man didn't have much, but he sure had an uncanny knack for predicting the future.'

The sound of the envelope tearing seemed unbearably loud. No way was the will meant for her.

With deft fingers, Schneider extracted one sheet of paper.

'Mr Schneider, I'm not sure—'

'Now that you're reading this, I'm gone, most definitely gone, most definitely murdered. In my life, I haven't accumulated much but lost a lot – a child, a wife and my dignity. In death, I wish to repair my wrongs, turn a stone I was too weak to in life. I won't find salvation otherwise. I'll burn in the pits of hell.

'There's one person who's proved her skill. From my research, she's a sharp sleuth, someone I can entrust myself with, someone who'd find me justice when my voice is silenced, deliberately.

'Ms Mackinnon, the cash in my wallet is for you to use. Use it to find my killer, use it to find the person who's robbed several families of their fullest life. Find them because only you can. Find them and my entire wealth is yours. I might not have much, not enough to measure against my lost child and wife, but enough to save an inn. Find the killer and get your inn back.

'Yours even in death, Mr Ken Macalister.'

Silence. A long gaping silence.

In her mind, though, thoughts raced, words crashing until one answer remained, 'No way! Stop this ridiculous scheme at once. I'm no detective. We have a skilled detective in Loch Fuar, Mr Schneider. You play your shenanigans with him and see where it lands you!'

Aileen turned on her heels, forgetting about the wallet, and ran out into the wintery dread, onto the slippery pavement. Her anger panted into clouds of smoke.

'Ms Mackinnon! I'm not jesting, I assure you,' Schneider shouted from the threshold of his office entrance.

She pulled open her car door and froze. A thin shiver of wind brushed against her exposed neck like the icy finger of death. A voice like smoke whispered into her ear, 'Salvation, Aileen. Salvation…'

Aileen hopped into the car, teeth chattering, hands fumbling with her keys. Then she floored the accelerator and raced away, ran away before a ghost pulled her into the world of the dead.

CHAPTER THREE

Callan stuck the image of the perp in a file. A dead end. IT couldn't patch a group of discoloured boxes and produce a coherent image.

Curling his wrists, Callan swallowed the temptation to punch the wall. He grabbed the phone instead and dialled the lab.

A monotonous voice came down the line. 'Please, Detective. You need to be patient.'

'Someone's dead and I need to know who and if there were others, damn it!'

The technician paused. 'I'm sure you know the evidence needs to be processed—'

'Haven't ye found anything?'

'We have, but not enough to write a report.'

Hell! This would get him nowhere.

Callan kicked his chair away. It was time.

Bloody hell!

He struggled into his coat then dragged his feet to his car. All other sources had run dry. And if they fought, he'd make it up to her. He'd just have to be gentle.

But when his car crossed the stone bridge and the whitewashed inn loomed ahead, Callan knew gentle wouldn't work, not with him.

And if Aileen got her back up, she'd skewer him.

He turned into the car park and frowned. No sedan. Where had she gone?

Callan parked his car to one side and clambered out. *She better not be getting involved in his case.*

Anger wouldn't get him anywhere though.

He trudged towards the back door and knocked for the sake of politeness.

No answer.

He reached for the knob, but it didn't turn. Good – at least she'd locked up. But what sort of inn closed doors during the day?

He raised his hand again when the door opened to reveal a smiling face. 'You must be Callan!'

'And you are?'

The hand she stuck out glittered with nail polish and fancy bracelets. She chirped, 'Bonnie. I help Ms Mackinnon clean the place. She's out.'

Callan nodded. 'When will she be back?'

Bonnie shrugged.

'I'll wait for her then.' And work out a strategy through gentleness and anger.

Who knew having a girlfriend would be bloody hard work? Callan sat in the dining area, alone with the cuckoo clock.

'I'm sorry,' he whispered to himself. 'But we need to talk about the inn.'

That didn't sound right.

'Is someone threatening to steal this place?' Hell, that sounded worse.

He tried again, this time in a calm voice. 'I ken about yer financial troubles.'

'You what?!'

The hairs on his skin stuck out like thorns. He faced the voice, eyes wide, hands up in surrender. 'Please listen to me. I-I... Oh hell!'

He rushed to her, seeing her reddened cheeks and nose.

'Does everyone know?'

'I... Stop crying. It'll be alright.'

'Crying?' Aileen faced him, her eyes angry. 'Does everyone think I'm some kind of blubbering fool? Let's give her a poke and off she goes.' Aileen gestured, stabbing a finger in his direction. 'I won't have this!'

Callan took a step back. Either he'd stepped on a live wire or bustled in at the end of a bad day. 'What're ye talking about?'

She marched up to him and slapped a card against his chest.

He tugged it from her grasp. 'Schneider and Associates. What do ye want with them?'

'So you know about them? Or were you following me?'

'What? No! Of course I ken who Schneider is, Aileen. What were *you* doing at his place?'

Aileen waved a dismissive hand. 'He's loony. How do you know about my financial situation?'

Callan's learned skill of interrogation fell flat in front of his girlfriend. 'Why did ye go to Garden Row?'

Crossing her arms over her stomach, Aileen spoke. 'It's strange...'

It took her a while to get the details across. Her thoughts shot off in tangents – the case-law books, an envelope, the email she'd sent him, Macalister having a wife, etc. – until Callan pieced together the important parts.

'I just don't get it. Why me? And where's the body if he's gone? Was it him in the car?'

Callan intertwined his fingers. 'When did Macalister leave?'

Aileen blinked, clearly at a loss for coherent thought.

'I'll check the cameras. Keys?'

He breathed in the relief of escaping almost unscathed. Every step up the stairs, his mind ticked. Things slotted into place as other pieces fell away.

The Control Room with its cameras welcomed him in a veil of musky humidity. Callan clicked the mouse to pull the footage from the cloud. It played until Macalister entered into view, heading out the front door.

He kept watching.

A two-seater pale lavender car drove past the backdoor camera. Callan checked the time, noted it down.

His heart grew heavier. Time to call Robert.

AILEEN SAT AT THE DINING TABLE, STARING AT HER FINGERS. She didn't pepper him with questions when he descended the stairs.

Her eyes clashed with his. 'Well?' She read his thoughts. Callan guessed his face displayed it all. 'You can't mean—'

'There's no one else.'

'But – but that's not even the car he drove. He rented out a two-seater because he came here alone. You saw the surveillance footage.'

Callan folded into a chair opposite hers. 'Who else can it be if it isn't a guest? Why would a car loiter in that lay-by so close to the inn otherwise? Unless, unless…' *Unless it's something got to do with you.*

'You think it's about the inn? Macalister didn't know anyone here. He didn't wish me any harm.'

'I know what you're going through financially.'

'Are you stalking me now? Am I a suspect?' Her words smarted like a whip.

He ran a hand over his face. 'No, darling – you left the rejection letter on the kitchen counter.'

Aileen's eyes met his, and he saw it, the hostility. 'I wouldn't, Callan. I would never kill someone and try to burn the place down for insurance money.'

He reached out to take her hand, but she pulled away. 'I thought you believed me.'

Damn it! Talk about assuming the worst.

'I never thought ye'd deliberately kill someone. But I wanted to ken if someone's put in a bid for this place.'

'And I killed them for revenge?' She pushed off the table. 'Get out.'

'Aileen.'

'Get out! Men, the lot of you, are such, such imbeciles. Why would I kill anyone to protect a life I've already lost? Why would I…'

Callan watched her – really observed her. Her hair was pressed flat on her head; the hat she'd worn lay discarded on the table. Her face was a deep red and her eyes – her eyes were the sole windows to her. And they looked panicked, scared.

Aileen Mackinnon was terrified.

He moved towards her when before he'd have run away from the tears lining her eyes. But in the past few months, he'd realised one thing: Aileen never ran away from the people who mattered to her. And now she needed help.

If he drew away, he'd rip them apart, tear Aileen apart.

Callan wrapped his arms around her and pulled her into his chest. 'I've got ye, darling.'

Her hands flew to his chest and grabbed onto his shirt until Callan swore he heard something rip.

'I-I'm sorry.'

'Ye shouldn't be.' He should've spoken to her sooner; offered help. As she sobbed into his chest, Callan realised what this meant.

If she had no money to stay here, Dachaigh would be gone, sold off to the highest bidder. And without Dachaigh, what kept Aileen here? Siobhan, her gran, was away at the nursing home. And Loch Fuar didn't need any forensic accountants.

Aileen would have to pack her bags, leave *him* behind.

He tugged her closer so not even air passed between them. If he crushed her, she didn't complain. She snuggled closer still.

'We'll figure something out. We'll—'

'You don't understand. If Dachaigh had burned down the other day, I'd've lost everything. Then this absurd offer. Why would Macalister want to involve me? I barely know him.'

Callan led Aileen to the dining table and sat her on a chair. 'Ye said the will mentioned yer *issue*.'

Aileen's reddened eyes cut through him. Callan focused on her words. 'He stayed here and saw I had no guests. It's easy to conclude the inn's struggling.'

Callan shook his head. 'It's the month after Christmas, downtime for most lodging businesses. He knew. Ken Macalister knew ye were struggling. Did ye tell anyone?'

'And risk them mentioning anything to Gran?'

'I'll run him, see if anything pops. Maybe we can go meet your bank manager—'

'No. I'll handle that.'

Callan took her hand in his. 'This is not the time to be stubborn. Besides, I want to ask him if anyone's eyeing the property.'

Aileen opened her mouth to shout another retort.

'I'm not blaming ye, Aileen. What I'm trying to imply is this is an extensive property. Not just yer inn, but the estate around it. It's all yours, or yer gran's. If that fire had spread, it would've burned the estate, the inn... caused a lot of damage. It would've driven ye out of business.'

Her eyes sparkled then. This time, she didn't direct the fury at him. 'And if the fire looked like arson, the insurance company would deny paying the claim, saying I burned it because of my *financial troubles*.'

Callan flinched at the phrase. 'Aye, ye'd have to surrender the place.' Callan huffed. 'This is just a theory until we confirm it. But first I need to ken about Ken Macalister and how he relates to ye.'

Aileen gripped the table. 'I never knew the man, Callan. He only stayed here ten days.'

Callan narrowed his eyes. 'Ten days in Loch Fuar? Alone? Doing what, exactly?'

'I don't ask my guests that. They pay for their stay, I'm happy.'

He stood. 'Perhaps I'll meet with Schneider then.'

'Can we trust him?'

Callan drew away, forehead creased in thought. Everyone knew Schneider, yet Callan's family had never needed his services.

Callan didn't trust someone based on their reputation alone. 'I'll run them both and we'll try to figure out what game they might be playing.'

Aileen's soft hand caressed his back. 'And until then, I'll speak with my bank manager and see if anyone's been asking about Dachaigh.'

'Be careful.'

She rose on her tiptoes and barely got to his jaw. Callan bent down and kissed her lips. 'I thought the one thing couples – *partners* – did was share things. Why did ye keep something so big from me?'

'I didn't want it to be true. I don't want to lose this.' She cupped his face. 'I don't want to lose you.'

Callan didn't want to lose her either. But if someone's will to destroy their piece of heaven stood stronger, then they were indeed toast.

Promising Aileen he'd be back after his shift, Callan raced to the police station. He had a few searches to run, starting with Schneider.

The scent of coffee hit him as if someone had poured a gallon all over the floor.

Robert bustled over when the machine spat out the bitter sludge. 'So I ran Ken Macalister's registration, from Aileen's security footage. It's a rental. Registered to—'

'Amy's Rental and Taxi Services.'

'Aye,' Robert pulled out his notebook. 'I called Amy, and she explained in exact terms: "Giant of a man with an ugly mug." He'd promised to hand in the car this morning, but—'

'He didn't turn up.'

Robert tapped a page on his notes. 'She called him up, no answer. She said, and I quote, "It's like he vanished into thin air."'

Callan pursed his lips. 'Not vanished, Robert. Ken Macalister evaporated into air. My gut says he's the man in the car. I just need to ken if he was the only one in there and' – he pointed at Robert's notes – 'why he didn't make a run for it.'

What a fool! She'd broken down in front of Callan after striving to always stay strong.

Aileen chewed her lip. When she'd saved an innocent life last time, she thought she'd grown strong.

'Aileen?' Bonnie peeked into the dining area. 'Er, is everything alright?'

Aileen nodded.

'Ye ken…' Bonnie sidled up to her. 'After spending the night with my boyfriend-troubled friend, I've gained quite the expertise.'

She smiled at the fifteen-year-old's attempt to lighten the mood. 'Have you now?'

Bonnie nodded. 'What did yer boyfriend do?'

'Nothing.' Callan had been a perfect gentleman, unlike the crude man she'd met the previous spring.

Without asking permission, Bonnie made herself comfortable on the chair. The mop dripped a staccato onto the floor. 'Is it about the wallet? Did you give it back?'

How much to tell the girl? She was discreet, but…

If everyone in Loch Fuar knew him, Bonnie would, too. 'Have you heard of a lawyer called Schneider?'

'Sure. He's a friend of my dad's. Everyone who needs a solicitor to do anything needs him.'

Not all solicitors did everything, but Aileen got the gist. 'And what does your father think of him?'

Bonnie frowned. 'Why are ye interested in him?'

Aileen leaned in, eyes narrowed. 'Let's just say I ran into him.'

'Ye need his services, don't ye? For the inn?'

'I need you to tell me about him, Bonnie.'

The girl sighed. 'There's not much to tell. He's good at

his job, keeps people out of trouble or helps them out if they're in the muck.'

Aileen sat back. Bonnie's intel had led her nowhere.

'Now, what happened to the wallet? Did you find Mr Macalister?' Bonnie's eager eyes pleaded for an answer.

Aileen shook her head. 'Not really.'

'But ye reached out to him, right?'

'Yes.' How could she explain this? 'I handed the wallet over.' Speaking to lawyers had taught her discretion for sure.

'What did he say? Why didn't he have his cards in it?'

And Aileen had thought the lass didn't gossip.

She pointed to the mop. 'Get your work done and go home. Don't you have homework?'

'I just want to—'

'Snoop? That's not good manners, especially for a housekeeper.'

'I work part-time.'

Aileen grinned at Bonnie. 'Get to work.'

The girl picked up the mop and stalked away, back slumped in a way only teenagers could accomplish.

Aileen huffed. She needed more on Schneider.

What better place than the trusty old internet?

Aileen frowned at her phone screen. The internet had only good things to say about the lawyer. He'd helped many people out of legal trouble, saved fortunes and families.

And now he wanted Aileen to solve a possible murder.

She leaned against the backrest. Not a *possible* murder, but a real one. If Callan believed it was Ken Macalister in that car, someone had murdered him.

He'd mentioned her in his will. What sort of person travelled to an inn and pledge their entire fortune to an unknown innkeeper?

Had Macalister kept tabs on her from afar?

She should've got a copy of the will. What did it bloody say?

Aileen tried. She scratched her head, shut her eyes and visualised. But all she recalled was confusion and a sense of strangeness.

Macalister had mentioned her name in his will; had it signed by witnesses before sealing it. He'd written about her financial situation and known about her sleuthing.

Aileen stared at her phone screen. She had solved a few cases with Callan's help, almost like a police assistant, but Loch Fuar was tiny – why would anyone bother writing about the crimes that had happened here?

With shivering fingers, she typed her name into the search bar.

In the couple of seconds it took to load the page, she almost hit the back button twice. She didn't need to see her face on the internet. How had she fallen in the crosshairs between Ken Macalister and his murderer?

First the how and then the all-important why. Why had he named her? Why *her*?

Her dormant social-media accounts flashed on screen, an old article about her success as a forensic accountant while she worked with her former employer and then there… Aileen squinted at the screen. She'd found an article hidden in the depths of the engine, on page four no less, that reported her helping a teenager to safety.

She clicked it open.

Amateur Sleuth Saves Doomed Teenager.

'Oh god. Zay!' Aileen moaned the girl's name. Andrew's roommate all but worshipped Aileen. No wonder she'd written a detailed account of Aileen and their case.

Apart from a couple of comments replying to that post,

Aileen found nothing else. Zay's article, though, held nothing back.

How could a man not only predict his murder, but also entrust an unknown sleuth on hearsay?

She needed more information about him.

Aileen typed his name and hit enter.

'What the…'

Ken Macalister, his profile read, worked as a manager in a security company. She kept scrolling, eyes darting across the screen, absorbing every designation he'd ever had and each case he'd ever worked. She reached the end and read the man's first employment on record.

Oh God! The man was a private investigator, someone bound to have secrets – and any number of enemies.

He'd worked with several governmental organisations, consulted for a few high-profile events and—

Brrrng! The phone screen lit up with an incoming call.

Aileen jumped in her seat. 'Oh!'

She fought the urge to shove the phone in a drawer somewhere and forget about it, but the sincere part of her swiped at the answer button. 'Mr Russell?'

'I'm so sorry for bothering you, Ms Mackinnon, but I have grave news.'

Her ears wanted to flip on themselves, so she couldn't hear the rest of it…

'I spoke with my boss and we… we're unable to wait any longer, ma'am. The unpaid debt is simply too much, and we need you to pay the overdraft right now…'

She'd tattooed the exact amount, right down to the pennies, on the back of her eyelids. There was no way she could scramble that money together in one day.

'What,' she scratched out of her parched throat, 'would help you buy me some time?'

'I'm sorry, Ms Mackinnon. I really tried, but my boss won't have it.'

'Is someone pressurising you? Does someone want my property?'

'Er, apart from my boss to get you to pay the overdraft?'

She would've shot him down for his jesting, but she didn't have the energy.

Russell cleared his throat. 'I'm sorry. But we're under strict orders ourselves.'

Was this it? Had the door locked before she'd had time to enjoy the breeze from the outside?

Back into a cubicle again.

Now that she'd smelled the fresh air, Aileen didn't want to go back to air-conditioning.

She gazed out at the scenery. Crisp, greenish brown grass glowed under the golden light of the sun. Those tall mountains dazzled every eye.

Could she leave this behind?

The cuckoo clock chimed – 3 p.m. Isla would just be taking out a fresh batch of chocolate eclairs about now. And Callan would come over for dinner in a couple of hours. She hoped.

Could she leave these relationships behind as well?

Aileen gnawed on her lip like a dog on a bone.

Bone.

Should she throw them a bone?

Her hands grabbed the phone in a death grip.

'Mr Russell!'

'Ms Mackinnon, I already told you. I cannot—'

Words spilled out of her before she digested their meaning. '£2,000. I'll pay you £2,000 tomorrow. Will that be enough?'

'£2,000... That helps, although considering the interest on the overdraft...'

'Great.' Aileen hissed from between clenched teeth. 'The rest will follow soon enough.'

Callan might hate her for this, but to hell with it! She'd rather he be angry with her than never see his annoyingly handsome face again.

Aileen jerked away from the seat, as if repulsed by the thought of sitting idle, and dived towards the small sheet of card, dog-eared from her worrying.

Schneider and Associates.

Every ring of the phone slammed into her heart.

Callan could keep his word, lock her up. What if Schneider meant her harm? Would she end up in jail?

'Hello?'

Aileen took a deep breath that did nothing to soothe her racing heart. 'Mr Schneider. I want to talk about Macalister's will.'

CHAPTER FOUR

'Aye, Callan. What've ye got?' Rory's candyfloss hair stuck out like Einstein's. His shirt sat skewed and there were dark circles beneath his eyes, like smudges made with charcoal.

'Schneider. Ken him?'

Rory raised an eyebrow. 'A friend of a friend. And the one my family will speak to when I'm...' He drew a finger across his neck. 'How's he linked to the arson case?'

Callan took a seat and told his boss the gist of his conversation with Aileen.

'Ken Macalister. Can't say I've heard of him. Did ye run him?'

'Ex-private investigator. Had applied to the force but worked with corporates. Perhaps for the money.' Callan placed a paper on Rory's desk. 'That's the report we have on him. He retired, shut down his firm fifteen years ago. He's a manager at a security firm now.'

'But no field work?'

Callan shook his head. 'No, he retired from it fifteen years ago, too.'

Rory plucked up a pencil and scribbled '2006'. 'Figure out if he was injured, suffered any ailment, got married or had a child. Any reason he would quit investigating and never get out into the field again.'

Callan had already planned to follow those lines of investigation but bouncing things off Rory kept him objective. If the perp had targeted Aileen, he needed to know and stay sharp.

And, Callan decided, until he caught them, he was keeping a close eye on her.

'I think I'll go talk to Schneider.'

Rory chuckled. 'And say what? Tell me how much the man left my girlfriend? For all we ken, Ken Macalister is alive and playing games.'

Aye, jumping to conclusions or assuming something at face value never helped. But until the lab came back to him, he had to do something.

Callan stalked out of Rory's office to his own.

Ken Macalister didn't have a long record. Not many spats with the police or pings on their radar. The man had a wife – an ex-wife as of three months ago.

Motive for murder?

The keyboard clattered under his inept fingers. 'Bloody hell! M, ye eejit, M for Macalister!'

Shaeline Macalister worked in accounting as a partner at what seemed to be a top firm in Stirling. Another close connection to Aileen.

Stirling... Where did Robert say Ken Macalister was from?

He dived into the work, dissecting every piece of information, every titbit, and plotted it out on the murder board. A private eye had enemies. But no one popped yet.

Callan dialled Amy's Rental and Taxi Services.

'Ready for the best ride of yer life?'

'Excuse me? This is DI Callan Cameron.'

'Hey! Did ye change yer mind about the calendar? I was thinking—'

'I wanted to ken if yer cars have a GPS tracker on them?'

Callan sensed the eye roll.

'Do you lot always work?'

For his girlfriend's safety? Yes. 'Can ye track the cars?'

'Nah.' Amy chuckled. 'I work on a cheap pricing model. I get more customers that way. Not enough profit to put fancy tech in. Trust is key. That's what I told the other sweetheart of a detective – that giant twit better not show his face here. I'll bankrupt him, I will. With one car up in flames, him taking off with the other, I'll be out on the streets by tomorrow!'

Chances were the man was bankrupt – bankrupt of life.

'Thank you.' Callan clicked the call off, not in the mood to listen to Amy moan.

He stared at the murder board. Two vehicles missing from Amy's Rental and Taxi Services. One had gone up in flames. Where was the other?

'The perp needed a getaway car. This one.' He pointed at the one Ken Macalister had rented out. A two-seater. 'This has to be it. They've got to have abandoned it somewhere. Hell!'

Footsteps pounded towards his office.

Callan swivelled and shouted, 'Robert, do yer exercise at the bloody gym!'

Robert peeked his head in, panting. 'Hey! MacNeill called. He says he wants ye at the garage.'

. . .

THE COLD AIR SMELLED OF ENGINE OIL AND GREASE. METAL creaked as it settled after a long day.

MacNeill waved from behind the hood of the vehicle. A bulb hummed overhead, just enough to splay sterile light over the wreck.

'We could've met tomorrow, but I've got to hustle. They need me at a scene in the next town.'

Callan nodded and took a minute to study the vehicle.

Its rear door appeared rusted. The fire had eaten the paint. Gaping jaws glared where glass had been, giving Callan a peek into the scarred skeleton of the interior. Grey matter glistened, highlighting the rubble, scraps of metal, and plastic the fire had molten. A haunted husk.

'What did ye want to show me?'

MacNeill straightened, a smirk on his face. His soot-covered white T-shirt and streaked blond hair meshed well with their surroundings.

'Since you're a friend of Walsh's and the lab technicians are driving you nuts, I thought I'd share my preliminary research.'

He pointed a finger at the front. 'As I said, our perp started the fire in the front after dousing the car in fuel. Petrol. But here's the interesting bit. From what I gathered based on the damage and photographs of the scene, the car had a single passenger.'

Callan narrowed his eyes. 'Passenger?'

'Aye, no driver.'

Callan peered through where the windscreen should've been. 'Why? Did ye find any rope, zip ties – anything that could have bound the passenger?'

MacNeill shrugged. 'I'm an arson investigator. But I don't believe there's much left – remember, the fire started from the front.'

He went to the other side of the car and pointed through the front void. 'The passenger sat on the left. If he or she had been bound, the fire would've burned zip ties or rope.'

He hardened his jaw. 'Based on the remains and my experience, the fire was intended to evaporate any trace of the person inside. The part diagonally behind the passenger's seat is better preserved than this bit.'

Callan observed the charred metal of the seat. Nothing tangible remained except for the seat's bones. Tufts of foam littered the back seat.

It was glaringly obvious the perp had come prepared. And the passenger... Ken Macalister?

He had no proof except for the circumstantial deductions he'd drawn. If only the lab would get back to him.

'Have ye concluded yer work, then?'

MacNeill nodded. 'I called you here for something else too. Strap in.'

Callan's gut grumbled with suspense, ticked off by the glint in MacNeill's eye. He didn't enjoy suiting up, but procedures were procedures, and he'd never contaminate a crime scene.

Dressed in scrubs, Callan hunched over onto the passenger side. The stale stench of chemicals and musk masked the horrid aftermath of the fire.

He'd never liked the remnants of a blaze, especially when it included murder.

Callan studied the metal rods, the exposed mechanisms and the burned dashboard. The floor lay in shambles. Debris from the destruction was scattered everywhere. Dust, scraps of metal, ash, substances Callan didn't want to name, and then—

'What the hell?'

He squinted when his shadow fell over the scarred

metal. He stuck his hands in his pockets and withdrew a small torch.

The brownish-gold metal glinted under the direct light, a sharp contrast with the grey dust.

Callan stuck his hand in the rubble and picked up the cylindrical casing.

'So that's how they kept the passenger from escaping? Bullets.'

MacNeill's smirk affixed on his face again. 'Here's the evidence bag. You might find a couple.'

Sure as hell, he did.

Callan dug around the muck, documenting it all as he went.

Bullet casings were made with brass, which withstood fire.

Callan counted three.

So their perp had had a weapon. A licenced weapon? If so, perhaps it could narrow down their suspect list – unless it was an illegal firearm.

Placing the evidence bags aside, Callan crouched beside the car again, keen to see if he could work out from which side the bullets had been fired.

Those damn lab technicians could take light years. He didn't have time.

Callan flashed the torch onto the left-side frame.

If the perp had shot the victim from the driver's side, that's where the bullet would've hit – assuming it had passed straight through of course...

He checked the left-hand-side frame again. Nothing, apart from the burn marks. No dents.

Callan stood up and went to the other side, the driver's side, and repeated the process there, but with the entire car so mangled by fire, it was hard to see anything.

At least they had bullet casings to study. That would also pinpoint the exact type of weapon used.

He flicked a glance at the interiors once again.

Shots fired from inside the car would cause a loud noise, enough to burst eardrums. Unless the perp had worn ear plugs.

MacNeill leaned against a nearby wall, typing on his phone. 'Satisfied?'

'Not until we catch the perp and clarify who the passenger was.'

Unfolding himself, MacNeill placed his hands on his hips. 'Good evidence collection and documentation'll get you to that goal.'

'I appreciate yer help, MacNeill.'

The man had a propensity to smile. This time, he spread his hands as wide as his grin. 'Anything I can do to help.'

Callan cocked his head. 'Did ye ken a Ken Macalister, too?'

'Ha ha! You're joking, right? The man can make you want to worship the soil he treads on and blast his brains out at the same time. Shame it all went to waste when he suddenly up and quit, you know.'

Callan blinked. He hadn't expected MacNeill to have a clue who he was talking about. 'And why did he do that?'

AILEEN'S FINGER TRACED THE EDGE OF THE CARD, HER teeth grinding against each other. The lamp's glow illuminated the cream paper. She studied the black ink again, tried to read between the lines.

'I really appreciate you staying on so late for me.'

He nodded in reply.

'What does he mean by "lost a child, a wife"?'

Over his steepled fingers, Schneider's beady eyes analysed her. 'What do you think, Ms Mackinnon?'

'He's a widower? He lost them in an accident?'

'I couldn't say.' He uncurled his fingers to reach for the tumbler of whisky at his elbow.

Night crept in through the windows. He'd left the curtains pinned to their holders. She had disturbed his quiet evening in, but the man didn't complain, saying his clients called with unusual demands any time of the night or day, and he catered to them.

That's what made him eminent.

She continued reading until every word hammered into her skull, etched into memory.

'"In death, I wish to repair my wrongs, turn a stone I was too weak to in life." What does that mean?'

Schneider shrugged. 'I was hoping you'd know.'

Hell! What *did* the lawyer bloody know?

'You said you've known him for a long time.'

'He had his will done twice in that time. Not exactly the premise for a strong bond of friendship. Acquaintance, yes. He and I were acquainted.'

The man spoke as if Macalister had indeed died.

Here she sat, reading the man's will.

Aileen held up the sheet of paper. 'Could I get a copy of this, please?'

Schneider leaned in. 'He might have confidence in your capabilities. However, you need to update me of your progress. As the will clearly states, if you find the person or people who murdered him, you get all his wealth. If someone else gets there before you, all bets are off.'

She clenched her fists into rock-hard stones. 'I have a track record, Mr Schneider. Don't worry – I'll find the killer and save my inn.'

Her grandmother's inn. The business she'd worked so hard to build after her own life had shattered.

Compare that to Aileen – terrified of losing her business, friends, and boyfriend. Siobhan had raised two boys without enough pennies in her purse.

And a fat diamond ring.

Aileen grinned despite the circumstances. Her gran was one woman even fate couldn't contend with.

Some of that resilience she'd passed on to Aileen – or so she hoped.

'What can you tell me about Macalister? You said he wrote his first will after he married. Who did he marry?'

Schneider chugged his drink and grimaced. He extracted the thick band he wore on his ring finger and held it to the light.

'Marriage, Ms Mackinnon, is fickle at best. It's more often wrenched by conflict than death.'

'You mean they divorced?'

'He didn't say so in as many words, Ms Mackinnon. But when a man reaches out to twirl the ring on his finger and it isn't there anymore… The sadness is as evident as a high fashion jacket in a small town.'

'What does his wife do? Former wife.'

Schneider ran a hand over his face, accentuating the tired circles and wrinkles. 'I never met her. I wouldn't know. When he first came to me, Macalister barely spoke. He couldn't string two words together. He handed me a sheet of paper with what he wanted done and sat there in silence while I arranged it.'

A picture of a broken man. That wasn't the person Aileen had hosted. Were they talking about the same person?

They were, Aileen knew, from Macalister's social-media

profile. A man with two distinct personalities. Which one was the real one?

She cleared her throat. 'Do you know anything about his private investigation firm?'

Schneider nodded. 'I filed some paperwork for him.'

Aileen raised an eyebrow as if to say, 'And?'

'I can't divulge client details—'

'You just said the man is dead. I need to know about him, more than an innkeeper does of her guests.'

Her questions didn't budge the man. He ducked under the table and squeaked open a drawer.

Something rattled, tinkled and ultimately: 'Ah!'

A shiny object clattered onto the desk.

Schneider straightened in his seat and passed the USB drive to her. 'All that I know about him is in there. And it's not much.'

Aileen didn't care. 'It's a starting point.'

THE DARKNESS CLOSED IN FROM ALL SIDES AS SHE DROVE home, steering the car from mere muscle memory.

When her headlights caught the stone fence, her heart thudded at a slower pace. Cutting off her car's engine let the deafening silence out to play.

Breath burned into smoke, fingers froze to icicles until her keys clicked in the lock and the back door shut with a satisfying click.

'Where have ye been?'

'Ah!' Aileen jumped back so far she slammed against the door. 'Oh God, Callan! Ye scared decades off my life.'

The man sitting at the counter didn't look amused or relenting. He stubbed one finger at the dark dining area. 'Last time ye left the inn unattended like this, a suspect waltzed in. And' – he stood up, every restricted moment showcasing the unused potential of his muscles – 'I sat right here, in this well-lit room, and ye didn't notice me. Is this what I've taught ye about self-defence?'

'Ca-Callan, please, I know how to—'

Bang!

Two iron-like palms slammed on the wall next to her ears. Those blue eyes, with their hint of grey, held a swirling storm. One that didn't bode well for her. 'If ye're so good, ye should've stopped me from caging ye.'

She hadn't even seen him move. Few 190-pound men moved with such agility.

'I saved the day last time!'

'And how do ye plan on saving yer arse and this inn from an eejit who plays with fire? Have ye thought about that? An eejit who might target ye, trap ye? Where were ye?'

Aileen raised her chin, trying to ignore the biceps almost bursting out of Callan's black T-shirt sleeves.

Their eyes met again. Aileen couldn't hide the emotion swirling around in hers and licked her dry lips. The fear had nothing to do with real fire and everything to do with the fire only he ignited in her belly. 'Callan.' It rang out like a moan.

They stood so close. If he dipped his head just a wee bit, Aileen could reach him and help him forget his temper.

A warm blush tickled her cheeks, evaporating any sign of the cold.

'Where were ye?' Each word whipped out like a leather belt, splintering through her daze. 'What were ye up to?'

'I-I…' Aileen's eyes darted around the room, hands reaching for her coat pocket, wanting to feel the USB drive.

Her hand slipped into the woollen fabric and wrapped

around the cold stick. 'Er, me? Nothing. Nothing. I headed out to meet Isla.'

Callan's smile resembled that of a tiger, right before it pounced on its prey. 'Funny. I didnae ken Isla had invited ye for a sleepover.'

Hell! She couldn't even lie. What time was it?

'One last time, where were ye?'

'I told you. Isla's.'

Aileen moved her hand an inch.

Wham!

An iron shackle clutched her wrist, the one holding Schneider's USB stick. 'What have ye got there?'

'No— Oh!'

His hand had found its way into her coat pocket. Pressed against the door as she was, Callan against her front, his hand inside her pocket sent her insides tingling.

A thumb stroked her fingers – a languorous, soothing stroke. Her grip loosened at his touch and the hand vanished.

Callan dangled the USB underneath her nose.

The grinding of teeth reached her ears. Aileen met hard, burning eyes.

'Oh, hell no!'

'Please, Callan! Don't be childish. Hand the drive over.'

'I told ye. It's dangerous, stay safe, and what did ye do? Took a bloody murder case when we agreed we knew nothing about that man!'

'He's dead! And I will not hurt myself.'

'Really?' The whisper echoed through the walls like smoke. 'Is that what happens every time we solve a case?'

'I need the money!' *I need to stay here, with you.*

'There are several ways to make money. Solving an unknown man's murder isn't one of them.'

'It takes time to build a business and a moment to see it shatter. I won't let my gran's efforts go to waste.'

'Good things take time, Aileen. Compromise is key. Understanding each other's needs and *honouring* them ensures survival. But you? Ye clearly don't care about cutting one to save the other.'

'What? That's not what I'm doing! I'm trying to save this life – this life that includes everything I want.'

'Do ye ken how much Macalister has left ye?'

'No, but it'll be enough to save the inn.'

Callan gave her a smirk, the one where he lifted the left side of his lips. It grated on her nerves. 'And ye believe him?'

She might've been a naïve woman clutching at straws, but she needed this. And Callan couldn't stop her. 'Relationships also take understanding and support.'

Callan's hands moved to her shoulders, squeezed. 'I can't let ye get mixed up in this. It all comes back to ye. It's like ye're the unextractable link in it all.'

'Then let me solve it. I'll consult with the police. *And* practise my defence skills every day.'

She sounded like a child making a deal with her parents. Callan did act like her guardian sometimes. Thick-headed eejit.

'Somehow, I don't believe ye. Because unlike someone, I have the facts. Ken Macalister isn't someone ye'll jump after from a running train because he said so. The man, while good at his job, proved unreliable in the end.'

Aileen frowned. 'Who told you all this? The lawyer I spoke to said he was a talented man.'

'Ah!' Callan held up a finger. 'What I think we agree on is that Ken Macalister was a man of contradictions. Things were never as they seemed with him.'

Aileen crossed her arms over her chest. 'How do you know that? How do you know anything about him?'

Callan held up his phone. 'I might have information.'

'If you share it with me, I'll share the USB stick.'

'Not good enough. The stick stays with me.'

Aileen imagined her fist connecting with those chiselled abs. 'I'll let you in on my investigation and my movements. Hell, you can install a tracking app on my phone.'

'All in exchange for information on Macalister?'

Aileen's gaze fell over the countertop, the darkness outside and the man in front of her. She drank him in and said, 'I'm willing to trade with the devil if it means I can save all that's dear to me.'

His tone softened then. 'And what's dear to you?'

Aileen swallowed the prickle in her throat. 'Please, Callan.'

Callan studied her for a minute. 'Ye won't stop, will ye?'

She shrugged.

He tucked a strand of hair behind her ears. 'Okay, *banlaoch*. Let's get cracking, shall we?'

CHAPTER FIVE

After catching a handful of criminals together and visiting too many hospital rooms, clutching flowers in one hand and his heart in the other, Callan knew when to resist and when to concede with his woman.

He might want to shake her like a bunch of flowers, but this was a Mackinnon woman. A special breed etched with stubbornness in their DNA.

Callan interlaced their fingers. 'If this case escalates and I tell ye to stop—'

'Callan.' Aileen pointed at the slick laptop on the kitchen counter. Her study, they both knew after the last time Callan had banged his head on the doorframe, wasn't ideal. Sitting in the kitchen – Callan munching on carrots and dip – satisfied his rumbling stomach and gave them space to spread out.

Aileen muttered to herself as she booted up her laptop. Various coloured pens littered the white countertop, cordoning Aileen's trusty yellow notepad.

He smiled. Aileen Mackinnon wouldn't be herself without her quirks.

Aileen reached for a pen, tongue sticking out, and in her neat non-cursive hand wrote '04/01/2022' in the top right-hand corner.

No margins this time.

Callan slotted the stick into place, and a folder popped up on screen.

Aileen tilted her head. 'Schneider appeared too prepared for someone being told I wouldn't take the case.'

'Perhaps it's a reason ye shouldn't. But deaf ears.'

'Excuse me?'

'Deft fingers. Ye're brilliant with the laptop…'

She shot him a glare, informing him she'd heard his original words, and squinted at the laptop again. Callan didn't bother reading the information as she scrolled through it.

He might've read up on some things, but he didn't scroll or read as fast. Some skills were best left to the tech expert, aka his girlfriend.

Callan pulled out his own notepad. Nothing like good old paper. It didn't go missing – he'd always find it under the stacks and stacks of it in his office. Eventually.

Elias Schneider stood first on his list of people to run through the database. Shiny shoes didn't guarantee clean soles.

Ken Macalister came up next. His dichotomic aura drew as many eyeballs as opinions of the man.

He'd known death was nigh, so he'd orchestrated an elaborate scheme. A game Aileen had to play on his terms.

What did people with no family do with their estate? Hand it to a stranger in exchange for salvation?

Why not employ a private investigator? Pay them a

fixed fee and that was the job done. Better yet, approach the police. He'd played it as if the problem at hand surpassed the enormity of his murder. What could be more important than that? Callan had an inkling he wouldn't like the answer to that last question.

He furrowed his eyebrows. 'Are ye sure the man who stayed here was the same man who visited Schneider?'

She answered with a single nod, a signal she was in deep. Judging by the brown locks curtaining her face and said visage almost kissing the marble counter as she scrolled and wrote at the same time, she'd behead him if he disturbed her.

A chime from the cuckoo clock informed Callan of the time. He scratched his head. 'Do ye have the copy of the will?'

A palm smacked against his notepad, fluttering the pages. 'Shut. Up.'

'Did ye find something?'

'Apart from the fact Macalister left everything to his wife in the previous will? He left that will unchanged for thirty-five years. And now he's given it all to me. After *thirty-five* years?'

'A sudden change of heart? I need to read the will.'

A dog-eared piece of paper slammed in front of him. He'd pulled the nib on that grenade.

If she was sauntering into a storm, he needed to assess the danger first. Prepare for it. Even if plans went awry, he would be ready.

His eyes traced the words, eyebrows joined until his head hurt. 'Ever considered this man might have been hunting a serial killer?'

Aileen twisted her head to throw him an incredulous look. 'Don't be ridiculous.'

Callan pointed to the last passage. 'I'm not sure ye read this, then.'

Use it to find my killer, use it to find the person who's robbed several families of their fullest life.

What did that bloody mean?

'Not a word in here makes sense, except for the fact that Macalister knew he would die.'

Aileen slammed the laptop screen down. 'Schneider's information is useless. There's nothing in there at all barring payment details and a draft of his previous will.'

Callan scratched his jaw, finding solace in the prickly touch. 'Who's paid? What's the amount?'

'I think those rates are justified for thirty-five years ago. Macalister's paid them himself.'

'With his wife?'

'A joint bank account.'

Callan reached for his notes again. 'Who did they consult for the divorce?'

'Not Schneider. He told me they met only twice.'

Macalister had another lawyer then, one not in Loch Fuar. Schneider he'd employed to get his will right. 'What if Macalister made more wills?'

Aileen swivelled in her chair so that her knees brushed against his thighs. 'Do we know where he lived? Macalister?'

'Stirling. Have his address right here.'

'Why would he have a solicitor in Loch Fuar, then?'

'For you?'

Aileen pushed away from the table. 'Oh God, oh God. I wasn't even born thirty-five years ago.'

'Hold on – bloody hell!'

She whirled around, fire burning in those eyes. Callan dropped his carrot baton back on the plate.

'Hold on? Hold on? Isn't it odd, Callan? The man lives

in Stirling and travels to the Scottish Highlands to meet his solicitor? How many solicitors would a city like Stirling have?'

Definitely more than Loch Fuar. 'Maybe Schneider and he were pals?'

'Pals know more about each other than what the man paid for your services thirty-five years ago. Schneider said they'd only met twice.'

'And he could be lying.'

Aileen wagged a finger. 'No, no. The man comes to Loch Fuar twice. Once thirty-five years ago to make his will when he marries and then now. Now we might have to consider he's left more wills. So why would someone leave multiple wills? Macalister came here for something, and that's what got him killed. We know that.' She panted, chest heaving like she'd climbed Ben Nevis. Eyes wide, fingers trembling, hair in disarray, she looked like the devil – a devil he wanted to grab and soothe.

Focus, Cameron!

'Let's not jump to conclusions. We need to ken more about Ken Macalister.' He stood and went to Aileen. 'There could be several reasons he chose Schneider. Let's see where he lived before he married, where they lived after. We'll talk to the wife and figure out if there are other wills.'

Aileen's shoulders drooped. 'Yeah, I want to know about his business, too. Private investigation can be risky. That's one area in his life he could have massive regrets about.'

'An unsolved case.'

'Yes, but... Hey! How did you know he owned his own private investigation firm?'

'A preliminary run on the man. Remember, I told ye I have an informant? He confirmed it.'

Aileen narrowed her eyes. 'Call him here. I make excellent coffee.'

'He's leaving soon. But I can ask.'

CALLAN GRITTED HIS TEETH AND LET THE PHONE CLATTER onto the countertop right next to his cold mug of coffee.

Aileen eyed him over hers. 'He's not coming, is he?'

'He can't. They needed him in the next town, so he left early this morning.'

Callan rubbed his eyes. 'He told me he has more, but insisted he'd tell me later. Bloody eejit loves suspense. He could've just told me everything yesterday.'

Aileen's coffee cup joined his. 'Well, at least he sent you the report.'

'How do ye ken about that?'

He didn't like her smirk. 'You griped about it all night while I, like any normal human being, was trying to sleep.'

'That was at 4 a.m.'

'That's not morning – it's the middle of the night.'

Callan sighed. Why did she always grumble about his alarm? Wasn't four a reasonable time to get up? He said as much to her.

'No, it's not,' Aileen whipped out.

Callan raised his cup. 'Coffee?'

'Perhaps if you slept, you wouldn't need it so much.'

She dumped the rest of the liquid from the coffee pot into his cup and waved. 'Drink up – we need to find out more about Ken Macalister.'

'And where do ye think we should go? The local library?'

He'd run Macalister in the system again, hope something pinged. After checking his record once, it was a long shot, but maybe if they found someone who knew him, personally or professionally, they'd catch a break.

Not bloody likely.

'What did I just say about sleep? It also keeps your brain sharp.'

Callan curled his lip. His brain had assisted in plenty of murders and could remember things better than most machines. 'I'm fine, thank you.'

When she tilted her head and smirked, Callan wanted to wipe it off with a retort. He failed.

'If you were, you'd recall someone in your backyard who's from Stirling.'

'Apart from Macalister?'

'Oh, yes.'

AILEEN BRACED HERSELF AS SOON AS THE SWEET FRAGRANCE hugged her. But the impact of a freight train on steroids that was Isla McIntyre never came. A voice boomed from behind the wall of people. 'Finally! Come here.'

Aileen hurried past the long queue, shielding herself from the dirty looks shot her way, and found her best friend practising her daily dance of packing goodies and manning the till. Aileen smiled at Isla's red-headed nephew.

'Hey, Andrew.'

The teenager gave her a smile and blushed until he resembled the red velvet cupcakes he was placing inside a box.

'Hey *Andrew*?' Isla slammed into her, her green eyes sparkling with such mirth, they put emeralds to shame.

Her arms tightened around Aileen.

'You're strangling me.'

'That's the plan.' Isla pulled away. 'You get that man

there' – she wagged a finger at Callan – 'and forget about me?'

'How could I ever?'

'Don't you dare joke about it! I'll kill you, right after I'm done with this crowd.'

Being the owner of Loch Fuar's only – and best – bakery, Isla was always hustling. The mother of one had enough energy to run the place and exchange hot gossip.

Aileen eyed Callan who, despite the full Scottish breakfast he'd eaten, was now chewing on a puffed pastry, the ever-present cup of coffee snuggled in his other hand. 'Isla threatened to kill me! You're a detective.'

'I come in after the act's committed. Sorry.' And off her boyfriend went, still munching.

'*Urgh!*'

Andrew pulled off his apron. 'I'll deliver these on my way.'

'Careful!' Isla called out.

'Aren't I always?'

'I'll help her out until you're back.' Aileen tied the apron behind her back and stepped up to the till.

Like every time she'd helped, Aileen fit right in with Isla's choreographed moves. She manned the till; Isla packaged the items.

The line thinned, right as Callan plucked out his second pastry.

Isla sidled up to her. 'Don't you feed him?'

Aileen narrowed her eyes. 'I don't know where he packs it all.'

'Ever seen those muscles?'

Aileen pursed her lips, her head tilted to a side.

Isla wiggled her eyebrows. 'Ooh, that fun, huh? Try getting married, fighting and making up. That's *really* fun.'

'Oh god, Isla. You're worse than Siobhan.'

'Ha! Don't compare me to a ninety-year-old.'

Aileen needed to reconsider the company she kept. Highly unlikely, she thought. Crazy women they were, but women Aileen would fight tooth and nail for.

'I'm here to talk about the car that caught fire near Dachaigh.'

Isla's amused expression turned into a devilish smirk. 'Oh yes! You're solving this with Callan?'

Aileen shrugged. 'Eventually, I hope. Ken Macalister. I need info on him.'

Frowning, Isla passed the package to a customer and held up a hand. 'Ken Macalister. Mac… Five minutes, my office.'

It took her ten, but Aileen didn't mind. The big playpen, which swallowed more than half of the office, lay empty. The miniature food showpieces and cream walls welcomed Aileen with open arms.

Another thing she'd miss if…

'Oh God, you won't believe the lad! You free him from potential imprisonment and now he wants to live his best life. God help me.'

Callan looked up from his cup of coffee. His third cup of the day. 'He's nineteen.'

'Eighteen and a half. But I need something to wipe that gooey-eyed look from his face.'

Aileen chuckled. 'Gooey-eyed? Hold on, is Andrew in love?'

Isla raised her arms. 'Crime. Tell me something that's not sweet.'

Callan set the cup down and raised a hand. 'I can't divulge details…'

Isla shut him off with a wave. They all knew she'd take precisely a second to find out from another source.

'Schneider likes my eclairs as well. I know what this is about.'

The queen of gossipmongers had proved herself.

Isla shot Aileen a glare. 'It's a shock, you know, when someone tells you things about your best friend and you don't know them already.'

'I was, er, busy.'

'Busy, my arse!'

Callan leaned in, cutting off their staring contest. 'What did Schneider say?'

'He's a nice sort of man. Predictable with his order. I've known him ever since I came here. He helped Daniel and me file permits for the bakery.'

'What did he tell you about Ken Macalister?'

Isla frowned, turning to Aileen. 'Ken Macalister. So I heard correctly. Schneider wouldn't betray his client's trust. He didn't tell me names, but when he asked me about you, I knew you'd met him.

'A car burned down near the inn. You don't come here after or call, but meet Schneider. I figured it's linked. But Ken Macalister. What about him?'

Aileen pulled out her yellow notepad. 'What do you know about him?'

'I'm not sure I know *your* Ken Macalister.'

Callan held up a hand. 'What do ye mean? How many Ken Macalisters would ye ken?'

'No one from Loch Fuar.'

'Isla.' Aileen drew her attention. 'I'm looking for a man named Ken Macalister from Stirling.'

Pulling out his phone, Callan sat it on the table between them. 'This man.'

Isla's eyes narrowed on the face before widening in horror. 'That's... It can't be... Oh God! He was the man in the car?'

'We've told no one there was a person inside.'

'Callan, please.'

Callan ran a hand through his hair, muttering curses. 'Isla, tell us about the man.'

She massaged her forehead before speaking. 'Ken Macalister. Aye, I know this man. He... He was best friends with my dad. They loved fishing together. He was always at my house. Him and his wife. Although, he was around more than her.'

Ken Macalister also knew Isla's father?

'Did he visit you here?' If Isla had put in a good word for Aileen, it could explain why he'd trust her to solve his murder.

Isla's forehead wrinkled. 'Why would I meet him here? He lives in Stirling. And I'm not sure he knows I live here either. We didn't keep in touch after Dad passed.'

Callan scribbled something on his notepad. 'Did he come to Loch Fuar often?'

'Not that I'm aware of. They moved next door when I was about five. He didn't have children, but loved to spend time with me and my siblings. Gave me piggyback rides and had this cool magnifying glass. Oh, he worked as a private investigator.'

Aileen would've noticed Isla's eyes turning into mossy pools if she weren't so stuck on what Isla had said. 'Hold on. No children? That makes no sense at all. He mentioned he'd lost a child.'

Isla blinked, a tear spilling down her cheek. 'No, he had no children. Just him and his wife. I know.'

Aileen scribbled down "children?" into her notes. Why would he say he'd lost a child if he had none?

'Maybe his wife had a miscarriage. Or could it be metaphorical?' Isla blew her nose. 'He had something like a child? Perhaps the firm he closed down? It changed him, that experience.'

Callan tapped his pencil on the notepad. 'I don't think so. But what do ye ken about the firm?'

'Not much. I didn't pay attention to those things as a twenty-year-old. One day he worked there and then I heard him say he'd found a job elsewhere. He had to commute longer for it, sometimes got home at midnight. My room faced their driveway and his car's headlights woke me up sometimes.'

Aileen wrote it all down, wondering if Isla might remember anything else. Anything of importance. 'How was he?'

Isla wiped another tear. 'A nice, happy man. He doted on my younger brother and sister. Brought us presents if he ever went away on business trips. Like I said, he had no children of his own but loved to spend time with them.'

'Where did ye say he lived?'

'I'll send you the address.'

LATER, AILEEN STARED AT THE ADDRESS. 'ARE WE GOING TO Stirling?'

Callan frowned. 'Why don't I call the ex-wife? She's kept the house, right?'

'And warn her so she prepares a nice sob story?'

'Aileen, I can't go. Not without proof this is our man in the car.'

Aileen smiled with an ounce of shrewdness. 'In that case—'

'I can't send ye off alone.'

'I'm not a child!'

'We don't know this man.'

'Isla does, Callan. Besides, you aren't the boss of me.'

He argued and griped, but to Aileen it was either find out who killed Macalister or haul her arse back to the city. She had no choice. She'd deal with Callan later.

'Let me plug the address into the GPS.'

Scouring the route to Stirling while your grumpy boyfriend argued in your ear didn't help. Callan refrained from plucking her phone out of her hands, though.

He knew the repercussions of her not solving the case first.

'Stay here just a wee longer. I'll come with ye after we get a match for Macalister.'

'I have to solve this before anyone else, Callan. That's the deal.'

'This is not a bloody video game!'

She zoomed out a bit; studied the map again. 'I fail at this, off I go to the city.' She faced him. 'Is that what you want?'

Callan ran a hand through his hair. Despite the close crop, his hair stuck out in all directions. 'When do ye leave?'

'In an hour. Chop-chop.'

She packed a weekend bag in half an hour. But by then Callan was insisting she took a train instead.

A train passed through Loch Fuar twice a day, and she would need to change at Glasgow. And the whole rigmarole would take twice the time a car would.

She'd driven herself here, hadn't she?

'You get yer things; I'll inspect the car.'

She let him be, checking if she'd packed her laptop, charger, torch and spare batteries. Isla had arranged for someone to take care of the inn while Aileen was away.

She'd go prepared and – she promised Callan – she'd share her location with him.

He kissed her, as if she were driving away forever. 'Come back in one piece. Any trouble and I'll lock ye up.'

Aileen pecked his lips again. Rough he was, but then again, that's what she liked about him, wasn't it?

She shut the door and faced Callan. 'I'll find something on him, I assure you. I'll find out who killed him and save Gran's inn. Save us.' She muttered the last bit to herself before pulling out onto the road.

What awaited her in Stirling?

CHAPTER SIX

Callan read MacNeill's report, struggling to get his mind off Aileen. He wanted to go see the ex-wife himself.

Damn procedures!

His email pinged. The bastards had woken up.

The lab technician, Callan was pleased to discover, had gathered the human remains and was running a DNA test on them. They had also sent evidence to a forensic odontologist. The DNA tests, unfortunately, would take two or more days.

He needed those damn reports right now, not tomorrow. Someone had died. Hell!

The phone rang, startling Callan. 'Bloody hell! It better be the lab—'

'Callan.'

Robert.

'I'm at the ELV yard. I think ye'll want to see this.'

Callan shut his eyes. Another case? 'I'll be there.'

. . .

LOCH FUAR'S ONLY ELV YARD SAT TWENTY MINUTES FROM the outskirts of town, close to the peatlands where a group of environmentalists had gathered to campaign for its protection. An entire police team, environmentalists and the Scottish weather never bode well for his dead best friend.

Blaine...

Callan's fingers fisted into blocks of ice.

They were to resume their search for Blaine after the holidays. That would be any day now. But with the winter mist blanketing the peatlands, their search would injure more than help.

Callan buried thoughts of Blaine Macgregor in a dark pit in his mind. A pit that needed a door with five deadbolts.

His SUV – his pride and joy – hugged the winding road. Its headlights failed to cut through the fog, but still Callan didn't slow down. Raindrops slashed onto the windscreen, muddying it and hindering his vision.

Bloody Highland winters! And Aileen planned to drive through this weather to the Lowlands.

Headstrong woman.

A jumble of red and blue lights surged through the grey.

The sound of metal and glass crunching as a machine crushed an end-of-life vehicle sent a tingle down his spine.

Callan thrust his fingers into gloves and pulled a beanie on his head to save his freezing earlobes before stalking over to the yellow-vested officer.

'Fancy salvaging a car, Robert?'

Robert turned, mouth agape. 'Not really. I've already been out here too long, and it's Baltic.'

The wind freezing his face didn't make him envy Robert. They had no time to complain. 'Get on with it.'

Robert pointed to one heap of reddish-brown metal; the mist swirled around its peak. 'The number plate stuck there...'

Callan had already spotted it and noticed the obvious. 'Far too clean and uncrumpled to belong to a recently crushed ELV.'

'Aye. It caught the manager's eye. They were to transport this heap to the recycling plant today.'

Callan memorised the number, then reached into his photographic memory and matched the sequence with Ken Macalister's car. The one he'd yet to return to Amy.

'Any sign of the two-seater car those plates belong to?'

'How do ye— Never mind. Ye want me to search for a two-seater in this weather?'

Callan shot Robert a look. 'Does this place have cameras? Where's the manager?'

Once they had their new crime scene cordoned off, Callan set to work.

Robert led him to a singular structure in the middle of the yard where the manager sat in his toasty office.

Hands in mittens, his orange vest discarded on the stacks of papers next to his desk, the man sat sipping from a metal flask. Callan could bet it wasn't coffee or water.

'Something ye're looking for?'

Callan hitched a hip on his desk. A desk littered not with papers but sweet wrappers.

'What made ye call the police?'

The manager, Bob, raised a finger dirty with grease, mud under the fingernail, to his temple and scratched. 'New plates. They don't look like that after we crush them. Besides, someone had broken the lock on the gates. Reckon it were a bunch of lads or Toby, the minced wee shite, forgot to lock up. I let it slide. Then I saw the plate and reckoned you lot would like to look at it.'

'Ye reckoned right. Have you issued a certificate of destruction for a car with that plate?'

'I checked and no, we don't have a car with that number plate, not in our database.'

So they wouldn't have anyone coming to pick up a certificate. But even if the car wasn't here, someone had still dropped off the plates.

'Does this place have CCTV?'

Bob snorted a laugh. 'In this mist? Ye'd be lucky to see yer own nose.'

He would leave no stone unturned and so he got Bob to hand him the footage.

Despite the fingers of alcohol Bob might've drunk, he was right about the mist.

Bloody Highland weather!

He wanted to tug at his hair, but he'd been doing that a lot lately, too. It wasn't as satisfying anymore.

Damn it!

Callan found Bob in his chair, now studying a file, his metallic flask stuck to one hand. 'Who kens which lot of cars are to be crushed next?'

Bob waved a hand. 'Toby's got a big mouth. He needs the cash. Hand him a tenner and he tells all.'

'This place is quite far out of town. I'm sure people don't just come and hang out. Anyone new been by recently? Any regulars asking too many questions?'

Bob shrugged. 'Nah, just the usual.'

Callan raised an eyebrow, indicating he should elaborate, but got no response.

'Who are yer usual customers?'

'Any person who buys old cars or scraps them, or the officers from the Environment Agency who come to inspect the vehicles.'

Callan huffed, his annoyance increasing with every word. Another dead end.

'If ye remember anything, get in touch.' Callan placed his card beside a half-eaten chocolate bar.

He headed out into the freezing cold and spotted Robert. 'Anything?'

'In these aisles full of rusted dump? Do ye ken people from all over the county come here to get rid of their ELVs?'

Callan rubbed his nose. They had all day. 'It's just passed noon. Let's make the most of the daylight.'

They split up, Callan taking the second aisle and Robert the first. Their mission: to locate a pale lavender two-seater. How difficult would it be to find such a vehicle?

Through the withering fog, with stacks of metal and lined cars disappearing into the mist, it was as difficult as it could be. The cold didn't help; neither did remembering that Aileen hadn't called yet.

His tracking app confirmed she'd get to Stirling in about an hour and a half.

'Sir!' A scrub-wearing crime scene technician ran up to him. 'We're almost done at the scene. Would ye like to have a look?'

The extra layer of white scrubs didn't help keep the icicles at bay, but the mask on his face thawed his nose somewhat.

He ducked under the police tape and went straight to the pile.

The pieces of metal at the bottom were a dark maroon. The glass from a crushed windshield created a kaleidoscope of criss-crossed strings. Someone had known these cars would meet their demise today. That meant the eejit had wanted to get rid of the number plate with haste.

Why just the number plate, though? Where was the damn car they belonged to?

The mist finally cleared out, thanks to the sun making a brief appearance. It also made things clearer to see.

A large yellowish-brown skip sat next to the stack, perhaps where the pile of cars Bob had destroyed yesterday had been.

The aisles of trash were piled closely together. If this was the only ELV yard in the region, it would be busy.

The number plates, two of them, Callan noted, were at eye level, tucked between two plates of rusted metal.

He raised his gloved hands to the metal and inspected the plate.

Brand new or recently cleaned. Two holes at the sides told him someone had unscrewed the plate with care. And ensured the plate didn't dent. Every number and letter shone back at him.

Callan studied the entrance.

Someone had broken the lock, gained access. Would a drunk eejit unscrew a number plate with such care and place it here without denting the plate?

Someone had assumed Bob wouldn't call the police over something so trivial.

They'd dumped the plates here for fear of being caught or they were smart and trying to lead the police astray. Why place these right here, where they'd stand out in all this garbage?

Callan left those questions reverberating in his head, ducked under the police tape, and stormed towards the entrance.

He saw the cut chain Toby or Bob had tied around the gate. The place didn't have state-of-the-art security. They didn't need it, considering ELVs came here when no one had any use for them.

Robert appeared beside him. 'I had no luck. I checked the third aisle as well.'

Callan nodded at him. 'Get some coffee. A crime scene tech brought a flask.'

'Had some already, or I'd be dying of hypothermia right this second.'

'I don't think this person left the car here. Just those plates.'

And why would they do that?

Callan pointed to the pothole-filled road. 'Someone drove up that road in the dark, cocksure the cameras wouldn't pick them up. Broke the chain, which leads me to believe they knew how this area's locked up, had the equipment to break the chain – not' – he held up a finger – 'pick the lock. Drove to the exact pile Bob would dispose of today and hid the number plates there.'

Robert crossed his arms over his chest. 'Either that's stupid or very arrogant. Ye think our man's done this before?'

Callan scratched his jaw. 'He or she clearly has no qualms about breaking rules. But disposing of these number plates tells us one thing for sure.'

Robert quirked an eyebrow.

'Ken Macalister is almost certainly the man in the burning car. And the person who likely killed him has his rental now with no number plate on it. Or a new fake number plate. Because they want that car hidden.'

'Wouldn't it be better to just ditch the ride, maybe light it up too?'

'Not if it's got evidence in it they want to preserve. Let me call the lab techs; let's see if they have Ken Macalister's records. They should be able to match the DNA quicker.'

❄

'HEAD STRAIGHT FOR 100 METRES AND YOUR DESTINATION will be on the right.'

Aileen's legs screamed to be set free. She'd been driving for what felt like five days but was really only five and a half hours. The frosty roads had slowed down traffic to a crawl in some localities, but at least she'd beaten the rush-hour traffic.

Her stomach let out a growl. She hoped Macalister's ex-wife would be hospitable and invite her in for tea.

Aileen rolled her eyes. If the woman was home at all.

The houses on either side of the lane were only one storey tall. Most had white picket fences, and children's bicycles lay abandoned in a few gardens, glistening with raindrops.

A couple of students trudged up the road, busy with their animated conversation. Most driveways sat empty. Not surprising, given it was the last working day of the week…

Running an inn made you forget.

Aileen slowed her car to a crawl, reading numbers on each door until she reached twelve.

The house gleamed a whitish-cream despite the grey light. The curtains were drawn, and there was no car in the driveway, nor any bikes in the garden. And not a sign of the Christmas season just gone. A letterbox at the gate announced 'Shaeline Macalister' in bold gold letters.

So she hadn't changed her last name after the divorce. What had caused their thirty-five years of marriage to dissolve? Aileen didn't want to dig up old wounds. She wanted data, facts to find the person responsible for a stranger's death.

Aileen pulled up the handbrake and cut off the engine. Car or no car in the driveway, she had to knock.

Her boots hit the concrete, and her nose wrinkled. What was that smell?

She eyed a car puffing out smoke. City air. It wasn't as bad as Glasgow or Edinburgh, but not as pure as Loch Fuar.

She'd not been in town a minute and already she was spewing off complaints. What would she do if she had to return to the city? Moan all day long?

Her car door clicked shut and Aileen had half a mind to lock the doors. This wasn't small-town Loch Fuar.

Aileen put one foot in front of the other, eyeing the wet footpath. Cobblestones in such weather glared at her like harbingers of doom. Slip and she'd be on her arse with no one to help.

The gate creaked as Aileen pushed it open to alert a resting dog next door. It reared its head and flashed its teeth at her.

She slunk lower until the dog stopped barking.

Cold gravel crunched under her feet, and a crisp breeze blew tendrils of hair into her eyes.

The air wasn't cool enough; the trees weren't inviting enough and the grey light... Aileen groaned.

'Get on with it!' she hissed to herself.

The buzzer, a circular button mounted next to the doorframe, twinkled in the light. Had the woman redecorated after the divorce?

Aileen pressed and heard the buzz.

No one was home. Maybe she should peek through the windows?

She tapped her foot to keep it from leading her to a window. Peeking into stranger's homes was stalker behaviour. And she wasn't a stalker.

Would a very brief peek count? Just a second...

Her tapping stopped. 'Urgh!' And her feet moved of their own accord.

Aileen caught sight of a large sofa set, a coffee table, a TV to match the—

'Excuse me!'

Aileen jumped, spinning round. 'Ms Macalister?'

The woman wore her hair in a strawberry-blond bob. She'd chewed most of her red lipstick off, and her wrinkled cheeks bloomed with a blush, her grey eyes wide. 'Who are you?'

One wrong word, and Aileen's arse would land on the cobblestones. She extended her hand. 'I'm Aileen Mackinnon.'

Shaeline tilted her head. 'And? Do you have another occupation than peeping into people's houses?'

'I wasn't... That's not what I... I'm looking for Ms Shaeline Macalister.'

A chic eyebrow rose. 'Why?'

'Er, it's a...' She'd driven for almost six hours and yet hadn't planned what to say. Should she say Shaeline's ex-husband was dead? Without evidence? Idiot! What happened to good old plans?

'Mr Macalister. I'm here about him.'

Shaeline flicked her hair out of her eyes. 'I've nothing to do with him. We settled our affairs fair and square.'

He's dead.

Aileen bit her lip. She couldn't say that. 'It's, er, I, er, I wanted to see his documents.'

The woman froze. 'Who did you say you were?'

'Aileen – Aileen Mackinnon.'

Shaeline looked at her with raised eyebrows. Then she raised her phone, her freshly applied pink nail polish glinting under the disappearing sun. 'You've got thirty seconds before I call the police.'

Aileen eyed the woman again. Her trouser suit, made with wool, hugged her figure. A pendant glinted at her neck and matched her earrings.

This is who Aileen would've been if she'd stuck with her old life. Distaste soured her tongue. She didn't want to be like this.

'I'm sorry to inform you, but I believe Ken Macalister is dead. I'm here to find out who killed him.'

'Dead? Ha! Why, that's the single most preposterous thing I've heard all day – and I've spoken to a politician today.'

'He asked me to investigate his death in his will—'

Shaeline's eyes sparkled. 'Will? Where did you get Ken's will? He's as warm and breathing as a bun fresh out of the oven. Now please leave before I call the police.'

'But, Ms Macalister…'

'You have no right to say such things. No right to anything. Will, you say? How did you get access to such a thing? Who are you?'

'I…' A flash of red and blue caught Aileen's eye. She whirled around to see a police vehicle halting right in front of the gate. 'You called the police?'

Shaeline curled her lip and pointed to Aileen. 'She's trespassing, officer, and saying the most absurd things. She tried breaking into my house!'

'No, I didn't!' Aileen's protest squeezed out of her throat in a squeak. 'You must believe me!'

The police officer stalked towards them. She had her hair in a tight bun, a frown on her face, her eyes hard. 'Miss, what's your name?'

Aileen opened her mouth to protest, but the officer raised one hand. 'Ms Macalister lives here. If she doesn't want you on her property, you can't force her.'

'You don't understand. I'm here about her husband—'

'She says Ken's dead! Dead?' Shaeline wailed. 'Who told her anything? And she's looked at his will! Investigate his murder? This woman's mad and she's a stalker, trying to break into my house…'

'I didn't!'

Aileen's protest fell on deaf ears – literally, as Shaeline screeched so loud a few curious heads peeked out from windows.

A blush crept from Aileen's neck to her ears.

The police officer, clearly not happy with the situation, stabbed her thumb at the car. 'Why don't you come with me?'

'I didn't break in…'

She waved her hands. 'We'll sort this out at the station. Ma'am, if you'll please follow us there?'

'Arrest her!'

What the—! Had this woman lost her mind?

Talk about mind and mouth connection. Aileen had failed.

A firm hand caught her arm. 'Mackinnon.' The officer led her to the car and, unlike Callan or Robert, opened the back door for her. The one made for criminals.

Lord, help her now and damn her tongue.

Crap! Hell! Shit!

DETECTIVE INSPECTOR SPIERS EYED HER OVER THE REPORT she'd been reading.

'Well, I have to read you your rights.' And so she began.

Blood roared in Aileen's ears, deafening her to the words. A criminal – Aileen was a criminal.

What did they know? Why was Spiers reading her her rights?

'Do you understand your rights, Ms Mackinnon?'

Aileen crossed her arms over her chest. 'You have to believe me, Detective, I meant no harm. I'm here about Mr Macalister.'

Spiers held up a hand. 'Let me get this straight. A car burns down in front of your inn.'

'Next to.'

'*Next to* your inn, and a guest who stayed with you was likely in that car? This guest then rears his head from the grave and leads you to a lawyer who reads his will. A will where he's mentioned you and left you everything.'

'Yes.' Aileen nodded. 'That's the gist of it.'

'Children's fairy tales are more believable, Ms Mackinnon.'

'I'm not lying! You can call Schneider and Associates.'

'I'll do that. But I'm not inclined to believe them either. For all I know, this Schneider man is in league with you to harm Ms Macalister.'

Aileen rubbed a hand over her face.

They sat in the interview room. She'd never been on this side except when she'd had to give a witness statement. She'd never been a blasted criminal. Oh God!

If they sent her to jail, Dachaigh would fail for sure.

She imagined strangling her mouth and chided herself for being ridiculous. Her ridiculousness had landed her here!

Aileen gnawed on her lip. 'I have a copy of the will, too!'

A knock sounded at the door. The police officer who'd brought her in stuck her head through the small gap. 'A word, please?'

Spiers left, leaving Aileen to her spiralling thoughts. She hadn't called Callan, partly because they'd taken her phone away and because she knew he'd lose his mind. She didn't want him driving down here to get her out. It would be a massive embarrassment for him and her.

The loud ticking of the clock felt like thorns pricking her skin. Sweat trickled down her neck. Had they turned up the heating?

Five o'clock. How much longer would she have to stay here? She needed to book a hotel. Finding decent accommodation at such short notice on a Friday night might be hard.

Just her damned luck. When would her stars align?

The door opened and in strutted Spiers. Not soon, judging by the expression on the woman's face.

She pulled out her chair. The scraping of metal on hard concrete grated on Aileen's nerves. She intertwined her fingers, scratching the back of her hand.

Spiers broke the silence. 'What did you say about Ken Macalister? He stayed at your inn?'

Her tone was nonchalant, as if they might've been chatting in the park, but something glinted in Spiers' eyes, something strange.

'Do I need a lawyer?'

'Have you committed a crime?'

Was it a crime to help a murdered man? Aileen shook her head. 'No, I haven't.'

Spiers nodded once. 'How do you know Macalister is dead then? The truth this time, please.'

Aileen blinked. So this woman didn't believe a word she'd said. 'A lawyer. I think I'll speak to my lawyer first.'

Spiers sighed and gave her a nod. 'Very well, Ms Mackinnon. Call your lawyer and let's hope he gets here post haste. Otherwise, you'll be spending the night behind bars.'

CHAPTER SEVEN

Thud!

Callan's fist connected with the papers on his desk. 'Finally!'

The words glared back at him. DNA samples found in the car matched Ken Macalister's perfectly. His ticket to Stirling.

He jumped up from his chair and strode over to Rory's office. His boss was on the phone.

'Hm… Are ye sure? Okay…'

Callan tugged at his jacket, shuffling his feet to kill time. One nod from Rory and he'd be off.

The receiver clicked home.

'Rory—'

'Ken Macalister,' Rory whispered.

'How did ye ken it was him?'

Rory gestured to the seat in front of his desk. 'Sit. Coffee?'

Callan shook his head. 'What's this about?'

He'd seen his boss stressed, angry but never dejected.

'Aileen Mackinnon's in Stirling. The police caught her snooping around Shaeline Macalister's house.'

Why couldn't she ring the bell like a normal person?

'What did she do?'

Rory intertwined his fingers and regarded Callan for a moment. 'Tell me what she's doing there.'

He'd never lied to his boss. Rory had been more of a mentor to him, someone Callan owed a lot to. 'The car that was torched…'

Rory listened carefully, his face turning grimmer with every word.

'That's why she's there. And now, the DNA proves it's Ken Macalister.'

'That's the problem, Callan. She went to Ken Macalister's former house *before* we knew he was dead.'

'But I just told you. Schneider—'

'Detective Inspector Spiers doesn't believe her. I got a call from them, asking about Aileen and whether she's ever created any trouble here…'

Trouble? Unless someone counted the times she'd annoyed the hell out of him, she'd committed no crimes.

'I can get hold of the guest who was in the drawing room the day of the fire. Besides, we spoke on the phone and she was at Dachaigh then. I heard the cuckoo clock.'

Rory sighed. 'Ye better tell Aileen's lawyer that.'

Callan stalked to the door, insides burning like the sun. They'd arrested Aileen. For murder.

Dammit!

He pivoted and— 'Ouch!' Callan glared at his elbow. Couldn't it see the bloody handle?

The day had gone to hell.

'Who did ye say the detective was?'

'I'm afraid ye're off the case, Callan. Aileen's a suspect at this point and, well, ye're her boyfriend.'

'But—'

'No arguments. We have to take the legal paths to—'

'Name please, *sir*.'

Rory didn't like the use of that title.

'DI Spiers,' came the quick answer. 'Cheryl.'

Detective Inspector Cheryl Spiers worked in Edinburgh. What was she doing in Stirling?

Callan flashed his teeth. His stint in Edinburgh had come to some use. A face he knew, a detective he respected and who respected him.

His phone dialled itself, that's how fast he moved. The front door of the police station swung behind him, and the wind wasted no time in assaulting his exposed skin. Damn his jacket. Important things needed done.

The phone rang and then cut off. Crap!

His car skidded on the frozen road. Callan steadied it and flashed his headlights to signal any eejit idling on the road. Then he floored the accelerator, not bothering about rules.

Quaint rays of the sun fought with the night, leaving behind a dark maroon hue. Night or day, he'd get to Aileen. Tomorrow was his day off. In fact, his shift ended in fifteen minutes.

Like hell he'd leave her to rot in jail. Annoying she might be, but not a criminal, never a criminal.

The sound of grinding filled his ears. He tried to relax his jaw, but when the whitewashed inn came into focus, he lost sight of sanity.

Tyres skidding over the mud, he turned the SUV into the car park, pulled the brake and leaped out of the car, all in a single breath.

The back door opened to a redhead with wide green eyes. 'Callan! What's happened? Aileen—'

Callan dashed past Isla and up the stone steps. A

resounding *click* signalled Isla had shut the door behind him. Her quick footsteps followed his.

'What is it? What's happened? Why isn't she answering any of my calls?'

Callan strode through the corridor to the last room on the floor, grabbed the doorknob, and pushed.

The door didn't budge, though the plate that read 'Control Room' rattled against the wood.

Isla ran up next to him, bent over and panted, 'What… Wait. Keys!'

She plucked them out of the depths of her trousers.

The sound of the door unlocking resounded like a death knell.

Callan let the door open and bang on the shelves behind. He rushed to the computer in the corner and then paused, unsure where to start. 'Shit!'

As any sister would, Isla shoved him aside and smacked his arm. 'If you'd bloody tell me what's wrong, I'd help.' Without warning, she let her fist fly, landing it squarely in his stomach.

Callan massaged the spot.

'I was holding my punch. Now, you were saying?'

Women!

'Aileen's been arrested. They think she killed Ken Macalister.'

'She didn't!'

'I ken that! I need evidence. Surveillance tapes to show she never left the inn and the name of the guest she served that day. I can vouch for her of course, but we need an airtight alibi.'

And they had it. They just needed to gather the bloody evidence.

Isla raised a hand. 'We'll do that, but where is she now?'

He didn't know. Spiers hadn't replied either. And he wasn't bloody thinking straight!

'Wait, let me call someone I know.' She dialled so fast, Callan's head spun.

'Hey! Isla here...' she spluttered.

Callan toggled through the surveillance tapes, not paying attention to Isla's call.

The weight of what could happen, was happening right this second, crashed into him. Callan leaned against the door and clutched his stomach. Not in pain, but in terror.

Aileen would spend the night in a cell.

A soft hand landed on his shoulder. 'I have this lawyer friend. If Aileen needs her, she'll help.'

Callan opened his mouth to say she wouldn't need a lawyer, but Isla squeezed his shoulder. 'And we're going to Stirling.'

'Ye don't have to—'

'Aileen's my friend. I'll arrange with Barbara for someone to come here for two days. You're in no shape to drive five hours into the night on these roads.'

'Daniel—'

'Is coming with Carly. A fantastic road trip, isn't it?'

Callan blinked at Isla. Women were mental, absolutely mental. Then again, some tension leaked from Callan's shoulders. 'Thank you. I really appreciate it.'

'Friends, Callan.' She patted his back. 'Now, why don't we get that data and get to Aileen?'

WORKING OR NOT, NO ONE EVER ACCUSED CALLAN OF NOT pursuing a lead with fervour.

Daniel studied him through the mirror. Callan couldn't remember his life without his best friend in it. They'd had their share of disagreements, but they'd follow each other anywhere.

He hadn't questioned Callan, simply strapped his toddler in the back seat, shoved a few clothes in a bag, and picked them up at Dachaigh.

Callan clutched the USB stick in his palm; the other held his phone. Why wasn't Spiers answering his calls?

He realised now what it must feel like when he didn't answer Aileen's calls.

He ran a hand through his hair. His stomach let a growl, loud in the car's silence. Isla raised a packet from the front seat. 'Granola bar?'

Like a child clinging to their toy, he stared at the small drive in his palm. He let it drop into his coat pocket and reached for the bar.

Had Aileen eaten? Why hadn't she called to ask for help? Had Spiers not allowed her to? Had they processed her?

He chewed on the sticky bar, not willing to go down that road. Like Isla had said, he needed a clear head to study the situation with a detective's eye.

Daniel cleared his throat. 'Ye got everything?'

Callan nodded. 'I, er, emailed but haven't had a response.'

'We should be there in an hour tops.'

Night-time meant little traffic and no road blocks. It might've been freezing outside, but they'd make it. Before it was too late.

Every second went by achingly slowly. Callan wished he had the steering wheel in his hand and his foot on the accelerator. Daniel was being cautious, of course, and far saner than Callan.

The moment Daniel pulled into the police station's car park, Callan unbuckled his seat belt. He'd have admired the size of it if he was here for any other reason; the police cars and officers working the graveyard shift.

He jumped out of the car, not waiting for Isla or Daniel. Puffs of smoke burned out of his lungs, his face bright red as he pushed his way inside.

The warmth hugged him, making him shiver, but still he didn't halt. 'I'm here for DI Spiers.' Callan placed his badge on the desk. One situation where he would pull rank.

His abrupt arrival flummoxed the officer sitting at the desk. He blinked at Callan and fumbled for a button. 'I-I... A minute,' he mumbled before pressing the phone to one ear.

'A DI Cameron here to see you? Aye – er, aye. Black hair, black clothes, blue eyes. Okay.' He replaced the receiver. 'She'll be out in a minute.'

More footsteps echoed behind Callan as Isla and Daniel, Carly sound asleep on his shoulder, stepped in beside him.

'Well?'

The arrival of another pair of footsteps saved him from answering.

'DI Cameron, what a surprise!'

He faced the blond woman. The suit she wore was wrinkled, and coffee stained the white shirt underneath, along with what Callan presumed was ink. Her hazel eyes furrowed, taking in Carly on Daniel's broad chest.

Callan reached out a hand. 'I'm here about Aileen Mackinnon. I have proof she isn't your murderer, Spiers.'

Spiers frowned and extended an ink-stained hand. 'You do?'

He pulled out the USB drive. 'Aye.'

Isla and Daniel couldn't follow him to her office, so they headed to a hotel to crash for the night. Callan thanked them, to which they reminded him to call if he needed anything.

'We've booked two rooms. Get Aileen to the hotel when ye're done,' Daniel reminded him. 'We'll ask the hotel to send a taxi for ye.'

Aileen's loyalty had stood her in good stead.

Spiers' fingers clattered on the keyboard. Her office boxed them in. A third officer would have to stick his arse out to fit. And yet, her desk was devoid of loose papers.

Was she a witch?

Spiers squinted at the screen. Callan pointed to the footage. 'The inn has two doors. She doesn't leave through any. Besides, I called her at three-ish. I heard the clock chime.'

Spiers turned to him. 'She knew Ken Macalister was the man in the car.'

'She knew that because of, er, her deduction skills.'

'Deduction skills? You believe her?'

Callan tilted his head. 'Why wouldn't I?'

'It's absurd! That's why. A detective like you should know that.'

He reached into his coat pocket and pulled out a folded piece of paper. 'A letter from her guest, saying she was in the inn. She barely knew Macalister. She had no motive to take his life.'

Spiers set the paper aside and regarded him like a bug under a microscope. 'What about the will? Why would a man who didn't know her leave all his wealth to her?'

Callan shrugged. 'I haven't figured that out yet. She didn't know him. I'm not sure if the opposite is true, though.'

'So you're willing to provide her with an alibi?'

'As is her guest.'

Spiers cocked an eyebrow.

Callan swallowed the lump in his throat that refused to dissolve. 'She's my girlfriend and I believe her.'

A loud silence echoed throughout the room. Spiers' eyes widened. 'I see.'

'And she has a clean sheet. No motive to bring harm to a man she barely knows. And an alibi.'

Spiers clattered the computer keys again. 'Be that as it may, Cameron, she still trespassed on Macalister's property.'

'Bullshit,' Callan snapped. 'We both ken all she did was knock and see if anyone was home.'

Spiers chuckled. 'Shaeline said she was attempting a break-in.'

Callan huffed. 'She goes a bit overboard sometimes. She's *passionate*. We both ken if we came across this case, a case where the perp has no history, we'd reprimand them for such a crime and let them go.'

Spiers raised an eyebrow.

HER STUPID MOUTH! HER LAWYER? WOULD SHE TUCK HER tail between her legs and call her uncle, tell him she'd been arrested?

The door to the banal room opened, and the blond woman sauntered in again. Detective Spiers crossed her arms.

'I told you, I want my lawyer present.'

The detective tilted her head. 'You don't need a lawyer at the moment. You're free to go.'

Aileen blinked. Was this some joke?

Spiers gestured to the open door. 'Please.'

Aileen swallowed the questions. It was past midnight,

and she didn't want to irritate this woman into locking her up.

As if manoeuvring through a field of landmines, Aileen put one foot out the door. She watched Spiers from the side of her eye. No handcuffs in sight.

Her other foot joined the one outside. Were they playing her?

Another officer handed her things over. Seeing her jacket and phone, it struck her how close she'd come to jail.

The door buzzed shut behind her, then: 'Aileen.'

She turned to find Callan, his eyes rimmed with dark circles.

'What are you doing here?'

He cocked his head. 'Someone almost locked ye up before me. I'm impressed.'

'Callan…'

'Let's get ye home.' Callan wrapped his arm around her waist before saying over her shoulder. 'Thank you.'

'Evidence, Cameron. It speaks volumes.' Spiers nodded at her. 'Ms Mackinnon. Have a safe journey home.'

Aileen followed Callan out into the dark night. A light smattering of snow was falling from the sky. The silent night acted like a balm to heal the inquisition Spiers had hounded her with.

Callan pulled her close. 'Ye okay?'

Aileen rested her head against his arm. 'I didn't book a hotel room.'

'Isla did.'

'Isla's here?'

Callan chuckled. 'You, Ms Mackinnon, have a superior ability to make people care for you. Must be that Mackinnon arrogance.'

Aileen snorted, wiping her running nose. 'So you care for me?'

He held up his forefinger. 'I'm an exception. You annoy the hell out of me.'

And yet here he stood, in Stirling, mere hours after they'd brought her in for questioning. She hadn't even called him.

The taxi pulled up, and when he opened the car door for her, Aileen stretched on tiptoes and pressed a kiss to his jaw. He dipped his head just in time to press warm lips to hers. 'My *banlaoch*.'

Female warrior. Hell, yes. She was a warrior, and if Ms Macalister thought she'd derail Aileen with this stunt, she had another think coming.

Aileen didn't argue when Callan urged her into the car and then pulled her into his warmth. Her brain had already shut off, her body on the verge of exhaustion.

Callan's large hand fell on her lap. He gave her thigh a squeeze before the taxi pulled out, leaving the police station far behind them.

Isla's green eyes met Aileen's over the rim of her mug.

'Da!' Aileen turned to the toddler strapped in her tall seat. The smells of bacon, coffee and fresh fruits drifted through the air. Dim chatter rose around them, but Aileen's mind settled on the people who'd driven through the dark to get her out of jail.

And they wouldn't let Aileen thank them. Isla took the definition of walking to the ends of the earth for a friend to another level.

'Solve the crime and stay put in Loch Fuar. That's payment enough.' She'd dashed away a stray tear and crushed Aileen to her.

Now, Isla wiggled one eyebrow, summoning Aileen back to reality. 'So?'

'So?'

She rolled her eyes. 'He lost his mind when he found out. I'm sure last night was—'

'I slept like a log. Thanks for asking.'

Daniel placed his plate at the table before taking a seat. Callan joined them, his plate brimming with strips of bacon, eggs, bread and fruit. 'I have the day off. What about you?'

'Owning your own business has its pros. Besides, now that I'm here after, goodness, six years, I wanted to show Daniel around. You can come along.'

Daniel nodded. 'That's a plan but…' He regarded Aileen. 'Ye went to Macalister's yesterday before the police took you in for questioning. But doesn't Shaeline stay next to where Isla's father did?'

Aileen nodded. 'Neighbours. The Macalisters never sold that house. The wife got it in the divorce settlement.'

'Andrew's mother stays in yer dad's old house, doesn't she, sweetheart?'

Isla's eyes lit up like jade. 'Why didn't I think of that before? Of course she does.'

'I'm not going back there again. Everyone got a look at me yesterday when the police arrived. They'd step on the street with pitchforks if they see me again.'

'Don't be daft,' Isla said. 'We'll just stick a hat on you.'

Callan placed the cutlery on his plate and took a sip of coffee. 'Neighbours ken things about each other. She might've seen Ken Macalister come over. Perhaps they argued, and his wife killed him.'

'In Loch Fuar?' Aileen's brows furrowed. 'And not here?'

'He changed the will in Loch Fuar.'

And in the previous will, Macalister had left all his wealth to the wife.

Isla had bent to feed Carly and said over her shoulder, 'What about life insurance? Does she stand to gain any money from his death?'

Callan shrugged. 'The police only know he was the man in the car so far. They should've seized his belongings. And' – he glanced at Aileen – 'I'm off the case.'

Aileen shut her eyes and sighed. Did the police really believe she was involved? 'I'm sorry I—'

'They'd have taken me off once they read the will, anyway.'

Daniel steepled his fingers. 'Let's go to Shelly's. She's stayed there for a while now. Let's see what she thinks of Ken Macalister. That might give us a lead.'

Isla grinned. 'Oh, Dan, you in this Bond mode is so hot!'

'Urgh!' Callan and Aileen both rolled their eyes, and Carly echoed with a gurgle of her own.

Aileen placed her coffee cup down. 'Why waste time, then? Come on.'

'I NEVER THANKED YOU ENOUGH, MS MACKINNON.' SHELLY wore her red hair in a bun. The toddler on her hip found one stray tendril and tugged. 'I wasn't able to get there, and my poor baby... He thinks he's a man, always thought so, especially after his dad left us and... Well, I told him to come down and he said he was fine. But boys...'

Isla cooed at the baby, holding Carly back when she reached out to grab her baby cousin. 'Andrew's fine, Shel.'

'Thanks to Ms Mackinnon.'

Aileen waved. 'Please, call me Aileen. And you needn't thank me.'

Isla set Carly in the playpen and intertwined her hand with Shelly's. 'We want to know more about Ken Macalister.'

Shelly frowned. 'That's strange. The police arrested a woman yesterday for breaking into his house.'

Aileen's eyes widened.

'That's Aileen.' Isla threw her under the bus with no remorse. Aileen's glare fell on blind eyes. 'But she wasn't breaking in. She rang the buzzer.'

The kettle whistled, splintering the tension in Aileen's muscles. Shelly eyed Aileen and then Isla, as if they were silently communicating. 'Why don't you all take a seat? I'll get us some tea.'

A few minutes later, five cups clanked onto the coffee table. The house, Aileen gathered, had three bedrooms, a study and a long living room, equipped with lots of shelves and toys.

A rounders bat lay discarded against the door, caked in mud. Next to it was a pink unicorn tossed carelessly by young hands. Some stray plastic pieces had clattered onto the floor, and more toys lay tumbled from their spots on the shelves. If not for the crime novels placed on shelves high enough to stay out of reach of curious minds, the area would've resembled a nursery.

Aileen sipped the aromatic tea. 'You see, Ken Macalister is...' She eyed the children before whispering, 'Dead. He was, er, killed.'

Shelly's eyes widened. 'Oh no! When? He was such a kind-hearted man.'

Isla leaned in to hug her cousin. 'He was, wasn't he?'

From one of the many pockets in her cargo pants, Shelly extracted a set of tissues. With three children, Shelly needed to be prepared. 'He loved to watch over the children while I worked. I work from home most days, but sometimes I have to head in.' Shelly wiped her hands on her thighs. 'He loved to come over and watch them for me.'

Callan set his unfinished cup on the table. 'When was the last time ye saw him?'

Shelly frowned. 'Oh, I can't recall. With the school just starting up after the holidays, days blur together with chores and homework.'

'Christmas,' a small voice drifted down the room.

Isla pivoted towards the stairs and smiled at a boy clutching the balustrades. With his red hair and green eyes, he looked the spit of Andrew.

Five sets of adult eyes landed on him. He contemplated the situation for a second and raced down the stairs in a series of quick footsteps before lunging behind his mother's chair.

Shelly leaned over to ruffle the boy's hair. 'Aye, Arran's right. Ken dropped by on Christmas Day. He'd brought gifts for the children like he always does.'

Tug! Tug!

Aileen looked down at Arran. He'd found his way over to her. He blushed when she smiled at him. The grip on her trousers tightened. 'Five-two-three-four, Murray parks his sleigh on the King's Road. Five-two-three-four, the King's crossed the street to dump the load.'

'What does that mean, Arran?'

Arran hopped up and disappeared towards the kitchen. His footsteps receded through the back door.

Shelly shook her head. 'He's awfully shy. He only talks with his best friend and Ken…'

'And you apparently.' Callan nodded at Aileen.

Daniel, who'd sat mum the entire time, finished his tea with a grimace. 'Say, Shelly, did ye hear any arguments from next door in the past three weeks?'

'Not that I can remember.'

When Isla beamed at her husband, a tinge of red stained Daniel's cheeks. 'Well, I just, since he came down here, maybe he visited his ex?'

Shelly crossed her legs. 'She's not usually... rude. Shaeline loved to come over as well. Loved children. I wonder why they never had any of their own. It was only since the divorce that she's become aloof.'

Isla's fingers danced over her thigh as her mind schemed. 'You could ask her about stuff but...'

Aileen shook her head. 'She'd never tell Shelly what we want to know. If she's a smart woman – and judging by her impressive employment record, she is – she'll piece it together in no time. A woman comes snooping and now her neighbour is suddenly interested?'

Shelly bit her lip. 'Well, what did you want to know?'

'I wanted to know about Macalister's private investigative work. Where he kept his case files, notes.'

'He would tell the children stories about it. I always thought he was joking. A private investigator! Oh gosh. You think... You think his past caught up with him?'

Callan sighed. 'We dinnae ken yet. But we wanted to know more about it.'

'In that case, I think you should talk to Mr Minh from next door. They were tight. However, Ken told us once he had to give up the work, his *adventures*, in autumn 2005. I just assumed he meant it as a tale for the children.'

Daniel frowned. 'Did he say why?'

'It was time to try new avenues he said. Safer alternatives for an aging man like him. That's when I'd assure him he was as youthful as any dashing young man. He'd grin and say, "Oh, Shelly, I'm young enough to be haunted by my regrets."'

CHAPTER EIGHT

Callan drummed his fingers on the steering wheel. He'd insisted on giving Daniel a break from driving, even though he was tired himself. He'd barely slept last night. They'd made it back to the hotel way past midnight and the morning didn't bring good news.

After visiting Shelly, they'd dropped in at Mr Minh's. He hadn't added much to what they already knew about Ken Macalister. His old PI office now belonged to a messenger company, all legitimate.

Mr Minh said Macalister had destroyed his files.

Callan's phone pinged, drawing him out of his thoughts. He peeked at it while at a red light.

More bad news.

Callan huffed. 'Ms M's got an alibi. She spoke at a week-long conference in York – 250 attendees.'

The light switched to green. He hit the accelerator with as much fervour as he gritted his teeth. A long silence settled in the car, only interrupted by Carly's grunts of awe.

At least one of them was enjoying their day.

Aileen faced away from the window. 'We should get lunch.'

'It'll be easier to feed this one in a stationary seat. She won't stop wiggling.' Isla cooed at her daughter and the car filled with giggles.

'There's a café here.' Callan indicated and pulled up outside a cluster of shops.

None of them had much of an appetite except Carly. They settled in with a sandwich and glass of lemonade each.

Isla sipped hers, eyes twinkling when they landed on her husband feeding their toddler. 'I wonder why Ken Macalister didn't have children of his own. He doted on them.'

Aileen sat back in her chair. 'I don't understand what he meant by that part of the will. Perhaps his wife suffered a miscarriage. And they divorced a few months ago. But how did he lose his dignity?'

Callan pulled out a crumpled sheet of paper from his pocket. 'A copy of his will.'

All four pairs of eyes and a curious toddler latched onto the paper. Daniel tugged Carly away.

That pulled the trigger. The girl who'd been happy all day opened her mouth and let out a scream. A fat tear cascaded down her reddening cheeks.

Daniel's eye widened. 'Oh hell no!'

Callan ran a hand over his face. 'Ah, hell. Does she have to cry?'

Aileen scoffed when Isla jumped up and grabbed the girl, striding outdoors while rocking Carly. 'Men six feet tall and broad, yet it only takes a single tear to scare you off.'

Daniel frowned. 'Have a daughter, then we'll see what happens.'

Callan would rather stay up all night solving a case or

watching a game with his pal. Or spend the night with his girlfriend. Not run behind a puking, screeching child. Even if the child had dark locks and fierce brown eyes.

Callan swallowed the ice water in his glass. 'Er, we should go. We need to get back to Loch Fuar.'

Daniel sat back. 'I'm sorry this trip came to nothing, Aileen.'

Aileen shrugged. 'At least we the know the wife's nasty. I'll look into her first thing.'

'No point in doing that.' Callan folded his arms. 'They already checked her out. She's alibied by 250 people, remember?'

Aileen's shoulders drooped, her face falling slightly. Callan itched to give her some hope, a lead. But he came up empty-handed. Their trip had really come to nothing.

He enveloped the hand she'd fisted on her lap. 'We'll figure something out. I'm sure there's something in his past, his will.'

'Not if we have no data to dig into his past. Schneider has nothing. The car told us nothing. His former wife almost sent me to jail. We're at a dead end.'

Callan knew what it felt like running into dead ends. Just as they had with Blaine. He gave Aileen's hand another squeeze. 'Ye're smart, *banlaoch*.'

He led the group to the entrance of the café. Outside, the sun shone onto the cobbled pavement.

Isla pointed Carly's attention to a bird chirping on the tree. The weather, unlike in Loch Fuar, didn't intend to freeze their insides in two seconds flat.

Callan reached for the door handle. His hand caught the leaflet pinned to the door, ripping it in two. 'Ah shit!' He plucked it out and waved to the staff behind the counter. 'Sorry.'

And ducked out.

A really bad day. That's what it was turning out to be.

He dumped the paper pieces in the cup holder, a symbol of their fragmented case.

Daniel leaned in to strap Carly into her car seat. She grabbed at him, tears long forgotten. Daniel placed a kiss to her forehead. 'Good girl.'

Carly squirmed, and her eyes landed on the colourful leaflet. 'Eh!' She made a grab for it.

Callan didn't dare a repeat of what had happened in the café.

He plucked the leaflet from the coffee holder and waved it at her. 'Hey, want th—?' His voice stuck in his throat, eyes latched onto the one sentence on the leaflet.

'Now serving the best cappuccino at King's Road!'

And below it, on the map, a bold strike showed King's Road and beside it, cutting right across, was Murray Park Lane.

Carly snatched the upper part of the leaflet and stuck it in her mouth.

'No! Carly, don't!'

'Callan? What is it?'

'Ye've gone pale, man.' Daniel grabbed the leaflet from his hands and read it. 'What's wrong with this?'

Callan squinted at Carly, now with a dummy in her mouth, before he unfroze. 'What did Arran say?'

'Arran? What's wrong with Arran?'

Callan growled, huffing when Carly startled. How could they've been such eejits? 'Arran' – he ruffled Carly's hair – 'got yer attention, Aileen. What did he say?'

'He sang a nursery rhyme.'

'It's not a nursery rhyme. Macalister visited Shelly at *Christmas*, didn't he?' Callan pointed to the torn leaflet. '"Five-two-three-four, Murray parks his sleigh on the

King's Road. Five-two-three-four, the King's crossed the street to dump the load."'

Isla shook her head. 'I'm sure it's just something silly he made up.'

'Not if there's a King's Road that crosses Murray Park Lane.'

Ken Macalister was a bloody genius. He'd hidden a clue with his neighbour's child, Isla's cousin's son. He'd known Aileen's tenacity would lead her to Stirling to question his neighbours.

Hell! In that case, Macalister had known he'd die *before* he'd headed to Loch Fuar at Hogmanay. And he'd taught the riddle to a child and perhaps asked him to recite it to Aileen.

His theory stretched sanity, but this whole case made little sense to begin with.

He manoeuvred the Saturday traffic, eyes and reflexes focused on getting them to their destination as soon as possible.

The GPS guided him to the left and onto King's Road. People milled about; some bustled into cafés or shops.

Banks, boutiques, and souvenir shops littered the road on both sides.

'What are we searching for?'

Callan could only guess. 'Shop number 5234?'

Daniel shook his head. 'They only have up to 106 here.'

'It's in seventies here,' Isla added.

And the map showed the road split into two up ahead. Callan circled back, eyes scouring for an empty parking spot.

Cars stuck to each other's bumpers until someone pulled away.

Callan slotted his into place and hopped out. No better way to explore than on foot.

Daniel, Carly hitched on one hip, surveyed the shops. 'These are random shops…'

Callan arched an eyebrow. 'So?'

'The rhyme said something about unloading the load?'

'Aye.'

'Well, what better place to dump something than in storage lockers?' Daniel pointed behind Callan. 'There's a storage locker company right there.'

Ah shite! Why hadn't he thought of that? The King crossed the road to dump the load…

They thundered to the shop. The man behind the counter sat riveted to the small television set chattering beside his desk.

Callan stepped up, ignoring the musky smell of the place, and slammed his hand on the bell.

The man startled, gaping at Callan in horror.

'Ye have storage lockers here?'

He nodded.

'Any belonging to Ken Macalister?'

'Er, I can't tell ye that. It's confidential.'

Callan's fingers moved towards his jacket, ready to flash his badge, but Isla stopped him.

She sidled up to the man, a wide smile fixed on her face. 'Say, you have lockers here?'

'Hmm.'

'How much do they cost? Do you rent them out on a monthly basis?'

'We have three sizes. From nine square feet up to something that'll hold furniture and things like that. Nothing more. Most people put up here temporarily.'

Isla leaned in. 'You see, I want to leave a parcel for my friend. Can I do that?'

'It ain't a post office.'

'She's travelling here from the States, and I won't be here when she does. And well, I haven't seen her in so long, I wanted her to feel at home. I got her these presents…'

If it had been anyone else, Callan would've asked Isla to zip it up.

But her rambling got the man to smile. 'You can do that. But she'll need a passcode.'

'That's so much better. Can we see the lockers please?'

'And let ye break into one? Nope.'

Callan gritted his teeth. He'd had enough of this. The eejit either led them to Macalister's locker or else. 'Locker 5234. We want to access it.'

'We don't have a locker 5234.'

'How about 25D? Have that?' Daniel piped in.

Could Macalister have chosen locker 25D for 25 December, Christmas Day? Could he really have planned that far ahead?

'Sure do.'

Callan narrowed his eyes. Maybe he had.

Isla turned to her husband, eyes bright. 'Oh my goodness, darling. You're on fire!'

'Let's see if the thing actually opens first.'

The man behind the counter was about to protest, but Callan's glare shut him up immediately.

They found locker 25D crammed between its neighbours.

Callan led Aileen to the front. 'I don't think we need to guess the pin. Want to do the honours?'

Her eyes twinkled, excitement tingling her nerves.

Every button pinged as she keyed in the code – five-two-three-four — then hit enter, and with a click, the locker opened.

Aileen's fingers trembled. She was accessing a dead man's locker. What had he left behind in here?

She extended her hand into the dark abyss.

'Um…' She frowned.

Callan squinted into the dark. 'What is it? His case files?'

'I can't feel anything. Can someone flash a… Thank you, Isla.'

Isla all but vibrated with excitement. Beside her, Daniel wore a frown.

Aileen stuck her nose into the space, to see what was inside. Her eyes roamed until they settled on a folder as slim as an envelope.

Was this a wild goose chase left by the man's killer for her?

Aileen reached into the folder and drew out an almost A4-sized sheet — as in *one* piece of paper. Four curious faces stared at it.

'These don't look like case files to me,' she told Callan.

'What the hell?' Isla shook her head. 'It's a bloody newspaper!'

An article clipped out from a yellowed newspaper.

'Man who cheated pensioners found dead. Suicide or murder?' the headline read.

'Why would he leave this here for me to find? It's an article from almost twenty years ago.' She perused the thing, finding no mention of Macalister.

Callan cursed. 'He's taken us for fools.'

Aileen bit her lip. The man had proven to be several steps ahead of them. Why would he lead them astray now?

Arran had led them here, so it had to have been Macalister who'd taught him that rhyme. They could confirm it. The boy was shy. If he'd spend enough time with someone, enough to learn a rhyme, it would be someone he knew, trusted.'

She glanced over her shoulder at Isla. 'Can you ask Shelly if Arran learned that rhyme from Macalister? If he did, we know this is a vital clue. And if it was someone else, we'll need a description of who it was.'

'On it.'

Aileen reached into her bag and pulled out another folder.

She slid the folder in her own folder – for safe-keeping – and placed it in her bag. 'We'd best get going.'

Four long faces and a gurgling one were soon buckled up in the car. The weather had soured, spoiling for rain.

And they had to drive all the way back to Loch Fuar.

But Aileen was ready for the long ride. Maybe she could think on the way.

When Callan – now driving Aileen's car – followed Daniel into the motorway traffic, Aileen pulled out the newspaper article.

This time she took her time with each word, noting the events it reported.

Beau Blanchet had conned plenty of pensioners in an elaborate financial fraud. He'd set up a scheme promising them high incremental returns. And he had delivered on the promise for about five years – until he couldn't convince a new set of pensioners to invest with him.

Aileen pointed to the article. 'This doesn't mention Macalister, but the French authorities caught this man, Blanchet, with £5 million in jewellery, cash, and art in his mansion. He had much more, some invested abroad and some in stocks and property.'

Callan indicated right, sped to the overtaking lane, and hit the accelerator harder. 'Who found him out?'

'A set of investors, pensioners, who did their due diligence better than the rest. The reporter hasn't mentioned a name, but Blanchet used a false broker number. They telephoned the broker whose licence it was and, well, the broker had no clue who they were talking about. Blanchet had forged the reports and the broker number for the sake of his scheme.'

'Daniel's father fell into one of those frauds. Luckily, he didn't invest all of his money with the sod.'

Aileen had seen it countless times, investigated such a case or two. And it broke her heart, more than any other time, when it was people's retirement savings down the drain.

She hissed. 'Blanchet died or was murdered. They found a body washed up on 1 January 2006.'

'When's the article from?'

Aileen found the date. 'Third of January. It's more about his death than anything else. I wonder if they figured out who killed him.'

She plucked out her phone, typed his name in. 'The police still don't know according to the internet. They think he killed himself rather than it being a murder.'

'Ye think he killed himself of a guilty subconscious?'

Aileen shook her head. 'Dunno. I once read a report that said schemers know they'll get caught eventually. It's about immediate gratification. They're not prepared to think that far ahead.'

'So it's possible he killed himself. What else can you find out about the case?'

She scrolled through the search results, trying to figure out which one was accurate. Aileen settled on reading three and connecting the common pieces.

'He defrauded people for about £45 million. The authorities found only five. They're not sure it's an accurate sum because they never traced all his ledgers.'

'Jeez. Not small change.'

'Why play it small when you can go bigger? He left a wife behind.' Aileen's eyes picked up their pace, searching for the woman's name. She tagged all the keywords she could, refreshed and read until her eyes hurt, but found no name.

'Well?' Callan arched an eyebrow, sparing her a glance. 'What about her?'

'No name. But the police cleared her of all wrongdoing. They concluded she did not know what her husband was up to. She'd been away to Germany for a year, studying. The husband took care of the books, sent her an allowance. His transactions account for it. There was an insurance policy in her name, although one article says they were separating. They'd almost finalised their divorce, a settlement where she'd get peanuts. He told her he'd lost most of the money.'

'Which was a lie.'

At least the wife had walked away from it unscathed, except for losing her marriage and a husband…

Callan scratched his chin, eyes still on the road. 'No name of the wife, the man's dead, no mention of Macalister. So why would he place the clipping in that vault?'

Aileen read the message Isla had sent her.

'Shelly came through. She says Macalister and Arran had a game going. He taught Arran rhymes while they played detective. Each rhyme cracked a puzzle. That was the last rhyme Macalister taught him. He told him it was one for a bigger adventure, one a brown-haired woman was on. That's me.'

All this elaborate scheming to reveal this piece of evidence.

Callan jerked the car to the left, cursed, and pointed at Aileen's thigh where the folder sat. 'You said 3 January 2006? Is that when the article's dated?'

'Yes.'

'But Shelly said Macalister's adventures ended in autumn 2005.'

She had. 'Could this be the tragedy he was talking about? After all, Blanchet had worked the scheme for five years.'

Callan reached into his pocket and extracted the crumbled will. 'Read them together again. See if it makes more sense now.'

Aileen traced the words. But no matter how many times she read them, she couldn't make head nor tails of the situation. '"Use it to find my killer, use it to find the person who's robbed several families of their fullest life." Could this be Blanchet?'

'They found Blanchet's body, right?'

They had. All reports confirmed it.

'Callan, there's no mention of Macalister in the reports, either. Nothing to say he was investigating this case.'

Aileen read through the information again. A sickening feeling settled in her gut. 'What if *he* was the accomplice? What if his past killed him?'

CHAPTER NINE

Aileen paced, not paying heed to her aching feet or pounding head. She'd barely eaten since they'd returned, her mind stuck on the man whose murder she was investigating. Was he the devil? Is that why he wanted salvation?

Or had someone coerced him down the wrong path?

She gripped her head, fisting her hair. The questions wouldn't stop. She just couldn't wrap her head around it at all. It was like a vicious circle, a broken record, beating around the same bush.

Callan had gone straight to work and hadn't come over after. At 7 p.m. she'd dumped dinner and sought out her notes. She added nothing to what she already knew.

Was Ken Macalister a good man?

He loved children, but had none of his own. Isla and Shelly both liked him, but his wife had almost sent her to jail. Isla was a good judge of character and she'd stressed the man would never do something like this.

Almost twenty years ago, another man had defrauded people of millions. A case Macalister was involved in.

She tugged her hair again. 'Urgh!'

A car approached the inn. The tyres crunched over a few stones and splattered through puddles. Headlights illuminated the curtains until the engine cut out in Dachaigh's car park.

Aileen peeked out the window.

A sleek, dark SUV with tinted windows, the metal on the bumper new yet muddy, blared an alarm. Her back straightened, the hairs on her neck stuck out and her ears perked up. Ready for trouble. She'd faced it often enough to know when it neared.

Aileen slid her phone into her pocket, Callan on speed dial and voice recorder turned on. She was no longer unprepared while on a case.

Two men, tall, muscled and broad, slid out of the car. They hid their eyes behind dark glasses, despite the blanket of darkness. Their black suits and shiny shoes matched, out of place amongst the silhouettes of mountains and meadows.

She stationed herself behind the desk as the pastel-blue door opened and two imposing suits loomed over her.

Aileen stood just over five feet, but she'd faced CEOs and seen her gran put fear in devils. 'Hi, I'm Aileen Mackinnon. How may I help?'

One man smiled, not bothering to pull off his glasses. He flashed a badge under Aileen's nose. 'I'm Detective Inspector Irwing from the Major Crimes Investigation unit. That's my partner, Sergeant Xin.'

Aileen nodded at the two men, smile still affixed. 'Do you need lodgings?'

Irwing shrugged. 'Seems like it. But we also wanted to speak with you about Ken Macalister.'

Her expression fought to turn into a grimace. She clung to her smile.

Aileen put on Isla's gossipmonger hat. 'Oh, of course, I'd be happy to help. But I thought the local police had the case under control.'

Xin stepped up. 'I heard you're chummy with the local detective. I'd say he's in your pocket, but well, a woman has better ways to entrap a man. So I'm sure you know how they're faring.'

The nerve of the man! She clenched her jaw, thinking of ways to show him his place.

Careful, Aileen. Be good to him.

'We might be more than friends, sir, but he would never sacrifice the integrity of a case by sharing things with me.'

Aileen made it a point to figure things out on her own, but she didn't tell them that.

'Well, we'll be taking over, and since we're checking in now, I wondered if you could spare a few minutes for us?' Irwing's smile had waned into something so forced, his wrinkled skin looked like it would crack any minute.

Not in a mood to be kind or forthcoming, Aileen nodded. 'Let me allot you your rooms, so you can get settled in. Then I'll put the kettle on.'

The moment the last shiny boot disappeared up the stairs, Aileen dialled Callan and hurried to the kitchen.

'Major Crimes, really?'

He sighed. 'Aye, I came in here to that good news. There are more coming apparently. Did ye install cameras in my office or something?'

'They're here, Callan.'

Cursing tinkled down the line, something crashed then a door slammed. 'Bastards. Hold on, I'm getting there.'

'No! Don't. They… I can handle them. I don't want you to put your career on the line. Besides, they think you share everything with me. Just... Let me handle them, okay?'

The oaf insisted until Aileen shut him down with a threat. 'You come here and hang up that badge, or stay there and see this case through. Keep that badge pinned to your waist.'

That settled him down, for now. He barked out warnings before hanging up. And rightly so, since the men in question hoofed down the stairs.

Irwing took a seat without Aileen inviting him to. She seethed but bit her tongue to hold the anger in.

'So, from what our colleague told us, Macalister stayed here before he was killed?'

Aileen nodded. 'Your colleague is correct.'

The sergeant didn't sit. Aileen didn't offer him a seat, either.

'How did he seem to you?'

'Like a tourist.'

Xin produced a notepad from his suit and scribbled notes with a black pencil.

This was going to be a long night.

They poked and prodded about Macalister. Did they know about the will?

'Did you know this man before he checked in?'

'No.'

'Then why were you at his will reading?'

Aileen huffed. They knew.

She shouldn't have opened her mouth with Spiers. 'Do I need to get a lawyer?'

Irwing eyed her. 'A detective's alibied you. You seem to have proof. Unless you've done something wrong, I don't see why you'd need a lawyer.'

'In that case, some things are private, sir.'

Irwing pushed away from the desk. 'Very well then.'

Xin snapped his notepad shut. 'Maybe we'll talk in the morning?'

Maybe they wouldn't. Aileen smiled, cheeks hurting, and watched them leave.

Ken Macalister's death had dragged the top dogs in, and with such haste.

Aileen bit her lip. Was he a criminal?

One thing she now knew for sure. She needed to know about the victim as much as she did his killer. Solving one of those mysteries would lead her to the other.

SHE BOUNDED UP THE STAIRS TO FETCH HER LAPTOP, NOTES, and pens. The marble countertop in the kitchen should be big enough. The police inspectors had turned in for the night, which gave her some freedom.

Aileen read through what she knew of Macalister yet again. How did Blanchet's case connect with him?

If he'd shut his firm to get a job with a security company in September or October 2005, why did he have a newspaper clipping from January 2006 in a safe?

She calculated using her fingers. He'd have been around thirty. He'd married early, at twenty.

Shelly had snooped a bit for them, asking neighbours without raising any red flags for Shaeline.

Aileen listed the timeline, murmuring to herself. 'He marries in 1987, starts up the firm two years later, maybe. And shuts it down in 2005, eighteen years later. Was it a question of money?'

It couldn't be. If the couple had money problems, arguments, surely they'd have divorced fifteen years ago. Why now?

Did this tragedy somehow relate to the incident in France?

Aileen bit her lip. How did fraud tie in with Mac—

'Hell!' She slapped her forehead. His wife was an accountant! Did she work on the case?

She found a social-networking website and searched for Shaeline Macalister. Her account popped up at once.

Scrolling through the woman's profile proved to be an educational trip through time. She had graduated with a degree in accounting in 1986, a year before their marriage.

With a 2:1 honours, she'd worked in a top accounting firm and then... Aileen frowned. She worked for seventeen years and then quit?

She'd been a partner and worked with the top dogs, handling double taxation treaties and such. Why quit suddenly?

Could she have fallen sick? Had the private investigative business gone south?

She couldn't find out what had happened in 2005, and she knew calling Ms Macalister would get her nowhere.

She worked through Macalister's other cases. There were a few high-profile ones, all restricted to the UK.

He'd worked well, was brilliant at his job.

'Urgh! Is there nothing wrong with this man?' There had to be. Why would someone kill him otherwise?

After what felt like ages, a stray headline caught her eye. *'Brilliant Mac hangs up his coat.'*

The article highlighted Macalister's work, puzzling over why he'd quit and what a loss it was to the private investigative world. Aileen scrolled to the bottom of the blog and found a name for the author. Lia Edwards.

Would this person know something about Macalister? She hunted around the ancient website and found an email.

Better yet, she found a phone number. While the old

Aileen would've hesitated, this one picked up the phone and dialled.

Like she'd said, losing Dachaigh came above all her other fears.

CALLAN IMAGINED PLOUGHING A FIST THROUGH THE WALL. Instead, he placed a hand over his stomach to gauge how much rage roiled in there. Plenty to go around...

He'd come in late last night to find Rory's email stating Irwing from Major Crimes would be around. And then Aileen had called.

Why did Ken Macalister's murder require the best of the best the force had? How had they spared him with such haste?

Rory had no words on the why.

Had Ken Macalister committed a crime? Perhaps murdered Blanchet?

Or was he part of a gang? Someone on the run? Callan had peeped at the gathered data. Nothing suspicious had pinged so far.

Why were the top brass sniffling into a small-town murder?

Heavy footsteps treaded down the corridor, fast disappearing into the other room. Rory had arrived.

Callan jumped out of his seat and reached Rory's door before the man had taken a seat.

Rory nodded without turning around. 'I knew ye'd be here first thing.'

'Why are they here?'

His boss rubbed his worn eyes. 'Ken Macalister used to be a private detective. A good one.'

When he didn't elaborate, Callan huffed. 'So?'

'I asked and got vague answers. I tried to be diplomatic, and they ran circles around me. Let's just say I'm not well-versed in diplomacy like them. I had little choice.'

His boss liked it straight, Callan knew, but the last thing he needed was people he didn't care for sniffing around.

His heart clenched.

Aileen didn't stand a chance against the likes of Detective Inspector Irwing.

'Ye ken I can handle this, Rory.'

Rory held up a hand. 'I do, but when they realised who it was in that car, yer pal in the Stirling police had Aileen in custody. There's little I can do to convince them otherwise.'

'What should I do then?'

The door to the police station opened and in swaggered the revered detective.

Irwing had his sunglasses fixed over his nose, but they didn't hide the wrinkles or the greying hair. Those threads of silver spoke of years of experience.

Callan nodded his greeting. Rory, putting on his rusty diplomat's hat, shook hands with Irwing and his partner.

'Detective Sergeant Xin.'

'This is Detective Inspector Cameron.'

Callan extended a hand, trying very hard not to crush the bony one placed in his. 'Inspector Irwing. Sergeant Xin.'

Irwing sized Callan up. He felt the intensity through those dark shades. 'I'm glad I caught you both here. I wanted someone to follow up on the number plates found at the ELV yard.'

Callan curled his lips. Rory elbowed him in the ribs and Callan smiled… grimaced, although he'd intended it to look like a smile.

At least Irwing hadn't cut him from the investigation.

'I'll get right on it.' Being in their good books could get them far.

'Keep me posted on your whereabouts. Remember, Detective, our job here is to be objective. And you aren't.'

Callan fisted his hands. 'I—'

'I need all hands on deck.'

'For Macalister?'

'Ask the right questions. Don't waste my time, Cameron. Chop-chop.'

What an arse! The ounce of admiration Callan had had for this man blew away with the wind.

Police officer or not, he didn't have to like Irwing. He liked justice, and if Aileen served that, he wouldn't let her lose, especially to a domineering man like Irwing.

Callan headed out to his car, sticking his hands in his coat pocket as the wind swirled up around him. If Aileen solved this case first and stayed, he'd have her by his side. She'd breathed life into him, reacquainted him with the Callan he'd lost fifteen years ago.

He paused, hands on the steering wheel. Last year, letting Aileen have the upper hand would've made him question his judgement. Now the warm feeling in his chest deflated any guilt that had ever existed.

Callan's eyes strayed to the paper on the other seat, flapping a picture.

Change – sometimes it snuck up on you. Sometimes the loss and gain of something unique changed you, like waves lapping at a boat, slowly drifting it off course.

Callan shook his head. Since when did he indulge in poetry?

Mad – the circumstances were driving him to insanity.

Blaine had pushed him over the fence, taught him the importance of friendship. And he hadn't found Blaine yet.

He pressed down on the accelerator, pinning his

swirling mind down to focus. Time to get his arse to Loch Heaven again. If there was one common link between the burned car and the missing one, it was Amy's Rental and Taxi Services.

Heading there would give him some definite answers. He hoped.

Like the first time he'd visited, the air hung heavy with engine fumes and grease. Detective Inspector Walsh tapped his hat. The familiar trench coat was wrapped around his broad form, the angular face underneath his hat barely visible because of the scarf he'd worn.

'Don't. The wife knitted it.'

'Christmas present?'

Walsh swallowed. 'Shall we?'

Callan fell in step with his fellow officer, an officer he admired. 'Where are yer folks with the car that went missing?'

'Not close. And we weren't expecting those number plates to turn up in the ELV yard. We traced the car, checked if it popped up on any surveillance…'

'That's like trying to find a button in a room full of cotton.'

Walsh frowned at him. 'Needle in a haystack. That's what I think you were going for. But you're right. It's a wild goose chase. For all we know, the sod used another car to transport the plates to the yard.'

Callan stopped before the garage doors. 'But then the rental car would be without number plates.'

With a point of his finger, Walsh indicated what he thought.

He followed the direction of the man's finger to where a gangly teen, his hair barely kept away from his face with a bandana, crouched, drilling number plates onto a car.

'Ah, you think the perp's fixed stolen number plates on the car?'

Walsh nodded.

Too much work and a high chance of being caught. Why not just dump the car? What was in there that needed protecting?

Callan huffed. 'Let's go talk to them.' His skin itched at the mere idea of talking to the owner of the rental company.

Amy's brother Callan didn't mind.

Walsh chuckled. 'She's already made you.'

Callan saw Amy – her blond hair in a weird up-do, her face caked in make-up – waving at them.

'Dealing with Irwing's better than this.'

'Ah, yes. That's something I want to hear about. How he's kicked you off the case.'

Their boots thudded against the tarmac. The smacks of Amy's heels sounded like gongs at his execution.

'My friend, she's a photographer, just called saying our December guy's cancelled. Bummer, ain't it? Now here you are, strutting that fine arse and those blue eyes.' She pointed at Callan and giggled.

He considered ignoring her comment. His recent dealings with a stubborn girlfriend had taught him a thing or two about women. Callan crossed his arms and drew the line. 'Why are ye looking for men to photograph for yer calendar in January? Isn't it too late?'

Amy waved a hand. 'She likes to prepare for next year before the handsome ones are all booked. Now you, blue-eyed babe, you—'

The hand he raised silenced her, as he'd hoped it would. 'No. *Now*, I want to ask ye about those cars.'

She pulled a face. 'Sure.'

Callan and Walsh followed her to the entrance, where three cars stood outside the corrugated aluminium gates. 'Tim's out, so the lad's've taken a wee break.' Amy rolled her eyes. 'Lord knows he's a slave driver.'

She stretched over the counter until she found something in the drawer. Bright red nails glistened as they held the silver packet. 'Gum?'

Callan and Walsh shook their heads. She shrugged, popping a chunk. A clunky ring rested on one finger. She used that finger to swirl the air. 'What would you like to see first?'

'The back door from where customers tread in.'

Anyone walking in through the back door entered undetected. Macalister's murderer had planned everything to a T.

Amy led them, hips swaying like branches in the breeze. The gum she smacked grated on Callan's nerves.

He fisted his hands, focusing on the rental side of the premises. The area had one camera trained on the reception counter; the rest of the interiors were timber, traditionally masculine.

Amy's prized calendar hung on the wall next to the back entrance. Pictures of various cars were lined up on the panelling. The varnish had peeled over time. Scratches from overuse stroked across the walls.

It smelled of grease and musk, more like a bar than a rental and taxi agency. Indeed, the door resembled one used in a Western's saloon, though Amy, with her sultry blue eyes and manicured nails, resembled Marilyn Monroe more than a gunslinging cowboy.

She pointed her finger to a gap in the concrete fence. 'That's the one. Nothing big.'

The road on the other side lay silent. Not the best place to base a rental company.

Once they stepped outside through the swinging door, Callan noted a sign running along the roof of the shop. 'Amy's Rental and Taxi Services' was written in dark yellow on distressed wood.

Sticking with the aesthetics, the sign had faded beneath the Highland sun.

Callan faced the alleyway. 'Strange ye face an alley.'

Amy dismissed Callan's comment with a wave. 'The internet helps find customers. And this place is ours. No need to pay expensive rent for a shop facing the main road, is there? Besides, Tim needs the added space, so customers can drive their cars in. This alley is too narrow to fit a Merc.'

Walsh, who'd meandered around with his hands tucked in his trench coat, spoke for the first time. 'What sort of customers do you cater to?'

Amy smirked. 'Not families. No family vans here. I like adults, not little pricks puking all over the seat. Been there, done that. It's a nightmare getting the car cleaned up later. And the smell…' She fluttered her hand over a glowering face.

'So ye do the social-media thing?'

'Aye, got a few thousand followers between my accounts.'

He'd read up on tech and decided he didn't like the social or networking part of social media. Aileen was far better at it.

Callan made a mental note to check up on her social accounts. 'Do you have any idea where Ken Macalister's car is?'

'It's like I told your man. Vanished like summer in October.'

Callan trudged through the frozen gravel to the back entrance, placed both hands on the iron gate, and pushed it open. It swung without a creak.

At waist height, the gate offered no protection. Either she didn't care about anyone stealing her stuff or it was an open playground for thieves.

No wonder two cars from Amy's Rental and Taxi Services had been involved in a crime. One had burned, and the other was either hidden or out there somewhere with illegal number plates.

Not to mention one of their customers had wound up dead.

Callan faced Amy, whose eyes studied him with too much scrutiny to be polite. Whatever happened to privacy and courtesy?

'Ken Macalister rented out a car, aye? Do ye have the surveillance footage for that day?'

'Why do you want to see his ugly mug?' She strutted towards the tiny office space. It had no door, just a string of beads cascading from the doorframe like a curtain.

Callan had noticed the area the last time he'd been here. It accommodated a chair, a narrow desk and stacks of boxes. The smell spoke of mould working its way through the room.

Amy sat on the only chair. It let out a puff of dust and a groan. The box-like computer, more ancient than the one Aileen used in the police station, whirred to life.

Her red nails clattered on the brown keyboard. They waited in silence.

Amy smiled, showing perfect white teeth. 'It's here.'

Walsh took the lead while Callan stood back, uninterested in catching a strong whiff of Amy's perfume, lest he gagged.

From afar, he watched the black-and-white video.

The back door swung open to welcome Ken Macalister. He wore jeans, a plaid shirt and a cap. A bum bag hung from his waist.

Amy stood there in a form-fitting dress, wearing a smile that made Callan want to run for the hills.

He rooted his feet to the spot and watched. A minute passed and neither Macalister nor Amy moved.

Then they leaned over the table. Another few minutes. Amy didn't reach for her keys or the brochure to explain anything.

What was she playing at?

Callan watched the clock ticking in the corner of the recording. Hell, why didn't they have audio?

Bloody primitive systems.

After twenty minutes and twenty-three seconds, Amy straightened. Macalister wore a sly grin on his face and grabbed the keys she'd placed on the counter.

The two strode out of the camera's range.

Callan waited for something, anything, to show the man had been in distress.

But neither Macalister's demeanour nor his clothing showed a man in town for business. He was dressed like a tourist and had rented a car to travel locally. So why had someone killed him?

What had he known?

Callan watched Amy re-enter the room alone. Another dead end. 'What did ye talk about for twenty minutes?'

Amy fluffed her hair. 'He's a man. I can't remember, but I'm sure it was harmless. It's a good break in the day – a bit of toying with clients.' The glint in her eye sent goosebumps running down his arms.

Callan had to get out before those red claws dug into him. He pivoted to step out and almost face-planted.

'Shit!' Callan grabbed the desk, glaring at the culprit. A

bag's handle poked out from underneath the table, a trap for his boot to entangle in.

His slew of terrible days was continuing…

Callan hissed curses until his boot wriggled free.

Amy's claws settled on his shoulder and her perfume shot up his nose like mustard. 'Are you alright, darling?'

'That could be a safety hazard.'

Her laugh grated. 'Oh, don't worry.'

Walsh chuckled. 'What's it doing there anyway?'

Amy swatted the air. 'Tim. He leaves his gym bag lying around everywhere. It's leather! Stupidly expensive. I gave it to him for Christmas. Now it's on the floor with cat piss and dirt.'

Callan plucked her hand off his shirt, contemplating soaking it in dung so it didn't reek of her perfume. 'Why's it in your section of the building?'

Amy plucked up the buttery soft tan leather bag and set it on the table. The bag had a luggage tag on it adorned with an illustration of Claude Monet's *Water Lilies*. 'As I said, he leaves it around.'

Get out…

'Thank you. If ye remember anything Macalister said that day, anything at all, get in touch.'

And he stalked off, ready to put as much distance between Amy's Rental and Taxi Services and him as possible.

CHAPTER TEN

'Hell!' Aileen's phone clattered onto the table.

'What's wrong?' Bonnie's head poked round the door. Then she entered, dragging her mop behind her. 'Ye've been on edge ever since ye returned from Stirling.'

Aileen shrugged. 'Someone's not answering their phone.'

'Ye ken my best friend? Her boyfriend sometimes doesn't answer her calls either. Yet she won't break up with him. What's wrong with us women?'

Aileen snorted. Teenage girls were amusing company. 'I find when you lead with a firm hand, people answer our calls.'

Bonnie tipped her chin. 'Never had one of those – boyfriends, I mean, so I wouldnae ken.'

At fifteen, her head buried in books and her hair in plaits, Aileen had had no friends, let alone boyfriends. Her troubles ended with textbooks and assignments. She never shed tears for anything else apart from when she'd been denied a seat at Oxford.

Aileen swallowed the memories, tasting the bitterness they still left on her tongue.

Bonnie crossed her arms. 'Ye don't seem like someone who dated a lot and ye turned out okay.'

'Why, Bonnie, I believe thanks are in order.'

'Oh well, I'll tell my best friend yer advice. After all, ye did fine and now ye're a detective and all.'

If she solved this before the actual detectives, she would be alright.

Aileen nodded. 'Thanks. It's time you got back. You don't want to be late for your classes.'

Bonnie pulled a face and trotted off. She had been spending more time at Dachaigh, waiting with bated breath for anything Aileen had to share.

The lass needed friends sorely. Just like Aileen. Hers had come for her in Stirling. She smiled. Not a year ago, she'd have laughed at the idea of such friendships. And now she'd experienced them.

Aileen pulled out the newspaper clipping. What about Beau Blanchet? Men like him seldom formed deep relationships. But didn't he trust his wife?

Ken Macalister. He loved children, had stayed in one community for decades, and his neighbours said only good things about him. How long could someone pretend they were good if they weren't?

Next to the clipping, Aileen placed her phone – where she'd been reading the only article about Macalister retiring from his private investigative practice.

Two disjointed scenarios. How did they tie together?

Aileen had telephoned the author of the blog several times. She'd also sent emails, only to receive no response.

Leads dried up, she sat back and rubbed her eyes. What wasn't she seeing?

She sought the newspaper clipping again when her phone vibrated with an incoming call.

Siobhan.

Aileen grinned as she answered. 'A bit early for you, isn't it?'

'Ha! I can call my grandwean whenever I want. Yer Christmas present's dried up.'

She'd gifted her gran a special ninety-year-old whisky. 'You didn't!'

'Ha! When every second could be my last, why would I waste such a treasure?'

'Don't talk like that.'

Siobhan only used pity when it suited her. 'Ah well, if I don't, ye'll never tell me about the case ye're solving.'

Asking her gran how she knew about it would be as fruitful as reading the article on Macalister again. Her old ears were stuck to the ground, and the number of gossipmonger contacts she had would put the best databases to shame.

'You'll know more about the case than I do.'

'Ken Macalister. Not yer average John Smith. And the talk is he's left ye all his money.'

Aileen swallowed. She hadn't really updated her business partner on the state of their accounts. 'Hmm, *if* I solve his murder.'

'Which ye will. Maybe ye can take all that, shut the inn and live a happy life.'

Aileen paused. She hadn't expected that, not from her gran. 'Are you unwell?' she whispered, not wanting to know the answer.

'Healthy as a whisky-drinking horse. And I'm no' a fool. I know the inn is a money-draining pit. Aileen, dear, I spent more decades taking care of it than ye've walked this earth.'

Aileen looked around the inn and all that it held for her and the guests who'd stayed there. 'If I'd wanted to make a fortune, I would've stayed in that drab job in the city, Gran. I'm here to preserve the best memories I have of my childhood and of you – us. Don't worry about all this. Dachaigh will be a home for us and many more guests to come.'

A long pause drifted down the line. 'Why do ye think I gave the inn to you?'

The reason rested the heavy weight of responsibility on Aileen's shoulders. Siobhan had chosen her. Believed *her*. And she wouldn't let her gran down – ever.

'Macalister,' she began. 'He's from Stirling. Ring any bells?'

'Ah, it's that surname... Just out of ma grasp, and what a firm grip I have on my memory. I've been thinking about it a lot, even skipping my horror nights! Bah! The bloody thing won't come to me.'

'Don't stress it, Gran. I'm sure you'll remember.' Aileen bit her lip at her gran's outburst. No matter what she said, she wasn't as sharp as she used to be. 'Does a fraud in France fifteen years ago mean anything?'

'Ye should know better than that. There's fraud taking place every damned day somewhere in the world.'

Aileen sighed. 'Why don't you stick to the Macalister part? I'll dig further into him, too.'

'Stirling, ye say? I've never lived there. But ninety years, lassie. I've met enough people in those decades. Hold on, I will get it for ye.'

Aileen smiled, happy to speak with her gran. They had met up for Christmas, but there was something about Siobhan's unbridled zest that always pushed Aileen to do better.

When she got off the phone, her mind had cleared. The stress morphed into determination.

She studied the blog about Macalister retiring again.

Amelia Downie had written the news article about Blanchet and... Aileen frowned. Lia Edwards had written the blog on Macalister.

Amelia Downie... Lia Edwards...

Amelia, Lia...

Now she dug in again, hands flying over her keyboard. She typed both names in and got a negative for Lia Edwards, but Amelia Downie was alive and well. The woman had her own talk show on the Loch Heaven radio, an online cookery show with thousands of followers and a business registered to an address in the next town.

Aileen grinned. Bingo!

HER SEDAN HUGGED THE ROADS, BUT SHE HAD TO ADMIT, Callan's rattly SUV did a better job.

She'd slid through these woods to the college and stumbled over a murdered body a few months ago. Now she crossed the peeking hills and ploughed through the forest until slabs of concrete replaced the bouquet of trees.

She followed the GPS into a part where one-storey houses had fresh coats of paint on the walls and a community garden ran alongside the road. Washing fluttered in some gardens, and a group of children in uniform marched down the footpath, singing some popular song.

Aileen parked kerbside and checked the gate of the fence to ensure it wasn't locked. Two cars, gleaming under the light, lined the short driveway.

She manoeuvred between them and pressed the buzzer of number thirty-four.

The door, a pale pastel green, shone as if someone had taken a duster to it fifteen minutes ago. Aileen twisted her fingers, not daring to peek through the side windows, not even when she noticed the netted curtains shivering.

The door creaked to reveal a woman wearing an apron. She had a fifties hairdo paired with bright red lipstick and nails to match. 'May I help you?' Her long lashes fluttered.

'Er, um...' Whatever she'd expected, it wasn't this. Aileen cleared her throat; tried clearing her mind. 'Amelia Downie?'

'Aye?'

With sweaty palms, Aileen held up the folder. 'I'm here about an article you wrote.'

Amelia's spine stiffened. 'Are you a journalist?'

'No, I, um, I'm investigating a death, in a personal capacity.'

With a flourish of her hand, the woman flipped an invisible strand of hair off her forehead. 'Forgive me, I'm in the middle of shooting my cookery show. What did you say your name was?'

Aileen groaned at her fast-depleting people skills. Last time she'd deployed them, they'd landed her in an interview room with a detective inspector. Not again, and especially not when it would be Walsh's office. 'Aileen. Aileen Mackinnon.'

A frown came over the woman's face. 'I might not work in mainstream media anymore, but I have contacts. And boy have I heard of you.' She let out an unexpected giggle and smoothed her apron over a slightly bulging underbelly.

'I'll put the kettle on. Gosh, it's cold enough to freeze a polar bear's arse out there.'

The house decor resembled a studio from the fifties.

Retro colours of pastel orange, green, and pink splashed over the walls. The furniture was all geometric lines with no flourishes.

A few blossoms livened up the living room and – Aileen almost chuckled – a car, fashioned like the ones used in spy thrillers, sat in the centre of the shelf running the width of the room on one wall. The rest of it held books.

The clicking of heels announced the return of her host. She wheeled in a tray with a kettle and two pairs of cups and saucers. Aileen's eyes rounded at the sugar cubes, milk pot and tongs. Tiny, precisely cut sandwiches would make it a tea party.

Amelia had lost her apron. She arranged herself neatly on the sofa as if she'd spent years at a finishing school.

Aileen's eyes darted around, searching for any pictures of the woman. She found none.

Amelia handed her a cup. 'Why are you so interested in that article?'

'I found this newspaper in the man's belongings. I'm investigating his death and wondered why he preserved it.'

Amelia took the paper from her and read it over as she took a sip from her own cup. 'Strange. Why would he preserve a newspaper clipping? Did he invest his money with Blanchet?'

Aileen pursed her lips. 'I don't have any information. Besides, he wouldn't have been a pensioner then. I was wondering if you could shed some light on what you found out? Something you didn't mention in the article you wrote, perhaps?'

Amelia gestured to the biscuits Aileen hadn't noticed before. 'Help yourself.' She skirted around answering the question for a long time. 'I destroyed all my notes. I moved, you see. After France, a brief stop here, and then to London. Freelancing, having fun, hungry to see the world. No place for notes in your backpack.

'Blanchet made quite the stir, but it's always the sort of hype that mists into nothingness as soon as the peak dies. It took a week, two at the maximum, for the press to move on from that case. I believe they never found out where the rest of the millions went.'

Aileen pulled out her notepad, asked if she could take notes and – when Amelia nodded – started jotting down the details.

'Who'd you interview for the case?'

'Oh, goodness me, that was years ago. Let me see. There was a dashing inspector of some sort, in his forties with a receding hairline, but well, French men... I usually wrote lifestyle columns, but the paper wanted an article on the fraud case and I was there, so they asked me to do it. The inspector spoke to me, an exclusive after they found the body, said I was more graceful with my questions, unlike the rest of them.'

'Anyone else?'

'Not really. Blanchet's butler. The man was half deaf. I don't think he'd be alive now. He looked about a hundred even then. Then there was a maid, someone from Eastern Europe. Blanchet had promised her a job. More like a slave trade and such. Illegal stuff.'

Aileen frowned. 'They think that's how he earned the rest of his money?'

Amelia shook her head. 'Blanchet never dabbled in anything that complicated. From what I gathered from the servants, he was pea-brained. Not someone who'd run this operation for five years. I'd be surprised if he knew his dollars from his pounds.'

Aileen had encountered people who knew nothing about the financial world. They were excellent scapegoats for someone smarter. So if Beau Blanchet had died accused of a fraud, that meant the mastermind of the scheme had likely got off scot-free.

Could he have travelled across the pond and settled in Stirling?

CALLAN SCOURED EVERY EVIDENCE AND REPORT, PURSUED leads – anyone who'd lingered at the yard – only to stare at his empty hands. The CCTV footage spat out mist, and Bob had his eyes closed. The technicians had found no fingerprints on the number plates, either.

Irwing, as the senior investigating officer, summoned his army in the reception area of the police station.

Officers from all levels of the hierarchy bustled. Murmurs and curious eyes tracked Callan.

'Detective Cameron.'

Callan pivoted towards the voice.

Detective Spiers wore a shirt soaked in starch.

'What happened to Stirling?'

She thrust a finger at Irwing. 'We investigated a murder of a private investigator once. He called me to assist, given the common undertones of the two cases.'

That Irwing had furnished a private bus to get all these personnel here raised red flags for Callan.

'And we're staying at your girlfriend's inn. She was, er, very welcoming.'

Welcoming, his arse! She recognised strategised surveillance when it sat in her own house.

Irwing clapped his hands, drawing everyone's attention.

He flanked Callan's murder board, a piece of his office Callan had surrendered only on Rory's barked command. With every second that passed, Callan's anger boiled at the precipice of his patience.

A case snatched from under his nose, where the detectives were pitted against his girlfriend.

'Cameron! What's the latest on Macalister's hire car?'

'No leads, sir.'

Irwing knew that car had fragmented their resources – as the perp had surely intended.

'Keep looking or hand the case over to Spiers.'

Callan set his jaw.

'As for you, Spiers, what did you find about Macalister's latest work?'

Spiers flapped her notepad open and began. 'He retired from fieldwork in 2004 and shut his private practice in 2005.'

'Amateurs seldom last long.'

Spiers trained her eyes on her notes. She wasted no breath on frivolities. 'He worked as a manager in a security firm. His last work, according to his boss, was supervising the security at a local museum in Aberdeen. He—'

'Any arguments there?'

'No.'

'Very well. Davis! Where are you with his personal life? What's the reason for the divorce? Any new lovers? Old scorned ones?'

Robert blushed, star-struck. 'N-No, s-sir. None so far. The separation seemed smooth.'

Irwing dismissed him with a wave. 'Thirty-five years of marriage. The divorce would never be *smooth*. My guess is the wife's richer for it.'

'I couldn't say, sir. But private security pays well.'

'Sure does.' Xin's mutter won a few chuckles.

Callan focused on Irwing's line of enquiry. His questions darted all over the spectrum – family, relationships, work, and lifestyle.

Mr Minh, Macalister's friend, believed Macalister

had lived like a hermit post his divorce, but more information couldn't hurt. He would get it all out of Robert later.

Irwing scratched a few questions on the board. 'I spoke to Ms Mackinnon, Cameron's girlfriend. She wasn't very forthcoming.' His bushy eyebrows furrowed, heat directed at Callan.

Callan wouldn't betray Aileen. He bit back his words.

'Mum's the word, eh, Cameron? I have no time for Poirot wannabes.'

Neither did Callan. But every day that passed pushed Aileen away from Loch Fuar.

'We visited the Schneider fella. He needs a warrant to show us the will. A lead into solving his client's murder and he wants a warrant! Bloody lawyers!'

Once Irwing snatched the will, he'd stop Aileen's investigation immediately. Shit!

Throughout the long briefing, Callan swayed from foot to foot, tracking Robert, who, like a sincere student, stayed focused on Irwing the whole time.

'Get to the van. We'll head for the inn in five minutes.'

Not a bus then, a van.

Callan stalked over to Robert and grabbed his yellow vest before he trotted after his master. 'My office – now!'

The door rattled behind them.

Robert propped his hands to the sides. 'I don't know what's got into you, but I did nothing!'

'Macalister's personal life. Who's yer source?'

'His ex-wife.'

'And?'

'And?'

Callan spent precious breaths teaching this eejit. 'And ye think she's telling the truth?'

'She – she was sure he hadn't moved on. They spent

Christmas together. Hence' – Robert gulped – 'I concluded their divorce was mutual. No bitterness.'

'Three weeks later, he's murdered, and she almost imprisons Aileen.'

Too cautious? Or perhaps spooked...

Robert punched his hands into his pockets. 'His wife said good things about him. Many people in their community also posted condolence messages on the wife's social media.'

Callan crossed his arms. 'Any strange comments?'

'Nah, just the usual. Sorry, rest in peace, a declaration of support. No mention of anyone else – no girlfriend, friends or family.'

Ken Macalister's isolated life would've spiralled him into obscurity post mortem. An ideal candidate for murder. A murder that Macalister had predicted.

Callan scratched his chin. This was a tougher case than he'd imagined, especially with Irwing in the mix. His manoeuvring had stuck Aileen in a fishbowl and deterred their progress, even if she would welcome the business for the inn.

They had to meet somewhere to talk. With Irwing's connections, the will stood no chance of staying private for longer than a couple of days.

Callan stabbed a finger at Robert. 'Find more from someone other than the wife. Isla's sister, Shelly – ask her son Arran. Ye ken how to talk to children. Just use yer loaf! Now get to it.'

Callan stalked out of the office towards his car. It was time to head home.

. . .

A spot beside Aileen's sedan welcomed him. Thank God for Irwing's van. It ensured ample parking space yet a full inn.

The sound of loud voices and laughter wafted through the chill air. Callan approached the back door and stepped inside.

'Ah! Callan!' Isla growled, a lid in one hand and a spatula in the other. 'You scared a decade off my life.'

'What are ye doing here?'

'Helping! Your arrogant arse of a colleague called an hour ago, commanding Aileen to ready beds and dinner for twelve police officers. She just returned herself.'

Returned? Where had she been?

He stalked into the room, shrugged off his jacket and followed the aroma to a sauce bubbling in the pan. 'That's one of Aileen's recipes.'

Isla smacked him with one hand while stirring the sauce with the other. 'She cooked; I'm helping. Go find her. She'd welcome the added hands.'

The gobsmackingly beautiful brunette behind the reception counter tucked a strand of hair behind her ear. An officer, his uniform stretched across broad shoulders, leaned over and smiled at her. She laughed.

Callan's boots thundered through the room, the rumble echoing off the stone floor.

'Callan!' Aileen smiled at him.

He puffed out his chest and snuck a hand around her waist. 'Hey, darling.'

She blushed a deep crimson. 'Officer Pataky was telling me about your arduous day.'

'Was he?' Callan flashed his teeth. 'I'm sure yers was no less taxing.' Aileen never spent her days shopping. Sleuthing? Aye.

Aileen cleared her throat and passed a key to the officer. 'That's yours. I'm sorry but I'm running out of rooms. You'll have to share with a partner.'

'Don't ye worry.' A second officer patted Pataky on the back. 'We're just happy to have a roof over our heads. I'm not for freezing me arse off out there. Come on, mate. Let's bunk together.'

She reclined into Callan. 'Your possessiveness is irritating but a turn-on at the same time.'

Callan raised his eyebrows. She smacked a hand over her mouth. 'Goodness! Between Isla and Gran, I've lost it. I'm sorry.'

'So no rooms, eh?'

'Twelve officers and ten rooms. They're paying extra for meals. An offer I had to take.'

'One taste of your meals and they'll never leave.'

She squeezed him closer and grinned from ear to ear. 'We need to get out, go somewhere we can talk without being overheard. I have questions and loads of things to tell you.'

Callan squeezed her in return. 'Me too.'

CHAPTER ELEVEN

Callan pushed away from the table. 'If Rory benches me for gaining a hundred pounds, I'm blaming you.'

'What did I do?' Aileen hid her smile as she piled the used plates on a tray. 'And you haven't eaten all day.'

'Ye're still to blame.' He hefted the tray from her hands. She tailed him, carrying more dishes. 'Ye cooked for fifty people, yet there's not a splatter left of that sauce.'

Aileen bumped her hip against Callan's. 'Detectives, in my experience, work up quite the appetite.'

'Do they?'

Aileen squealed when Callan tugged her to his chest and poked her in the ribs.

'Let me see.'

'Callan! I need to do the dishes!' Aileen swatted at his arms. 'And I'm sure you don't want to give my guests an impromptu show.'

Losing his warmth sent a shiver through her.

'I can't wait to see the back of that van. Want my help?'

'If you do the dishes, I'll have to wash them again since you can't—'

'Ye're OCD, not me.'

Callan jumped away from her swinging arm. Hands up in surrender, he headed for the dining room. 'I'll be in the library. Let me know when ye're done.'

'Library? You?'

'Why?'

Aileen frowned. He secreted himself away from her whenever they weren't doggedly pursuing a case. It tickled her self-doubt. 'Nothing…'

She eyed the stack of dishes, staring down the barrel of a long night. A financially profitable one, though. Maybe Midas had laid a hand on her head.

Footsteps headed towards her, their gait unfamiliar. 'Need help?'

But the voice was familiar. 'Detective Spiers.'

Spiers had swapped her suit for jeans and a shirt. 'I worked at a restaurant before the badge. It was a few years ago, but I'm sure I can handle drying the dishes.'

She'd never fit all these dishes in the dishwasher anyway. 'I'd appreciate your help.'

True to her word, Spiers handled the task with efficiency. Their routines fit into silent unison until Spiers reached for a plate and said, 'I worked with Cameron for almost five years and never saw him smile as much as he did tonight.'

'He doesn't smile – he, er… It's a lift of the lips, almost like a grimace.'

'Eyes don't lie, Ms Mackinnon. I never saw that glint, not even when we rid the streets of a serial criminal preying on the old. He breathed the job. Now he doesn't.'

Aileen straightened her shoulders. 'And that's a bad thing?'

Spiers set the plate aside and tilted her head. 'It's change. A change I never imagined for Cameron.'

A question crowded Aileen's throat. A doubt…

'No, Ms Mackinnon. We were never more than colleagues, never entertained the idea. Cameron doesn't make friends – at least, the man I worked with didn't. Now…' Spiers sighed. 'I think it's you.'

'Me?' Aileen hadn't pegged Spiers for a talker. 'What did I do?'

The detective's chuckle rang through the room. 'I think you're the catalyst and the reason for the change. I'm happy for him. The man I worked with, he had no future except for running himself into the ground with every case. This man, he has a purpose beyond that. And that's healthy.'

She placed the last plate away and smiled at Aileen. 'I really don't like you as a suspect for being involved in this crime. It's not because I know you; it's because I know Cameron. And he's a great judge of character.'

Aileen blinked, then stared after Spiers as she headed out the room. She shook her head. What had just happened?

She'd *changed* Callan?

Aileen toed off her shoes – she'd crammed her feet into them over twelve hours ago – and went in search of the man in question.

He was, like he'd said he would be, huddled in the library. Not dozing off, like she'd imagined, but tucked into one of the high-backed chairs. The lamp illuminated a square notebook resting on his arm as he attacked it with a pencil.

Long lines shadowed his eyes, veiling him with an air of mystery. She stood on the threshold, just watching, sharing his silence.

'Ah shite!'

He scribbled something in the notebook. The sense of purpose in him captivated her. He'd carried that notebook with him since November. And he'd refused to share its contents.

Aileen froze when his blue eyes pinned her. 'Aileen.'

His husky voice tingled her nerves. 'What're you doing?'

'Nothing.' The notepad snapped close.

Hiding, again.

'Callan.'

'Should we head out?'

'What's in the notebook?'

'Aye, we'll head out.'

Aileen took a deep breath. 'Is it about Blaine?'

Callan narrowed his eyes. 'Are you snooping on me now?'

His reserve and anger caught her unawares. 'I only want to help, Callan. It's easy to guess. I don't have to snoop to know. Blaine's all that's been on your mind.'

The notebook was slipped into his coat pocket. The pencil followed.

'Are you trying to map out a possible location?'

Callan's eyebrows drew together in a frown. 'Aye. Shall we?'

AILEEN TUCKED HERSELF INTO CALLAN'S CAR JUST AS THE clock turned midnight, Cinderella in reverse. He revved the engine, cranked up the heater, and drove out of the parking spot.

'What did ye do today?'

'I went to Loch Heaven. The person who wrote that newspaper clipping lives there.'

'Yer bum's oot the window!'

'No, really. This woman…' He listened, eyes on the winding road but his sharp ears absorbing every word she uttered. 'Ye didn't ask her about Ken Macalister?'

'I didn't name him. He's on the front page of the newspaper today and, well, I didn't want her to zip up, thinking I'm someone posing as an undercover agent or something.'

Callan let the silence drone on. 'Alright. But she might talk if it's gossip.'

She might but then… 'And I didn't want to alert Walsh either.'

Callan huffed. 'About that… Irwing's closing in on the will.'

Him staying at Dachaigh, despite the welcome income, would hinder her investigative work. She uncurled her spine. 'I don't care about him. I *will* investigate, and he can't stop me if I don't bother him.'

'He hasn't stepped on yer toes yet.' Callan shrugged. 'He's a big deal in our world. But he isn't open to suggestions. My take? Drill into this French case.'

'We're colliding against one dead end after other.'

'Just like I told Robert today, ye can't trust just one source. Ye need to cross investigate.'

Aileen stared out into the nothingness, her heart cracking more with every passing day. 'Cross investigate with *whom* exactly?'

'Ye're a tech whiz. Ye'll find someone.'

Finding Amelia Downie had stolen much of her time. Now she had to find someone else? An idea struck her. 'Amelia mentioned a French police officer. If I find his name in one of those articles, I can ask him.'

'What about Blanchet's ex-wife? Who was she?'

'An innocent, apparently. Someone who remained nameless in the case. Lawyer magic.'

And poor luck for them.

Diamonds glittered in the sky above.

'Somehow, I think solving this fraud case is the key. That's what he said in the will, didn't he? Find my killer and save families. The fraud case hurt many people.'

Callan hummed. 'Right up yer alley.'

'Aye.'

Armed with a talent for prediction, Macalister had obviously carried a brain in his toolbox as well. 'I need data to investigate and I don't know who might have it. Amelia doesn't either.'

'I'll look into that. See what I can find.'

The car's headlights lit up a foot of road. 'Where are we going?'

'What do you think the fortune is? The one that's missing? Is it in cash?'

'Can't say. For one, they aren't sure if there *is* a fortune. It's all speculation but... But if Blanchet was a puppet, I'm thinking whoever sacrificed him has the money. What if it was Macalister?'

When Callan didn't pitch in, she continued. 'For one, they never found all the ledgers, and after Blanchet died, whatever he left in assets was stripped to pay his victims. But as is always the case with Ponzi schemes, the process takes years and you get peanuts back, if anything.'

'How much do the authorities think Blanchet spent?'

Aileen huffed. 'From the reports I found, the figure is a bit murky. On the surface, it looks like he's a genius. No one except Amelia hinted at his lack of brainpower in their articles.'

'Why would she claim that?'

'That he's stupid? His staff told her that.'

Callan drummed his fingers on the steering wheel. 'What if he hid the unaccounted-for treasure?'

'Maybe. But then, a search warrant for his belongings would've found a key or something, you'd think. Unless... Well, unless he hid it under another name.'

'The wife?'

'No. He planned to leave her, dupe her out of money. The last person he'd use to clone his accounts would be her. She'd disappear with the cash.'

The car turned right on the bend until they entered the market square, now as desolate as a haunted house.

'This was fifteen years ago. Why did Macalister come here now? Who would murder him over an old fraud case in Loch Fuar?' Callan pulled up in the empty car park and threw his hand over Aileen's seat. 'We have a lot of questions.'

'And no answers.' She chuckled. 'We always find ourselves in this position.'

His hand resting on the headrest, Callan's thumb caressed her hair. 'There's more at stake now. Especially with Irwing on site. He has the best record of closed cases ever.'

'Well, he can take the credit for it. But I'll solve it.' She reached across to envelop Callan's hand. 'There's a reason Macalister thought I could do this. He didn't write to you or to anyone in the police. He's worked in this field all his life. I'm sure he knew detectives much more experienced and better than me.'

'He gave it to a forensic accountant because he kens ye're good at it.' Callan pointed to her satchel. 'And dedicated to a fault. Take that notepad out. Let's start from the top.'

Heads pressed together, they read the will and article again. Referenced what they knew. 'I'll reach out to Amelia for her source, although she used to be a journalist and anonymity of sources is usually sacred.'

'Fifteen years later, she isn't one.' Callan placed the notepad on his lap.

Aileen reached for the light. 'She's shooting her own cookery show. Currently, she's doing a series about brownie recipes. She's called it Amelia Downie's Brownie Recipes.'

Callan stilled. 'What?'

'The name cracked me up. Downie, Brownie. Get it?'

'Bloody hell.' Callan started up the car. 'Why didn't ye tell me her surname before?'

Pastel green faded against the grey clouds. The person at the door lost his smile, in sync with the weather.

'Detective Cameron! What are ye doing here?'

Heels clicked from inside the house. 'Who is it, darling?'

Amelia Downie's hair was curled like corkscrews, her jeans faded with age and her T-shirt sporting a vintage car. 'Oh, Aileen!'

'Hi, Amelia.'

Callan nodded his greetings, unamused. 'I think we should take this inside, don't you, Tim *Downie*?'

The silence blared louder than horns. Good – the more uncomfortable he was, the better.

Porcelain cups and saucers clinked, yet no one spoke.

Pure, unadulterated rage radiated off Callan like a radio signal. Tim Downie, his red beard shrivelled, sat twiddling his thumbs, looking anywhere but at Callan.

Aileen had strutted into his house alone.

Tim slinked away when Amelia sat beside him, teacup in hand.

Callan discarded his on the coffee table, uninterested in

dainty tea and pleasantries. His jaw was fatigued from the clenching.

Callan's anger bounced right off Tim and lasered in on Aileen. How did she find her way into trouble every damned time?

Amelia cleared her throat. 'What is this about?'

'Ken Macalister,' Callan gritted out through clenched teeth. 'The dead man.'

'Ah! Is that why you were here yesterday?' She gestured at Aileen.

Tim scowled, beard twitching. 'This is harassment! How can you send someone in here to question my wife? We've nothing to do with that man's death! He fooled us, robbed from us! We are the victims here.'

Callan didn't interrupt him, because it would mean hurling something at the pastel walls. His rage choked him into silence.

He shot Aileen a glare.

She'd pleaded innocence, said she hadn't known Amelia was a suspect's wife. Yet she'd failed to mention Amelia's last name. A coincidence, she'd tried to joke. But coincidences were as real as unicorns…

Damn it!

Beside him, Aileen sighed. If she had another trick up her sleeve, he'd strap her in handcuffs. Callan had vowed as much when he'd dropped her off at Dachaigh last night and left her alone.

'Amelia Downie. What was your surname before you married?'

Amelia smiled. 'You catch on quick, Ms Mackinnon. Yes, I wrote an article on Ken Macalister as Lia Edwards.'

Aileen powered through before Callan could vent his frustrations. His death glare lost against her will. 'You told me you didn't report news then; you wrote about lifestyle.'

'It was about lifestyle – a career change, and a very surprising one at that.'

Tim cleared his throat, comprehending the undercurrents and pressing into the cushions like he wanted to camouflage himself amongst them. 'She was living in Stirling then.'

Callan leaned in, gaze directed at Tim. The man swallowed, eyes darting around like he wanted to poof into thin air. 'And yet ye didn't say a word.'

'I-I didn't know! How would I have known?'

Amelia set her cup aside. 'Look, we met in 2004 at a trade show. I was living in a small flat in Stirling. He was in town to see cars, and I was interviewing car enthusiasts.'

'We dated long distance until we married in 2005.' Tim smiled. 'So I didn't know her day-to-day projects.'

Callan hissed. 'Anything else ye'd like to disclose?'

Tim gripped the cushions until his knuckles faded to white. 'As a matter of fact…'

Callan braced himself, imagining himself pouring a litre of truth serum down the man's throat.

'Speak!'

Tim wrung his fingers, still not making eye contact. 'Ken Macalister. He… He…' The feartie jostled his wife.

She, sitting as regally as a queen might, didn't seem the least bit perturbed. 'Ken Macalister was here for us. We'd employed him.'

Callan curled his lips. 'And unicorns fart money.'

'No, no, she's telling the truth!' Tim jumped up. 'I'll show ye.'

Callan gestured to the door before Tim inched towards the car model on the shelf. No way he'd let the man hurl an object at them and make a run for it.

Tim held his hands up, the meagre wind knocked out of his sails. 'I'll show you!'

For a short fellow, he walked like a giant. His wife followed, head held high and a smile on her face. 'Right here.'

They headed to the kitchen, which was decked out with a centre counter and dark granite worktops.

Aileen trailed behind him, eyeing the shining silver appliances with doe eyes. Envy radiated off her. She had eight stoves at Dachaigh, for God's sake!

Amelia reached for the top cabinets, perfect for her height, not her husband's. The room had yellowish-pink walls and camera equipment sitting in the corner – was it a working kitchen or a studio?

A cabinet clicked open next to the back door. Callan cursed at the box inside, armed with a shiny handle and a keypad to enter the passcode. A safe? They had a safe in the kitchen? Right next to the back door?

Amelia's smile morphed into a grin that split her face in two. 'Marvellous idea, isn't it? You'd never think to look for a safe here.'

Callan crossed his arms. 'Yet I'm assuming someone did.'

Her shoulders deflated, and she clutched her husband's hand.

Tim spoke up, having regained some semblance of self-esteem. 'I wake up at about five. Couple of weeks ago, I came downstairs to make coffee, and it stank of cigarette smoke in here. The windows and doors were all locked, and none of us smoke.'

'But' – Aileen had wandered over to the fridge where magnets held up pictures – 'you have a daughter.'

'Pamela's fifteen!' Tim spat, swishing his hands around him. 'She'd never.'

At fifteen, when freedom of adulthood lurked around the corner and extra money from weekend jobs dripped into their pockets, children turned into their evil doppelgangers. After processing his share into custody as a patrol officer, he knew.

Callan pointed to the picture of a girl standing between Tim and Amelia. 'Have ye asked her?'

'N—'

'Yes,' Amelia cut her husband off. 'She denies it, and she doesn't lie. Besides, she shows no symptoms. No smell of smoke on her clothes, stained teeth or anything like that. And I know as a mother.'

Tim blushed. 'I used to – got back into it last year and Lia spotted it. I denied and well…'

Callan steered the conversation away from the breakdown of their relationship. 'And? I'm assuming that wasn't the only reason ye called in an investigator from Stirling.'

'A few days later, I found a cigarette butt and then some money from the safe went missing. There was a muddy footprint – a man's boot, huge. As I said, we felt unsafe.'

'Why not call the police? Ye ken Walsh.'

'We had nothing to show for it except a couple of misplaced items. The last thing Declan needs is us sending him on a wild goose chase.'

'Did yer sister ken about this?'

Amelia snorted. 'Amy? Her opinions don't go much beyond whether she prefers magenta or dark pink.'

He saw it in her eyes and in the subtle lift of her chin – Amelia and Amy didn't get along.

Tim cleared his throat. 'Amy and I, we'd lost contact until she moved back. We're not that close.'

'Except she works right next to you and lives next door.'

Aileen treaded over to the safe, perhaps as eager as Callan was to cut the tension. 'And Ken Macalister? Why did you employ him for the job? He wasn't doing fieldwork anymore.'

'I wrote articles on him. Heard good things. We asked for a consult over the phone. He said he'd come here.'

Callan scratched his chin. Some missing change, a footprint and a cigarette smell had tantalised a seasoned security worker to travel miles to Loch Heaven? Macalister's job paid well, so something apart from money must have drawn him here.

Callan uncrossed his arms, surveyed the safe one last time, and bobbed his head. 'If there's anything else, ye better fess up. It won't look good in court when ye've withheld information. It's obstruction of justice.'

They swore Macalister had kept them in the dark. Except for a phone call, the day he'd disappeared.

'He called Tim to say he'd solved it. And then he gets killed.' Aileen snorted, burrowing down in her coat to shield herself from the gushing wind as they headed to the car. 'Looks like we have another mystery to solve. Another route that might lead us to the actual killer.'

Or lead them astray.

'So you're the lucky one. Faithful as a pup, your beau is.' Amy waltzed up to them, wearing a pink fur coat. 'Hard to find such a man.'

Aileen blinked, then smiled flatly. 'Er, thank you?'

Amy stuck out her hand. 'Not well trained in manners though, is he? I'm Amy, Tim's sister.'

'H—'

'If ye ever get bored—'

'Amy,' Callan butted in. 'We have to go.'

His words didn't seem to register. She leaned into him, so her lips brushed his ears and her perfume made him gag. 'I live right next door and cook a mean steak.'

Words said, she winked and sauntered off to her house.

Callan just shook his head and sighed as he opened the car door.

Aileen stayed mute while she buckled herself in. Crossing her arms, she stared out at the hurtling scenery. No questions about the case, no nothing.

Callan let it go, focusing on the road.

When the signpost indicating Loch Fuar flashed past, Aileen dropped her arms. 'Pink fur – did you like it?'

'Fur's never pink, is it?'

'Expensive fur can be. Not in fashion with those who advocate sustainability though, is it?'

'Amy Downie mustn't care for sustainability.' He floored the accelerator.

'No, she doesn't seem to be very… mainstream. After all, who throws herself at a man when his girlfriend is standing right next to him?'

Callan licked his dry lips. 'I'm not sure she threw herself at me.'

Aileen crossed her arms again. 'Oh, I'm sure you never noticed her wandering hands—'

'Geez, Aileen! For all I ken she's a suspect.'

He pressed the brake outside Dachaigh and the car screeched to a halt.

The dust settled. Aileen snarled, eyes spitting fire. 'Of course, but look at us. Wasn't I a suspect to begin with?'

She hopped out of the car before Callan formed the words. What the hell was that? What had he done wrong?

He ran the scenario through his mind. Amy had accosted him. He'd peeled her off him from the first time they'd met. If she crossed the line, he'd stop her, hands down.

Where had this green-eyed monster come from? Aileen never acted this way. And they'd dealt with a lot of female suspects.

Callan chalked it up to stress. She'd come around tomorrow. He had other matters to worry about.

He turned the car around and made for the police station.

IRWING STANDING BY THE COFFEE MACHINE WAITING FOR Callan's arrival threw him off stride, farther than he already was after the argument he'd had with Aileen.

'I hope you were off looking for the missing car.' Irwing assessed him from top to toe.

'Aye. The case, that's all that's on my mind.'

Irwing trod over, shorter than him by a couple of inches, eyes hidden behind sunglasses. 'I hope you know which side you're on. Not with that girlfriend playing amateur sleuth. I heard she's got you on a leash, dragging you around to do her bidding.'

Callan curled his fingers into fists. First Aileen and now this man. Did he look like a damned punching bag?

'I have assured ye, several times, that I'm my own man. And she kens what she's doing.'

Irwing dangled a sheet of paper before him, the photocopy of a document he'd perused so many times now, his eyes bled just looking at it.

'So you got the will.'

'Easily. What's to say she didn't convince him to write a will in her name before murdering him?'

'If that's yer theory, it's piss poor in logic.'

'It's more objective than what your tiny brain's comprehended. Listen carefully now, Detective Inspector. You best be autonomous. And as is, you're off the case.'

Callan let out a chuckle then a growl. 'I wasn't on it anyway. Which makes me wonder: why pull in the top dogs to investigate an almost retired man's death?'

'We're dealing with—'

'Aye, aye, I've heard that silly excuse. But even my tiny brain sees crap and comprehends it.'

Callan leaned in until his fury clashed against the other man's ego. 'I'll let you know, *Inspector*, no matter yer opinion, I see more clearly and independently than yer myopic eyes do.'

And this time, he stormed away, vibrating like a raging bull! His stack of unfinished cases awaited investigation, and if Irwing decided he could flick Callan off the case as one might shove away a puppy looking for attention, he'd have another think coming.

CHAPTER TWELVE

Aileen paced the kitchen, happy with the silence given the police officers were out working. She loved the cooking and chatter of a full inn, just not Irwing's assessing gaze documenting her every move.

Nor did she care about women like Amy, who smelled of expensive perfumes and waltzed towards her boyfriend like he was the designer handbag they wanted.

Urgh! Amy shopped not just for pink furs, but also at jewellery stores. Aileen shied away from such baubles, but, thanks to her mother, she recognised expensive jewellery when she saw it.

That ring she'd been wearing was too fancy to flash on a working day. Unless Amy had spotted Callan enter her brother's house and had just decided to irritate the hell out of Aileen... Or try her hand at Callan.

Isla said it right. Men were oblivious, and Callan led the pack.

Neanderthal, blind oaf...

'Urgh!'

She stalked out the back door and to her car. She needed a keen eye.

Isla McIntyre's emerald eyes could peruse a pink fur coat like a quality control officer. 'Are you sure you it couldn't have been fake fur?'

'I told you the ring was real! Big enough to take out someone's eye.'

Isla hummed. 'Jewellery's useless in determining someone's worth. It could be an heirloom or a gift from a rich lover. Did she look well groomed?'

Aileen sneered. 'The gold jewellery shone so bright it blinded Callan's senses.'

'Phew! That's saying something.'

'It sure is,' Aileen seethed, still unsure why Amy had irked her this much. Her reaction kindled from something more than stress. 'The ring shone, so she'd polished it recently. So I'm thinking it's either new or she gets it cleaned regularly. That means she cares about it. But... Her hair's seen the hands of a hairdresser. And her whole physique. She must be fond of the gym. That's a lot of work for a woman who owns her own business.'

Isla held up one finger. 'It's not a crime to take care of oneself. And she clearly does that. Are you sure you aren't... you know?'

Aileen huffed. 'Sometimes you're just useless!'

She bristled at Isla's snort. 'You need a tub of ice cream, a spa and some chocolate eclairs. And grooming. When was the last time you had your hair done?'

'No way! I've real work to do. Callan can go admire as many—'

Isla drew Aileen into a hug. 'He's not that sort of man. Whatever you think, you haven't seen him every time you're in trouble. That's not the sort of man to shop around.'

'He's no loyal dog, Isla!'

Her friend chuckled. 'No, he's a wolf.'

SOME ICE CREAM DRIPPED STRENGTH INTO AILEEN, boosting her to take on the day. She had dinner to cook and rooms to clean.

She set Bonnie to work on arranging the toiletries and headed in to dust and make the beds herself. Ten rooms in order, she hurried into the kitchen, hoping one day she could hire more staff to manage a full inn.

A girl could dream.

By six, Aileen had set the table for her twelve guests, knowing they wouldn't be in until after seven, and set a curry to simmer on the hob. Despite the labour, she wasn't hungry for food either. She'd kill for some peace to do her research.

Schneider's message notified her Irwing had laid his paws on the will. Either he'd question her about it or eat his dinner in peace and postpone the interviewing until tomorrow.

She hoped for the latter.

Aileen sighed. More funds would let her break these walls and… 'Enough dreaming for today, Aileen. *Work*.'

She focused on the data before her. Should she give Shaeline Macalister another call? And risk that woman setting the police on her again?

Half past six. Experience told Aileen to call her office.

Aileen bit her lip, reached inside herself to rekindle her earlier anger, and dialled the phone number on the website.

'Fox, Krishnan and Maxwell, how may I help you?'

'I'd like to speak with Shaeline Macalister.'

A pause. 'Who am I speaking to?'

'Aileen Mackinnon. Ms Macalister knows me.'

A tune played down the line. Aileen didn't care for the baroque notes. She imagined a stuffy, dark timbered office.

'Ms Mackinnon, I must stress this is harassment.'

'Please, Ms Macalister. I'm trying to find justice for your ex-husband.'

A pause came down the line. 'I spoke with Schneider. He trusts you, but I don't. I don't see why Ken would leave it all to you or change his will days before he… All I can say is, I'll see you in court.'

The line went dead. 'Crap!' She tugged her hair, annoyed by it all. Damn the day; damn this case!

'What's wrong, Ms Mackinnon?'

He was the last person she wanted to deal with.

Like a robot, she replied, 'I presume you'll be ready for dinner in fifteen minutes?'

Irwing smiled. 'Sure. I could help.'

'No—'

'My wife says I should've taken up hotel management with my skills at setting tables.'

Aileen gestured to the dining table where empty plates and glassware already sat.

'And you should be the one teaching the class, I see.'

He sat at the kitchen counter, on the same seat Callan always occupied. 'You're as efficient as your CV suggests.'

Aileen froze. He'd run her?

'You're a suspect. I must know who's who.' He read minds, yet he didn't pick up on her annoyance at his presence. 'I must investigate, even if the local police seem disinclined.'

The pan she'd just picked up crashed back down on the hob. Another retort aimed at Callan.

Her boyfriend's silence after their brief fight might frustrate her, but the man in front of her was testing her patience more than Callan ever did. He'd strutted in here for a reason, and it wasn't to be polite.

Aileen stirred the curry, ignoring the eyes drilling into her back.

'Wine?'

'I don't drink; never gave in to its temptation. I've seen a few colleagues fall from grace that way.'

Alcohol dimmed the senses, and he wanted to stay sharp.

She switched off the heat and placed the pot on the marble counter.

'Ah, curry! I haven't had one of those in a while. My wife's idea of a curry is water and curry powder. Yours smells lovely.'

A bowl of steaming rice joined the pot. 'I hope you like it.' Curries were her comfort food from her accounting days, a reassurance that next time she wouldn't let her colleague or boss steamroll her into taking work home.

She cooked a mean curry but still struggled with saying no.

Irwing pushed away from the table. 'Let me plate it up for you. Those bowls there, they're for the curry?'

Aileen let him be, reaching for the spoon when *slap*! His hand caught her wrist. She startled, before sending him a scowl. Her heart hammered and the glint in his eyes infused fear.

'I'm sure your loyal boyfriend,' he spat, 'will have told you I have the will.'

Aileen tilted her head. 'I haven't spoken to him in a while. Besides, as I'm sure I've told you, we leave his work at the door.'

'Ms Mac—'

'It might be difficult for you to wrap your head around.' Aileen leered at him despite her racing heartbeat. 'But murder and crime aren't the best topics for pillow talk.'

Aileen snatched her hand back, pulled the pot away from him and plated the curry into bowls, dismissing the man.

Irwing chuckled. 'Looks like I've been sucked into a domestic. No wonder you haven't spoken to your beau.'

Aileen's neck prickled. Beau?

'But know this: you can trot around with your little magnifying glass and hat all you want. Impede my investigation and you'll be in handcuffs. I'm not looking the other way like your lapdog does.'

'Excuse me? Who's a lapdog?'

'You know exactly what I mean.'

That nasty piece of —

'I know what it says in the will. Leave the murder to the police. That fickle piece of paper won't hold in court. The former wife's bound to contest you and win. So please, stay out of it – stay off the killer's radar.'

Aileen sneered. 'Oh, you poor men. You think you can patronise a woman into doing your bidding. You think Callan hasn't tried various versions of that same line on me? Well, think again, Detective Inspector Irwing. A man's been murdered, yet all you can do is poke my boyfriend and me. What concrete data have you found yet?'

Irwing curled his lips. 'Why, the way you're spewing curses at me makes me believe it is you, after all.'

CALLAN RATTLED HIS DOOR CLOSED. EVERYONE understood not to mess with him, not now.

He'd been shunned twice that day. Aileen hadn't said it in so many words, but he'd known what she was getting at. Hell, was he some wanton teenager?

He stalked to the back wall where his murder board used to be. Bloody Irwing had hijacked his life.

Old Burn's barn beckoned to him. An hour of kick-boxing sounded refreshing, but he had other plans. His notebook, the one for his eyes only, slid into the bottom-most drawer, followed by the pencil. Callan then kicked the drawer closed and locked it.

He plopped into his chair – an item he'd fight tooth and nail to keep in this office – and shut his eyes in thought.

Amelia and Tim's lack of truthfulness jeopardised their word. Macalister had answered their invite. Had they killed him?

Too much of a paper trail, too much trouble to kill a man. And what would their motive be, anyway?

Amy, Tim's sister, knew nothing about his problems. She didn't remember what she'd spoken to Macalister about in those twenty minutes. That woman would flirt with a rat. Besides, he had no proof she'd interacted with Macalister before that day. Again, no motive for murder.

The ex-wife. Her relationship with Macalister was strange. Thirty-five years of marriage and yet they'd gone their separate ways with no altercation or bitterness. Sure, separation bruised, but what had created the rift? Had one of them been unfaithful only to have their affair and marriage both fall apart?

Their divorce papers, according to Robert, cited 'irreconcilable differences', yet they'd never approached a therapist or marriage counsellor. And two months later they'd shared Christmas dinner together.

Shelly, their neighbour and Isla's sister, didn't

remember any fights between the couple. She'd shrugged it off, saying they'd grown apart. The wife, according to her, went on several work trips and Macalister kept late hours at the office.

But the Macalisters' schedule would have been nothing new.

A couple of days ago, Shaeline had set the dogs on Aileen for knocking at her door. Who called the police on a stranger at their door? They might've exchanged words, but calling the police?

Was Shaeline Macalister afraid of someone?

Had Ms Macalister committed the fraud? Was that the reason for the divorce?

'And so she kills him, not in Stirling, but miles away where no one suspects her,' he murmured.

The only dent in his theory? The woman had a solid alibi.

Back to square one. Callan pursued two other tangents. Ken Macalister's death had something to do with Beau Blanchet or the man stealing from the Downies.

Since the first case required accounting skills and data he didn't have, Callan focused on the latter.

He pulled up the list of dates the stranger had allegedly entered the Downies' residence.

Random days. He cross-checked them with the calendar, but there was no obvious connection.

A thought came to mind, a stray memory of his sister sneaking out the back door to meet her boyfriend.

Callan smirked. He'd caught her and sent the eejit packing.

Now he knew just what to do.

He grabbed a pair of binoculars and some peppermints then headed to his car.

A stakeout meant long, lonely hours of precious silence.

CALLAN BOUGHT A SANDWICH AT LOCH HEAVEN'S supermarket. Fury had kept his body going so far, but now it craved real food.

Residents of Loch Heaven liked the night as much as the day. Different patrons crowded the streets now, the kind he'd encountered when he and Aileen had gone in search of Marley Watson's killer in the lesser privileged areas of this town.

He stuck to the GPS, legible in English now.

His car lumbered down the road at a pace that drew no attention. Close-knit communities, like the ones he was en route to, stayed vigilant.

The speaker asked him to turn right. His destination lay on the right. He found a parking spot and cut the engine.

His black clothes matched the long shadows. A gold beam from the street light stretched towards the Downies' place, falling shy of his car by an inch.

A car gleamed in the driveway next to theirs. Amy was most likely home.

Minutes ticked by and Callan's eyes adjusted to the darkness. Shadows moved inside the Downies' house.

At eight o'clock, the family would be winding down for the day. It was the perfect time for the teenage daughter to sneak out or let someone in.

His assessment was that whoever entered had to walk through the gate at the fence. And that sat right in front of the house. The fence was too high to allow entry through the back garden, and the neighbour's garage blocked any other access point. And now, shadows ate up the dark space, making it easy for someone to enter undetected.

Callan caressed his chin.

A man's footprint, Tim had said. And the smell of a cigarette.

Could a lad fill out a man's shoe at fifteen? Highly plausible. But Callan had a feeling the perp could legally buy his cigarettes.

Classic case of why she'd sneak him in. Or steal the money.

Callan cursed himself for not asking the Downies where the girl studied. Such predators hung out near schools, casing their next gullible prey.

But could that man have committed murder, too? It seemed unlikely, but curiosity had wrapped around him like a puppet's strings and bewitched him to come here.

Callan's lips parted for a yawn. Hell, it was hardly nine!

His penance for spending last night worrying, dissecting and running the facts of the case in his mind.

Yet nothing had slotted into place.

The French fraud case had nothing in common with the Downies except for Ken Macalister.

Well… He had another connection. Amelia Downie had written an article on Ken Macalister and on the French case. Still, she had no motive to want Macalister dead that he could see.

Whoever it was had known how to set a fire, enough to destroy evidence. And Aileen… Had they wanted Aileen to find the crime scene? Had they known about the will?

Bloody hell! Bloody Macalister was proving to be the biggest mystery of them all.

A light flickered on in front of him, drawing Callan from his thoughts.

Someone had switched on a golden lamp on the first

floor in the Downies' household. Amy's house remained shrouded in silence, even though lights brightened the ground floor. He'd never met a more flamboyant woman.

Callan ran a hand through his hair. Flamboyant enough to get Aileen's knickers in a twist.

He wasn't apologising to Aileen. He'd done nothing wrong.

He'd deal with his personal life later. Foremost, he had to find Macalister's killer so Aileen could—

Ah, there was Amy at her window. She was definitely in then.

Callan examined the Downie household, or more importantly the back garden, where trees created a convenient canopy.

The house next to his car lay empty. One thing on his side. He didn't want eyes trailing him.

Back in her house, Amy was still peering out the window as if she was waiting for someone.

Hell! Callan sank into his seat, hoping the beanie and turned-up coat collar hid his identity.

The sound of a car engine drifted through the closed windows. A second later, headlights highlighted the houses, and a car drove past Callan's.

No guesses where it stopped.

A minute later, a man with a silver jacket, white shoes and a dark hat shadowing his face swaggered to Amy's door and—

She yelped and jumped into his arms.

So she *had* been expecting company.

Callan rolled his eyes and refocused on his mission. The Downies'… And he waited.

At Amy's, they didn't bother drawing the curtains. If Callan's eyes moved an inch from their spot, he'd see things he'd never be able to erase.

He watched the Downies' house until his eyes watered, his arse frozen from the cold seeping into his idle car. Yet nothing happened.

Time passed – an hour, two and...

Crap!

He'd just been about to give up, resigned to failure, when something rustled.

A second rustle emanated from the darkness near the Downies' back door. Shite!

The eejit had climbed over their neighbour's garage and jumped into the back garden.

Nothing moved – nothing except the grass in that dark patch of yard.

Callan elbowed his car door open and stepped out.

CHAPTER THIRTEEN

The chill enveloped him first, and then the icy wind found its way through his thick scarf.

Bloody hell!

Just when things couldn't get any worse... Callan shivered.

Ensuring he'd locked the car and stuffed the key in his pocket – so the perp didn't use it to get away – he blended into the darkness.

The shadows between the dim street lights crafted perfect hiding places. No wonder he'd managed to sneak in.

Callan skulked around a stray patch of light, a cat hurtling past into the hedges.

Dry twigs tugged at his woollen beanie and caught into his scarf, so he ducked, tucking his chin into his chest. One hard tug and the bushes would rustle. And on a still night, he'd give himself away like a searchlight.

One noiseless footstep in front of the other, he never inched into the periphery of the light. Callan eased through the gate until his feet dipped in the grass.

Soft earth, frozen grass...

Warm air from his lungs misted the air, so he tugged the scarf up over his mouth and felt his way to the edge of the wall. The rough concrete scratched his back as he eased his way around the building.

He slid an inch, and then a squeak fragmented the silence.

'Shush! You'll wake them up.'

'Sorry!' a female voice gushed. 'I didn't mean to—' She trailed off.

'Not here,' a male voice countered.

Callan didn't pick up his pace. He needed to catch the eejit red-handed. Tim's daughter had held the door open for him. Sneaking in – when invited into a house – wasn't a crime. He had to wait.

And Callan had patience in spades.

Another click announced the perp had slipped in, the parents asleep in their beds.

Callan crouched lower until the grass tickled his knees. In the darkness, the cold grew denser, making it harder to draw breath.

He studied the garage – it had to be ten feet tall at least. Either the perp was after more cash or he wanted something else – something Callan didn't want to think about.

The kitchen windows would give Callan the perfect opportunity to observe. But he was no stalker.

Before heading to the windows, he dialled Walsh.

'Cameron, don't you get any—'

Callan rattled off the address. 'I have the perp under observation. He could be a killer. Come prepared, no sirens.'

Without waiting for a reply, Callan crept towards the back door. One more step, then he peeped through the window and saw them.

The eejit appeared about twenty. He sat on top of the kitchen counter, back slouched, a cigarette burning in his hand.

Pamela – not as innocent as her parents claimed her to be then – opened the window to let the smoke out, then stood back and wrung her hands, clearly uncomfortable with her boyfriend's arse being plonked on her mother's pristine counter.

She wore jeans and a sweatshirt. A curtain of dirty blond hair shielded her face, and her slouch suggested waning confidence.

Callan rested his phone on the sill, recording the video for evidence. He had no jurisdiction here, but he wanted a record just in case.

The lad mumbled something. Callan couldn't read his face; he'd hidden it under a cap. And they hadn't switched on the lights, so he only had moonlight to see by.

The lad puffed rings of smoke before tipping the ash on the counter.

Callan watched him gesture into the air.

The girl jerked her head up, eyes wide. 'Money? I-I…'

'Your parents have it in that safe, don't they?'

'They'll know it's me. I told you they got that detective to investigate us.'

A long silence drew more puffs.

Then he curled his fingers around Pamela's chin and jerked it up. 'You know I love you, don't you?'

'I-I do,' she whispered.

Callan fought the urge to punch a wall. He didn't appreciate adults preying on young, impressionable girls.

'I just need the help, babe.'

Her chin wobbled, and she swallowed. 'I'm not sure…'

'You'll do it for me.'

Callan didn't appreciate his tone. But he had no grounds to barge in and make an arrest yet.

'I... How much d-do you...?'

'A couple of thousand? Aye, two grand.'

Her eyes widened — watery grey orbs that reminded him of a scared pup's. 'Johnny, if they find out!'

'Shush, honey!' The man couldn't even coo without it sounding like a leer. 'If they hear you, no more fun.'

'Last time you said...'

'Last time was a different day, different night. I took you out, didn't I? Twice to that fancy restaurant in the other town? Even while that man sat right outside, spying on us like a perv?'

Pamela's hand trembled. She raised it to swipe a tear. 'I'm sorry for not being discreet enough. It's just that... He's gone now.'

'Aye. Oh, come 'ere.' Johnny didn't stop puffing away — he just used his other arm to tug her in.

The smoke, stronger now, wafted through the window. It had no other escape from the room. The kitchen door stayed shut to keep the smoke and sound trapped in.

But that meant Callan swallowed the bloody fumes. Hell, he'll deal.

Half a minute passed before Johnny shoved her away.

'Now, the money?' Sleazy bastard!

She rubbed her palms against her arms and traipsed over to where, only hours before, Amelia had boasted about her ingenious safe.

Not so secret, was it?

Callan adjusted the phone to document Pamela's movements. It wouldn't pick out much through the darkness, but it would have to do.

The cabinet door swung open, and Pamela raised her hand to type in the pin. So the pin wasn't a secret.

Beep!

The door of the safe clicked and Pamela thrust her hand inside.

Despite the darkness, Callan could tell Johnny's eyes were twinkling.

Where the hell was Walsh?

Callan crept towards the back door and slowly turned the knob. To his surprise, the door was unlocked.

He had no jurisdiction here, but he had evidence of coercion. Should he wait?

Callan checked his holster. He suspected the lad was a killer. It was good enough.

Callan gripped the butt of his gun and pressed his shoulder to the door.

'That isn't two grand! Can't you bloody count?'

'I'm sorry – sorry!'

Something thudded, and a yelp caught Callan's ears.

'What did I say? Shush. Not a word. Understood?'

Callan left his position at the door and peeped through the window to see Johnny's arms were now wrapped around Pamela, so he had her in a chokehold.

Damn it!

A knife glistened at her throat. 'But now that you've opened that pretty box, I guess it's mine for the taking, eh?'

To hell with Walsh and jurisdiction.

Callan crashed through the door, gun raised. 'Drop the knife now!'

He startled Johnny enough that the knife clattered to the floor.

Pamela gaped, rooted to her spot.

'Move, Pamela!' And Callan lunged, not for the girl, but for the man drawing another knife from the rack.

'You called the damned police?'

Callan ducked out of the knife's range but— 'Urgh!' It nicked his arm.

He slotted his gun back in its holster and let his frustration at the day fly. His fist caught Johnny in the gut. One kick sent the knife skidding under the counter.

A fist flew at his face. Callan swivelled, cold muscles warming up.

A warm trickle slithered down his forearm. Blood. This was much better than kickboxing at Old Brun's.

Callan crouched and knocked the lad's feet from under him. Johnny fumbled, flailing towards the counter.

Pamela screamed, the sound blasting Callan's eardrums.

'I'll deal with you after I deal with this bastard!' Johnny thrust a knife at Callan. Callan deduced Johnny hadn't a clue how to wield one.

But he could do more harm that way.

Callan leaped away, avoiding the razor-sharp edge by a millimetre.

'Drop it!'

'Ah!' Johnny kicked and punched, knife clutched in his hand.

'Ye're going to hurt yerself.'

'I'm going to kill you!'

And he lunged straight for Callan's heart.

Callan sidestepped, caught the eejit's wrist and—

The door to the kitchen crashed into the back wall.

Tim stood there, hands raised. 'What the hell?'

'Move!' His wife, silky pyjamas rustling, stormed inside. 'Stop it!'

Callan would stop it if the eejit stopped. Otherwise, he'd die for sure.

He faked a kick then punched Johnny square in the

face. Callan's foot skidded over the knife on the floor. 'Hell!' Johnny went in for another kill shot.

Using all his might, Callan pounced and dragged Johnny's arse down. He pressed his knee into the eejit's back flattening him on the floor.

A prey caught by his predator, the lad flailed his legs, almost dislodging Callan. Bloody hell! He had to be above 300 pounds.

Callan grabbed his wrists, holding him down.

Where the hell was Walsh?

'Stop!' Amelia shouted.

Freezing water smacked into Callan. It stung his arm, before seeping through his clothes. 'Jesus!'

Then the water changed direction towards the perp underneath him, smacking him in the face and ending any attempts at a fight.

Callan kicked the knife away then strapped him in cuffs 'What the hell was that?'

'I could ask ye the same!' Tim raced into the room. 'Johnny! What the shite are ye doing here?'

Goosebumps smattered Callan's arms. Water mixed with blood dripped onto the wet floor.

Callan faced the Downies. Amelia clutched a hose to her chest. Pamela burrowed into her father.

Water dripped down Callan's face.

'Ye ken him?'

Tim nodded. 'He works at the garage, damn it!'

Crack! The back door hit the wall and there stood Walsh, dry in a trench coat, hat in place, dark skin glowing and his eyes... Callan didn't like the glint in them or the hint of a smile.

Walsh beckoned to the police officers behind him. 'Get the perp checked out by the paramedics before hauling his arse in.'

Callan handed the eejit over to the officers, glad he'd done something worthwhile that evening.

'You look nice.' Walsh smirked.

'Yummy, he looks yummy. All wet abs and muscles.'

Amy stalked in, clad in her nightgown and heels.

'Amy!' Tim barked. 'What—'

'I saw him.' She pointed at Walsh. 'My date just left.'

Despite the glare Amelia fired her way, Amy clicked towards Pamela and hugged her.

'Aw, Pammy, what is it?' she cooed as Pamela cried into her shoulder.

Callan's shirt would dry under the heated gaze Amelia shot at the duo.

Undercurrents...

Amy soothed a hand down her niece's back. 'It's alright, alright... A nice tea is what you need. Come on.'

Walsh stopped them. 'I'll need a word with her.'

Tim crossed his arms. 'No! She's done nothing wrong.'

'Yet we have a video of her taking the money out of the safe.'

Callan frowned. 'How do ye know that?'

'You video-called me, didn't you?'

He had no clue how to video-call someone – he thought he'd just been recording to his own phone – but either way, technology had finally done something right.

Amy shook her head. 'She's just a wee girl!'

'I'll speak to her with a guardian present. That's either parent.'

When Amy's sultry eyes turned on him, Callan backed away. He didn't care for her attention any more than he had the hose.

Walsh jerked his head towards the door. 'A word?'

They stepped out into the cold night air, unmerciful to a man in wet clothes.

'Fancied a bath with the perp, did you?'

'Shut up!'

'If it's any consolation, Amy's looking at you like you're a slice of pizza after a gruelling day.'

Callan curled his lips. 'Keep yer trap shut!'

Walsh held his arms up. 'I won't tell Aileen! You can have all the fun you want. But first, what the hell are you doing here?'

He didn't make friends often, but Walsh was solid.

Lights from the kitchen flooded the yard. He saw the sleep lines on Walsh's face and the T-shirt sticking out from his trench coat. Callan grimaced. 'Sorry, it's hell when someone wakes ye from sleep.'

'You think? Next time, a warning at least fifteen minutes *before* you barge in would be appreciated.'

The tips of Callan's hair had frozen. He shivered. 'It wasn't planned! When my new boss plus my girlfriend decide to use me as their personal punching bag, I've got to do something.' And so Callan ranted, explained it all, cursing in between words and sentences.

Walsh listened, not interrupting even when someone blanketed a towel on Callan's shoulders and pushed coffee into his hands.

'Okay, I get it now. So you think this eejit killed Macalister?'

Callan considered their wrestling match. 'I'm not sure. He had motive. Macalister caught them together.'

'A man observed them from afar, that's what he implied.'

'Aye. The day he died, I think Macalister was coming here to inform the parents. If Tim knew Johnny was fooling around with his daughter, he'd fire Johnny on the spot.

'From fighting with him, Johnny kens crap about

combat. And he scrambled over that roof; didn't lock the back door. Compare that to the premeditated nature of the crime scene, I just can't see him doing it.'

Walsh crossed his arms and leaned against the wall. 'Well, didn't you say the killer shot Macalister first? So he or she didn't give him a chance to fight back. Johnny avoided the parents for a month.'

He didn't seem like a cold-blooded criminal. His crime had most likely just been to lure a youngster and steal from her parents, not murder.

A paramedic trudged over to them. 'The perp is cleared. But you, Detective, are bleeding.'

Callan raised his hand to wave the medic away and ended up grimacing. 'Hell!'

'Go on, Cameron. I'll deal with that eejit now.'

He let Walsh be and followed the paramedic.

'It's a wee bit deep – might need stitches,' the medic informed him. 'Hold on.'

It hurt, despite the anaesthetic. The cold didn't help. Callan hated needles, hated them so much, he contemplated making a run for it. 'Ouch!'

Damn it!

'Hold still, sir.'

Easy for him to say. He wasn't being stitched up like a torn teddy bear.

He gritted his teeth, sure he razed off a millimetre of enamel.

A couple of minutes later, the paramedic stepped back, grinning at his handiwork. 'Done!'

Callan wanted to stick his tongue out, but, well, he'd made enough of a fool of himself.

'Your clothes are wet – don't sit out here.'

Callan waved the medic away and stalked off.

'Sir!' The man ran after him. 'If the pain intensifies,

take this painkiller. Not on an empty stomach, though, and not before you drive back; it might make you drowsy.'

Callan stuck the tablet in his pocket and strode to his car.

'You're welcome!' the medic called after him.

Callan hissed. Hadn't he dealt with enough bampots for the day?

Apparently not. Amy sauntered over. 'Aw, blue-eyed babe, are you okay?'

'You're not needed—'

She threw her arms around him. 'Oh, I was so scared, especially when I saw the blood on your arm!'

Callan's breath hitched. The woman hadn't bothered to cover up. How she survived the cold, he couldn't tell. But that wasn't the reason he couldn't breathe. She'd slapped on so much perfume, Callan's senses dizzied from its fumes.

He peeled her away, afraid the smell would linger. He didn't want to face Aileen after their last conversation reeking of women's perfume.

'I have to get to work.' He dodged her wide arms and found Walsh. Behind him trailed Johnny.

The perp lashed out, feet not connecting with anything. The poker-faced officer clutched him in a tight grip.

'I'll get you for this! Mark my words!' Johnny screamed until several more people peeked out of their windows. 'You won't make it!'

The officer opened the car door and shoved him in. 'We'll get you for this! You'll never—' The door slammed in his face.

'Loony,' Walsh remarked, hands stuffed in his trench coat. 'And a piece of work.'

'Your work, not mine. But I'd like a word with the parents.'

'All yours. I have to forgo sleep because you had a pissing match with your girlfriend. I've never seen eye to eye with her and this certainly doesn't improve my opinion of her.'

Callan sighed. He'd caught an eejit at least. He hunched over against the cold and headed for the house.

Questions echoed in his mind. It was time he got some answers.

CHAPTER FOURTEEN

Callan found Tim in the living room, pacing a hole in the floor and spewing curses. Officers and medical staff had cleared the room.

He paused, seeing Callan at the threshold, before gesturing to the chair.

Callan was grateful for the distraction from his smarting arm.

'Thank you. I don't... To think a man I paid, *hired* wasn't just stealing from me but leading my daughter on!'

'It's hard to spot predators sometimes.'

'Hard to spot! I shoulda known. The lad couldn't keep that leer off his face, the tobacco stench off his clothes. Twenty, but what had he to show for it? No manners, no kindness, no nothing! If I wasn't around, he'd be the first to take off with a car, and to think he's been messing with my baby!'

The turmoil dancing in Tim's eyes exploded into the room. 'He came to my house! Coerced my baby to steal! And... Oh god, I hope he didn't make her do anything else...'

Sandals slapped against the tiles, and Amelia entered the room.

'No, he didn't do anything else. Otherwise that bastard wouldn't have left here alive.' She faced Callan. 'And I have no qualms about saying this in front of a detective.'

'I hope your daughter is alright.'

'As alright as she can be.' Amelia rubbed her arms. 'It's a lesson she had to learn one day, although I'd have preferred not so soon and in such a way. The police will question her, won't they?'

Callan rubbed his palms against his thighs. 'We don't yet know if Johnny was involved in anything more sinister.'

'He wasn't,' came a whisper from behind him. Pamela, pale and slouched, trudged over to the sofa her parents sat on and sank between them, looking five years younger. Her dirty blond hair was drawn back into a ponytail and she'd changed into sweats.

Skin and bones with not much self-esteem. Or perhaps Johnny had scared the living daylights out of her.

'Johnny wouldn't hurt someone, not deliberately. No matter what it looks like.' She swiped a tear. 'He wouldn't have hurt you. He'd fallen on tough times and I just wanted to—'

'Pamela, you cannot defend him!'

She shrank away from her mother, burrowing into her father again as if he were her blanket. Tim draped an arm around his daughter and pecked her on the forehead. 'Darling, you need some sleep. Your mum and I'll talk to you tomorrow.'

'That's what got me here in the first place!' She pushed away from him, sat up straight, and set her pleading grey eyes on Callan's. 'He isn't vile. He was the only kind guy around. He's only ever been kind. Then... Then his brother got into drugs and such. Johnny only wants him to get help, so he needed the money.'

Callan folded his arms. 'When was this?'

'Some time ago. But he's never asked for money again. Not until… until tonight… He works at my father's and helps around to make some extra cash on the side. Johnny's never hurt anyone – ever!'

He had to look into her story, ask other people Johnny had worked with, and check his rap sheet.

'He's never raised a hand to you before?'

Pamela shook her head. 'He ghosted me a few days ago. I didn't know what to do. He wouldn't answer my calls, messages, or emails, just silence… I—' Her eyes flitted between her parents. 'I don't have many friends, and no one really looks at me. I don't go out much.'

She wrung her hands, not meeting Callan's gaze or that of her parents. 'And he talks to me, notices me in a room full of people. He's different. So when he wouldn't reply, I wondered if he'd lost interest and, like, forgotten, or found someone more beautiful.'

Amelia opened her mouth to interrupt, but Callan silenced her with a shake of his head. He needed the girl to talk.

'So Bonnie told me – she's my best friend; she's from Loch Fuar but we go to the same school – Bonnie told me how her boss at the inn told her to be a bit more assertive when boyfriends ghost you and stuff.'

Callan's ears caught the keywords. Boss, inn, assertive… Aileen… How did she slip into conversations that weren't connected to her? Wonder of wonders…

'And were you? More assertive?'

Pamela nodded. 'I told him if he wanted to keep seeing me, he had to reply to my messages and answer my calls.

In turn, I promised not to call in his work hours unless it was urgent.'

Callan intertwined his fingers. 'And that was it?'

'Yes, we discussed it – like adults!' She glared at her parents. 'He works hard.'

'He hates working, Pam. I know,' Tim countered, red with the rage he'd bottled up for the past hour. 'Those boys never come to any good.'

'Not Johnny!'

'Darling—'

'No, Dad! You never understand, never see I've grown up. You've kept me in this golden prison. I've never had a weekend job—'

'You don't need—'

Pamela wasn't having it. She stomped her foot, faced Callan and spat. 'That detective followed us from the first night. He knew the first day he came here – he just looked at me with a grin on his face. He followed us around for a week, but never butted in. You know why? He told me it was alright for young girls to have fun, be reckless, but to know how to defend themselves if they needed to. He told me that's how I'd learn. Johnny might not come from a private school, Dad, but he comes from integrity.'

And she stalked up the stairs and slammed her bedroom door behind her.

Silence descended over the entire house. And one question reverberated in Callan's head. If Macalister had known for a week, why did he wait to tell the parents?

CALLAN DIALLED WALSH FROM THE CAR, UNSURE HOW TO deal with the contradicting opinions he'd heard about the lad. He had *seen* Johnny attack Pamela, *seen* him steal, and then he'd tried to murder him.

'He confesses to taking money from the daughter. Says she gave it to him willingly. He just asked her for it. He isn't lying, unfortunately.' Walsh sighed. 'He didn't break in – she let him in. And since you didn't identify yourself, we can't say he knowingly assaulted a police officer. But he tried to choke the daughter. So we have him on that.'

'Any run ins with the law?'

'Not him, but his brother has. He visited the station a fortnight ago for sulking around spots known for drug dealing. We found nothing on him and let him go.'

Callan considered what Pamela had said. 'Does Johnny have a record?'

'What the daughter said while we were handcuffing Johnny holds true, Callan. She told me, rather forcefully, that he's innocent. Based on what Tim said, the lad's just lazy. Not very friendly either, but never caused us any trouble.'

Which meant it was highly unlikely he'd jump to murder until provoked.

'Why did he hurt Pam?'

'He's saving to send his brother to rehab. They've got a history of abuse in the family.'

Ah, shite!

'Most importantly, he's got a tight alibi for the day of the murder. He was in the shop, working. My police constable saw him when he took his car in and waited for him to repair it. About an hour. The cameras will show him there too.'

Callan fought back a yawn as he ended the call. He'd worked his anger off – this drowsiness afterward was the consequence.

With questions and exhaustion weighing him down, Callan started up the engine.

Johnny was scrambling for money – he could hardly hire someone to kill Macalister.

Callan considered giving Aileen a call then checked the time – 2 a.m. Hadn't he decided not to grovel?

The car rumbling underneath him shifted his thoughts to the drive ahead of him.

Frosted roads didn't bother him; neither did the dark. He relished the silence of it, the shapes of nature unveiling themselves like a shy child as he passed through it.

He pressed down on the accelerator, grateful for the lack of traffic. A police car passed by, sirens blaring. When he stopped at the light, Callan peered into the shadows.

Several Johnnys would be brooding around; youngsters like his brother tasting the forbidden fruit.

The never-ending cycle of life.

He put the car into gear and sped away towards greener territory.

With only himself for company, Callan breathed his mind empty. A good night's rest followed by a pre-dawn jog would help him crack this, and forget about Irwing and Aileen.

The road curved left, and Callan's car tracked it with ease. He pumped the accelerator again, craving his warm bed.

Perhaps he'd fall flat on his face as soon as he shut the front door.

Callan steered right, mentally inventorying the contents of his fridge as he did so. Eating at Dachaigh was out of the question for a while.

Lights flashed in the darkness ahead – moving lights disappearing behind a cluster of trees.

Callan's forehead furrowed. Who, apart from him, took a deserted road to Loch Fuar this late?

Not many.

His car hugged the bends, maintaining the pace.

Up ahead, his road companion swayed left before straightening again.

The driver could cause an accident if they were falling asleep at the damned wheel.

Callan sped through a stray patch of moor. The moon, almost full but not quite, spotlighted the road and the frozen grass lining either side.

The car in front ascended a wee mound right into the brightness. Under the moonlight, it gleamed a pale grey.

'Bloody hell!'

It had no number plates and would only seat two people. A useless vehicle in this terrain, but... Could it be?

The glow of the moon had turned the pale lavender into liquid silver, but yes – it had to be.

The car's tail lights cut off, and Callan gritted his teeth. That tiny piece of metal was no match for his SUV.

His foot hammered the accelerator and the SUV lurched forward, almost flying into the air, gravel spitting in its wake, as it charged towards the tiny two-seater.

He'd driven this road several times and his memory had catalogued every inch of it.

The landscape ebbed and flowed along with the distance.

They began the steep climb up a hill. In the valley beyond sat Loch Fuar, the lake and the town.

Callan felt for his phone, patting his trousers and the passenger seat.

'Bloody bastard!'

He swung right, almost catching up with Macalister's former rental. They climbed higher, the road growing steeper, the turns sharper.

He skidded on the next bend but managed, thanks to the slope, to hone in the curve. One hand on the steering wheel, his foot unwilling to ease up from the accelerator, Callan willed his car to go faster. Faster and faster still.

How the hell did that tiny thing still have a lead?

Callan grunted as he bounded over a stray rock, skidded, and charged straight ahead.

He swatted the wallet and badge on the other seat away, grabbed his phone, and tapped on it. 'Bloody hell! Wake up, damn it!'

His phone spluttered to life.

Teeth clenched, he tapped the buttons as he jostled his way along the stony road, eyes focused on the route ahead, hoping Robert would pick up.

They'd reached the summit. Any minute now, they'd race to the bottom – and he'd be damned if he let the bastard give him the slip. He'd almost got away, travelling like a cat in the night. It was a true stroke of luck that Callan had taken the same road.

And now he'd catch Macalister's killer.

Lights still off, the car in front hobbled to the top, then whirled left, heading for the descent.

At that speed, the driver needed skill or they faced a drop to their death.

Callan flew over the summit, snapping at the eejit's heals. Lights from Loch Fuar flickered down in the valley.

The sun was still hours away, the sky shaded black. Yet the farmers would soon be hefting tools to begin their gruelling day.

Blood pounded in his ears, his heart clenching as he trained his attention on his prey. The car bumped along, straying from the path. The driver clearly didn't have a clue how to drive well.

A death wish they had.

The car wavered again, scraping the hedges barricading the drop to the town below. Tyres on the right kissed the edge. Gravel loosened, cascading into the valley, just before the driver steadied the car. Was the sod drunk?

Nope, just agitated and poor at driving.

Loch Fuar, a slate grey mass of mercury-like water, lay ahead. The dark shapes of trees surrounding the road stood petrified, not a single leaf shivering.

Absolutely still, absolutely silent. Except for the roaring in his ears and the rumbling of the speeding cars…

Callan kept on its tail. Five metres more.

He cursed, pushed harder.

Four and a half.

'Come on, ye bastard!'

Three.

His phone clattered into the seat beside him. He had no use for Robert if he lost this sod and plunged into the valley himself.

Two and three quarters.

Two and a half.

Callan inched towards the bumper. Another ten minutes before the road ended…

The perfect opportunity to corner the killer.

Unless a startled wild animal ran onto the road. At this speed, they would have no option but to hit it and lose control.

Harder! Callan gritted his teeth.

Two and a quarter…

The tiny car didn't have a grip like his.

Another bend and— 'Ah shite!'

Bright light blinded his eyes.

He blinked. 'Damn it!'

An ambush. Macalister's killer had kept the car to lure them in.

A car, bigger like his, roared up behind him, squashing him in the middle.

The headlights glaring into his mirror hid the identity of the driver.

Another curve to the left and a drop to the right.

His phone slid onto the floor and smashed against the door. The car almost overbalanced, and Callan pulled his weight to the other side. A save…

They rolled downhill, beyond control, like a rocket with no—

Callan switched to the brake and hit it once. The car didn't slow.

He tried again.

Oh no, no, no… His ride couldn't give up on him now.

Callan pressed the brake again. Still, the car didn't slow.

Shit!

An ambush could lead to one thing only.

He clamped his teeth together, thoughts torn in every direction.

He clutched the handbrake, but nothing would save him now.

How soon did the road even out? Five minutes? Seven?

'Crap!'

Headlights flashed right into his orbs, stamping his retinas with two burning circles.

Again, the headlights flashed.

Callan squinted into the side-view mirrors.

Blind and without brakes.

He had just one destination.

The car in front of him manoeuvred another bend, promising a deep dive into Loch Fuar.

'Come on, come on.'

He neared it, a metre and—

Blind. The car behind charged at him like an angry bull in a fight.

He couldn't slow down.

Callan tried to balance, to stick to the road.

The other driver nicked his bumper.

And he lost control.

The loose gravel gave way, the tyres lost their grip – and he lost his.

He veered off the road and the lights behind him vanished, leaving only a wild roaring in his ears.

The car shuddered as he ploughed through the hedge, the thorny shrubs scraping against the windows.

Callan popped the seat belt and smashed a hand against the steering wheel. Where the hell were the airbags?

A horn blasted in the night; the light from his own car disappeared.

And then he tumbled into the nothingness – down, down, down towards certain death.

CHAPTER FIFTEEN

Aileen rubbed her forehead. She'd taken a pill, but the headache hadn't eased, just like sleep hadn't come.

She stared at the screen, eyes almost bleeding with fatigue.

Amy Downie.

She'd searched that woman until she was sure there was nothing left to find.

The newspaper clipping, which she'd photocopied, sat next to her yellow notepad and pens.

Amy Downie came from money. Her ancestors' several business investments had reaped the Downies a healthy income, which she spent on the nicer things in life.

Her mother, a businesswoman in her own right, had started several enterprises and succeeded in them.

Both parents had died in an accident somewhere in Asia while on a business trip.

Judging by the eulogy, their deaths hadn't been a huge loss to the two surviving children.

Aileen pursued Amy's trail across the pond to the US

where she'd dropped out of university and spent a year living the good life.

And in 2004, the woman had gone to Germany to study fashion design.

Why not study in France, the hub of fashion? Where Beau Blanchet had committed fraud and died.

If only she could connect Amy to the French scene in 2004. She'd been studying just over the border then.

But when her sister-in-law had published the article on the French case, Amy had been on a trip with fellow students to Austria.

Nowhere near France.

Aileen bit her lip, perusing her handiwork.

Amelia was in the centre of all the hubbub. What if Tim had gone over to visit her?

Very possible.

That placed the entire Downie family, save for the fifteen-year-old daughter obviously, in Europe.

Yet there was no evidence, especially regarding Macalister's death.

Aileen sighed a long breath. And still her tension didn't ease.

She'd start by apologising to Callan and cooking him a good breakfast. The green-eyed monster had sneaked up on her.

Perhaps her past had scorched deeper than she'd thought. She'd never cared about someone so much to ever notice before.

Aileen swallowed. She had an inn full of guests. Two hours and they'd be prowling about needing breakfast.

She clicked off the lamp and headed for her bedroom.

Her socked feet padded on the floor.

She trudged towards the bed and let out a groan; 4 a.m. – Callan would be starting his day and here she was, a ghost reaching for her blanket. But the soft shade cast by the dull light didn't invite sleep.

The stomping of footsteps on the floor below evoked another groan. Callan wasn't the only early riser.

No sleep for the wicked. Maybe she could get a head start on her day, too.

Aileen pivoted towards the bathroom when someone shouted. More steps pounded on the floor; doors opened, slammed; voices spluttered.

Her robe fastened at her waist, she raced down the stairs.

Chaos raged on the first floor. Officers in all stages of undress hurried from door to door. Some stepped out with sleep-flushed faces, asking what was going on.

A tremor zapped her. Something had happened.

Was it another body?

She braced herself and climbed back up the stairs to seek Irwing over the sea of heads.

Not in his suit, Irwing hunched over a notepad, phone clutched at his ear. The hard lines on his face spoke of terrible news.

'What's happened?' She rushed over, shoving a police officer aside. Xin was barking directions, buttoning his suit with one hand.

'What's the matter?' Aileen raised her voice over the hum. 'What's happened?'

Irwing's slate-grey orbs found hers. 'Ms Mackinnon, let us do our jobs.'

'You're up in the middle of the night in my inn, causing this hullabaloo. You'll tell me. Now!'

He narrowed his eyes, which deepened his wrinkles. 'I can't say. We don't know yet.'

Urgh! She hated being in the dark. But the mask on

Irwing's face had crumpled. He spoke the truth. They'd had a call. That's what she gathered.

Another car burning?

Another murder?

Aileen bit her lip. Callan would know.

She tightened her robe en route to the kitchen. One thing her gran had taught her: always have ready-to-carry snacks on hand.

Aileen stacked containers on the counter and placed the coffee pot under the coffee maker.

While the coffee maker worked away, she hauled the snacks to the reception counter, where dressed officers were making their way out into the cold.

'Granola bars and energy balls. Grab whatever you need.'

Racing back to the kitchen, she found a flask to dump the coffee into and handed it to another officer. 'I'll make some more.'

'Sure appreciate it, miss.'

Irwing sent her a glare when he reached for a bar. 'Your boyfriend here?'

Aileen frowned. 'Why would he be? He's an early riser. He'd already be out and away.'

'Likes his jogs then?'

'Aye, he goes out on one almost every morning. Why?'

The inspector shrugged it off. 'Curiosity.'

Aileen paced, listening to the clock tick, then paced some more and checked her watch.

She hit the call button. Callan.

A pre-recorded voice from the operator came down the line. Why had Callan switched his phone off?

Aileen paced again, checked her watch again and another ten minutes later gave up. She had nothing to do. She couldn't sleep now, not after that ruckus.

Vibrating with too much energy to sit still, she headed to the kitchen and filled up two more flasks with coffee.

A good excuse to loiter at the crime scene.

She'd heard the location officers had yelled over each other's heads. Right at the edge of town, below the cliff.

Had the killer chosen a secluded spot this time?

She bundled into the car in a fresh pair of jeans and a jumper. Two flasks full of coffee, another with tea, and a box full of biscuits stacked in the back.

The GPS guided her at a snail's pace. At almost 5 a.m., the sun was still hours away, and winter had left a thin layer of ice over everything. Her sedan's tyres weren't made for these conditions.

No one stirred – only a slight breeze sent the grass waving, then a rabbit scuttled past.

The edge of town it may be, but given Dachaigh's location it stood close to the inn.

Blue and red lights danced in the darkness far ahead. She saw the ambulance and her heart clenched. Someone had either been hurt or died.

She pulled the car into the lay-by, far enough to keep out of trouble, and perused the scene.

No sign of a stretcher or body bag.

A sigh left her lungs. No rushing paramedics, either.

But the firefighters had arrived. Water hosed down on something tucked into the trees.

They might've just reached the scene in time to stop the flames spreading. Was the perp playing with fire again?

A chill breeze found her naked face. She'd need a litre of warm tea to feel human in this weather. Aileen saw now why curiosity killed the cat. It knew no boundaries.

The police officer flanking the blue-and-white police tape spotted her and shook his head. 'It's best you go home, miss.'

She held up the flasks. 'I brought supplies.'

'Miss…'

'Ms Mackinnon!' The sound whipped towards her, as did the owner of that voice. Irwing curled his lip. 'I won't ask how you located this area, but you need to go home!'

'I'm not traipsing all over your crime scene. Anyway, I brought supplies.' She gestured to the flasks. 'So a thank you is enough.'

'Officer Kirkpatrick, take those flasks!'

A brunette, her hair tucked beneath her chequered cap, jogged over, radio crackling. She managed a small smile and gave Aileen a nod to say thanks.

At least someone had manners.

Aileen peeped over the officer's shoulder, eyes zeroing in on the scene.

Water battled the flames. Grey smoke billowed from the blazing heap of metal that had once been a car.

Pop! An explosion sent debris flying from within the heap. Something had exploded. For the first time, the definition of blazing intensity registered its severity in her mind. Nothing inside would survive.

An inferno engulfed the tyres, and the scent of burning rubber wafted towards her.

Flames raged, holding their own against the water, the grey smoke obscuring much of the scene.

The firefighters worked in tandem, snaking around the rocks and trees to get to the fire. Water splashed, sizzling against the metal until finally it claimed victory. Metallic skeletal remains emerged from the smoke, a battered phoenix from the ashes.

It looked ancient, a husk; the fire had robbed it of everything…

Aileen tracked the swarm of officers, yellow jackets flashing around the rocky terrain.

She spotted a white shock of hair. Rory.

Beside him stood Robert Davis.

Where was Callan?

In answer to her silent question, Rory turned, eyes a window into his thoughts.

She heard the gasp, a mile away from the roaring in her ears. But it hadn't come from elsewhere. It had come from her. A gasp that petrified the oxygen in her lungs, robbed her of strength.

That wasn't just a car. That was *Callan's* car.

'Shit!' Rory made his way over.

Quaking, Aileen watched her hand shiver, as white as a ghost's. She took a step back.

'Aileen!'

She took another step, head shaking.

Callan's car. Callan had been driving the car. Her boyfriend had been driving the burning car. It was nothing but a husk now... The fire had left nothing but a husk. Nothing could survive that inferno.

'Aileen!'

Her retreating foot caught on a loose stone, and the earth tilted.

Car burning... Callan in the burning car... No one could survive... The smell, fire and rubber... The smoke... The metallic husk of the car... No sign of Callan... Robert's face, Rory's face... This is real...

Pinch me!

Her legs gave in, a house of cards tumbling. Her knees crashed against the tiny stone; shards of welcome pain pierced her.

Callan was in the burning car.

Pain failed to breach the searing of her heart.

Aileen placed a palm over the sharp rocks and pushed. She didn't move. Her elbows buckled, and she crumpled to a heap on the ground.

Arms wrapped around hers, beefy and unfamiliar; unwelcome. 'Let go of me!'

'Miss! Miss, I'm sorry. You—'

'Aileen! What are ye doing here? Kirkpatrick, Pataky, help her to the chair – she's in shock.'

She flailed her arms, wanting to see, wanting to speak. But her teeth chattered, and any words she mumbled made no sense.

'Ms Mackinnon!' Irwing moved in, eyes level with hers. 'I asked you to step away. Stop making a scene!'

'That's my boyfriend's car. Where is he? Where is Callan?'

'Aileen!' Rory appeared in her field of vision, hair askew, eyes drooping. 'Please – please sit down here.'

'Don't lie to me. Callan was in the car, wasn't he?'

She saw Robert in the background watching her, yet not meeting her eyes. That was one man who couldn't lie, not to her. Whose drooping shoulders answered her question.

That car was Callan's, and he'd been in it when it had gone up in flames.

Aileen shrugged out of those entrapping hands. 'Leave me be. Please.' She fumbled away, stumbling towards her car.

The rumbling of the engine beneath her felt light years away. Air closed in on her, the world out of reach as she drove. Then her foot slammed the brake, her head lolled onto the steering wheel and the dam broke.

Callan was gone. She'd never see him again. *Never*.

CHAPTER SIXTEEN

'Aileen, eat up.'

Isla had tried it all: sweets, meals, tea, water, and snacks. Aileen stared at her fingers, intertwining and untangling them.

'That's the third cup of tea I've warmed for you. You need to eat something.'

Aileen pushed away from the table.

Isla would never understand. She and Daniel had knocked on her door sometime that morning, followed by a few more of Loch Fuar's citizens. Everyone had a sad face and words of consolation. She didn't need bloody words.

Without a glance at Isla, she thundered up the stairs. The door to her chambers clicked shut.

Exhaustion kicked in now, at last, when all she could do was see the entire scene, feel the intensity of the fire, the heat of it.

Aileen trudged towards her bed and, without a thought, crashed into it, face first.

Spreadeagled with no strength in her limbs, no coherent thoughts in her mind, she just lay there.

The bed sheets slammed the cold into her. Such frigid sheets... Aileen shivered, then her face heated, pressure popped into her eyes and the pent up-frustration broke.

Her fist crashed onto the mattress. So alone, so painful.

'Urgh!' Another fist and another.

She hit the mattress until she couldn't feel her knuckles. Her fingers had turned red.

The phone on the nightstand lit up, beeping until she let out a roar of frustration and smashed it to her ears.

'What?'

'Ah, dearie. I'll come down there—'

Siobhan.

'You don't have to come, Gran.'

'Callan's a strong lad, a good boy.'

'Gran.' It sounded like a moan to her own ears. 'He was... He was in it... Oh, Gran!' she sobbed, unashamed, just like she had when she was a little girl, right on this bed, two decades ago.

'He's the best detective I've dealt with, and good to you, too. Such men are hard to come by.'

Never in her twenty-nine years on this earth had Aileen heard Siobhan sounding so sincere, a catch in her own voice.

'Isla's here with me but... but she doesn't understand. She doesn't understand, Gran.'

A loud silence descended on them, both women thinking of their lost men. 'They say time heals all wounds. But when you've lost the other part of your soul, that's never the case. Not a day later, and certainly not five decades later.'

'At least I wasn't married to him with two boys,' Aileen whispered.

'And you think that matters? Marriage doesn't form the bond – the people in the relationship do. You've shared it all with him: murders and heists, fights, and times of joy…'

Aileen's bottom lip trembled. She chewed on it, trying to stop the avalanche, but the first sob wreaked havoc on her heart. If she'd thought she'd cried herself dry, this time she ruptured.

Tears and tears, sobs after sobs; pain, such awful pain. She buried her head in the mattress, right where she and Callan had spent many nights just being.

She heaved when the tears wouldn't fall, whimpering. The day moved on; the sun inching towards the horizon.

Siobhan didn't hang up.

'I argued with him… I didn't even kiss him bye when he left.'

'Aileen.' Siobhan cleared her throat. 'You have a task ahead of you. Now is not the time to break. You've done it, the crying. That's enough for now – you have something more important to do. More important than Dachaigh and Ken Macalister.'

Siobhan's words took root, grew and gave Aileen strength to wipe her tears. Something gripped her heart, something steel-like. 'Aye, I need to find out who did it. I need to find out who hurt my boyfriend.'

'And ye've got me, lassie. Ye've got me and there's nothing I cannot make happen. Leave it to me and I'll get what you need.'

Aileen swallowed her tears. For one moment, she wrapped herself in Siobhan's bubble of care. 'I'd appreciate any help I can get. But I don't know what I need.'

Siobhan's dry laughter cracked like a whip. 'Macalister. You need Macalister.'

'He's dead too.'

'A day. I'll be there tomorrow, and I'll get you what you need.' And then the call disconnected.

In all these years, they'd never had such a serious conversation, and Aileen had never heard her gran sounding this strained. What did she mean by getting her what she needed?

Aileen let it go. She didn't have a spare room for her gran to stay, but Aileen would sleep on the floor if Siobhan could be here. The ninety-year-old had more guts in her than ten warriors put together. And enough muscle to shove some of that strength into her grandwean.

Aileen pushed up and saw her reflection in the mirror: the splotchy face, the wild hair and the hollow eyes.

Find the man, Aileen, she told herself. *Find the man and get Callan justice. You can cry later.*

THE MOON, A FULL ONE, SWEPT THE LANDSCAPE IN monochrome. The inn's walls gleamed white.

None of the officers returned to inform her about anything. Not Rory, nor Robert. Were they hiding from her?

Aileen pressed her palm against the window and peered out. A shadow fell behind her and a soft hand massaged her shoulder.

She'd acted like a moron with Isla, a child throwing a tantrum, yet her friend had moved heaven and earth for her, uprooted her family again to come help. 'I'm sorry.'

Isla drew Aileen to her, the familiar hug like a protective shield. 'Rory's on his way.'

'What... Why?'

'He has something to say, but he said it would be best if he came here in person to tell you.'

Aileen wrung her fingers. She'd sat with Isla and

broken down the case, discussed what she knew, what she didn't.

Isla had drawn it up in a diagram to comprehend it all. But they hadn't found anything new.

Aileen hoped Rory could enlighten them, tell them something.

This was a case now, her case. To hell with what Irwing thought.

She leaned against the wall and turned towards Daniel, who rocked Carly, blabbering sweet nothings to her. 'Callan's family. D-Do they know?'

His eyes were just as hollow when they found Aileen's. He nodded. 'His sister wanted to come over, but their mother needs her now.'

Aileen ran a hand through her hair, disturbing her ponytail. 'I must go see them.'

Isla hugged her from the side. 'You don't need to – they don't expect it. But they want to reach out to you. Tomorrow is soon enough.'

Callan hadn't ever introduced her. Was it because their relationship was still new? Hadn't he wanted her to meet his family?

Rory plodded in, his face etched with worry and hopelessness.

If she'd been herself, it would have been her, not Isla, placing a cup of tea in front of him. But all she wanted to do was ask questions.

'Rory, the police processed the other scene quicker than this.'

The man tugged at his frizzy hair, nodded a thanks to Isla and took a sip of the hot tea. 'Lord knows I needed this before my brain froze.' He raised the cup to Aileen. 'The car – a farmer found it on the slopes. We hacked through the shrubs and trees to get there. The fire, the firefighters inferred, was caused because of the fall. It's a steep drop from where the road winds downward.'

Aileen shut her eyes. 'What was Callan doing there in the first place?'

'Detective Inspector Walsh told us he left Loch Heaven late last night. He'd been to the Downies', caught a perp after a brief scuffle. Nicked his arm on a knife. A paramedic stitched up the wound and gave him a painkiller. Eaten on an empty stomach, it can make the patient drowsy. And Callan left way past midnight – he would've been tired. And if he took the pill…'

Daniel placed his sleeping daughter in the crib and settled in a chair. 'That's not like Callan. He's not that careless. Are ye sure there wasn't something wrong with h- his car?'

'Not really. We're still trying to get to the bottom of it. But the scene's a mess. Our priority was to collect the evidence and then investigate. So we…' Rory sighed and sought their eyes again. 'We found the remains of a badge, a wallet and a phone.'

Aileen gripped the chair's arm, squeezed it until it dug into her palms. Callan went nowhere without his badge. His phone? Yes. He hated the bloody thing, but not his badge.

'Do we know when the car crashed?'

'Approximately fifteen minutes past three this morning. The farmer heard a crash. He hadn't yet begun his day.'

Rory finished his tea and took another minute before leaning in. 'I'm not here to tell ye all this, even though it's important. When was the last time ye spoke to him, Aileen?'

She didn't want to remember. Didn't want to tell them that the last time they had spoken, she'd argued with him. But she had to.

Isla squeezed her shoulder. And Aileen told Rory all.

'He drove away in his car then?'

She nodded.

Rory scrubbed his eyes. Aileen felt a twinge of guilt for not being more polite. They'd been working since before the day had dawned.

'Callan left the police station in his car in the evening. He made it to Loch Heaven, as far as the Downies'. Case closed, he started for Loch Fuar again.'

Rory ploughed on, arms splayed wide as he addressed the three. 'Callan had to be driving that car. He had to be! Ye know as well as I do, he'd never take off his badge. But Walsh said one of the Downies hosed Callan down. So he changed. He changed and left his damp things on the car seat to dry.'

His palm slapped against the chair's arm, almost startling Carly awake. 'The right-side door, the driver's side door, was found on the hill, dangling from a shrub. And – and they searched the wreckage, but found no evidence of a body.'

'No evidence of a body? Ye said the car caught fire. How will ye find a bloody body?'

Rory's eyes cut to Daniel's, his reply just as vicious. 'There are always traces, things that can lead us to form an opinion. And the smell! With Ken Macalister, the crime scene stank. This one didn't. There were no signs that Callan was ever in there except for the wallet, badge, and phone.'

A gasp escaped Aileen. Rory had to be joking. It had to be wishful thinking. He cared about Callan; theirs was a tight-knit team and still...

'No evidence of a human body? And the driver's side door was found away from the car?'

'Aye, Aileen. Someone can't hack a door off a moving

car, but the driver can open the door and leap out. It's dangerous and it'll hurt, but it's a possibility. And timed right, it could work, if he's smart.'

Siobhan's words whispered in her mind. *The best detective I've dealt with...*

'Callan's smart.'

For the first time in hours, hope, the faintest flickers of it, stuttered in her heart. It kick-started her dead muscles, and her head sparked into action. 'The hillside!'

'We're searching, but it's a vast area. We need resources.'

All he had to do was utter those words. With Isla's contacts and power to bring everyone together, they had a search party organised in under an hour with plans to canvas the entire hill.

No one cared about the freezing temperatures, the wind, or the rain. Nor did they mind shoving their feet into boots and jackets over their pyjamas to find a man who'd given the community so much.

The stinging in her eyes came from sheer pride. Callan had told her not long ago she had a knack for building strong ties. And here was a sea of people from Loch Fuar: Mrs Douglas, cat in one arm, and Lieutenant General Warren hunched over a map, torches in hand, not arguing for once. Old, young and everyone in between spread out until the dark night lit up with torchlight.

No way could Callan evade them now.

Dead, alive or injured, they'd find him and bring him home.

Resolute, Aileen lit her own torch, joined her group and started, not bothering with the storm overhead or her aching limbs.

Callan would be by her side soon.

. . .

They searched all through the night and into the dawn – hours with no shouts of victory or evidence of a man.

More skilled rescue officers, some from the team Walsh had picked from Loch Heaven, had started working their way from the top.

Done with her designated area, Aileen descended the hill to report to Rory. The man, eyes still downcast, nodded. 'They haven't found much. The damn wind and rain isn't helping either. It's the easiest way to lose evidence.'

He held up a plastic bag containing the tiniest scrap of black fabric.

'That could be Callan's, Rory!'

'It's all we've found. Any blood or other evidence will have been washed away.'

The last few hours had given Aileen hope, an ember of a chance that Callan was still alive – hurt but alive.

She circled her fingers around that hope and held on tight. She'd need it to fight this, to catch the person who'd done this.

'You should head home, Rory. Get some rest. You're been up over twenty-four hours now.'

'Aye, I'll head off.' He placed a hand on her shoulder. 'You should too.'

She conceded and hiked back, quads and hips aching like they did after her and Callan's self-defence sessions.

Dachaigh's pastel door brought her no joy, though seeing the faces of officers lugging themselves off to bed after a long shift tickled her empathy.

Aileen headed to the kitchen instead of her chambers. Her hands moved of their own accord, taking out eggs and bacon. She wanted something to do, she realised. Not because she didn't fancy shutting her eyes, but because she felt the stress overpowering her.

Salty, sweet aromas wafted through the kitchen, the demands of cooking soothing her like she was being rubbed down with exotic oils.

Aileen sprinkled some pepper into the pan, then flipped the bacon with her other hand. The coffee maker dripped a rich aroma into the room.

Just a wee sense of normalcy.

Officers filed in as if entranced by the smell, in want of something warm.

Irwing picked up the plates, arranged the tables. He didn't bother with his taunts, and Aileen didn't bother interrogating him.

'You can take that plate of bacon out; I'll get the next batch when it's ready,' she told a waiting officer.

Aileen set the coffee pot onto the dining table and returned to make another. The feeling of a houseful of guests washed over her. Hope…

The back door slammed against the wall to reveal a blotchy-faced Isla. 'Aileen! I thought you spent the entire night… Never mind.' She jostled Aileen and picked up a plate. 'I'll help. I brought some fresh bread and Danishes.'

With a mouth-watering aroma to match.

Isla had had to return home with Carly in the middle of the search, but here she was, bright and early, perhaps having given the reins of the bakery to Andrew.

Aileen drew Isla into a hug, hoping the prickle behind her eyes didn't manifest into tears. 'Thank you.'

'I could ask you why the gratitude, but hey.' Isla smacked Aileen's butt. 'No slacking. Put that booty in the chair. It's time to fuel up.'

Another smack had Aileen grunting. 'Hey! My glutes are killing me without your slaps!'

'So eat and get some sleep. You'll scare Carly from a mile away.'

No energy to hold her head up, let alone argue with Isla, Aileen listened and ate until her stomach protested.

'Isla! Let me do the dishes!'

'Off you go!'

'Is—'

'Oh, you've got a visitor.'

Aileen frowned, staring out of the kitchen window and into the car park. 'What is *she* doing here?'

The front door of the inn flew open less than a minute later. Siobhan, her walking stick poised in the air, frilly frock fluttering in the breeze, threw Aileen a smug smile.

'What are you doing here?'

'I told ye I'd come today, didn't I? And I've been successful too.'

Her gran didn't elaborate, waltzing in like no ninety-year-old should. Her nurse, Nancy, clomped in behind her, holding two suitcases. Aileen hurried over, thanking the kind woman who, by the looks of it, could do with a gallon of tea.

'Harried me she did, worse than a toddler's tantrum, to get here.'

'Ha! You're young. Barely sixty. What are ye complaining about? It's time to solve a case!' the former jewel thief sang out. 'Where is she?'

Aileen frowned. 'I'm here, Gran.'

Siobhan flicked her away. 'Not you.'

A shadow fell over the front door and a minute later another woman sauntered in, hair in a bob, grey eyes sharp and trouser suit sharper still. A woman Aileen never expected to see again.

'Shaeline Macalister?'

Ken Macalister's former wife blew hair off her face and nodded. 'Aileen Mackinnon, we meet again.'

She lifted a cardboard box labelled '2003–04' and thudded it onto the reception desk. 'There are three more. I'm sure your younger arms can lift better than mine.'

Car keys dropped next to the box.

'How... You said you'd contest me for the will in court and you'd never—' Aileen turned to her gran, who'd swiped a stray piece of bacon and a mug of coffee from the kitchen. 'How did you sort this?'

Siobhan grinned until alarm bells chimed in Aileen's head. 'Aileen, meet your aunt, Shaeline Macalister.'

Her *aunt*?

'When ye said Macalister, I knew it was something. Ha! Ken Macalister, that wee bastard! I'd heard that name before. And then I realised I'd swatted that eejit's bare bottom once when he was a wee bairn. Macalister...'

Aileen waited for a better explanation but didn't get it. 'You still didn't explain how that makes Shaeline my aunt.'

Shaeline sat on the other chair, crossed her legs, and sent a flat glare at Siobhan. 'My husband's mother was your grandfather's sister.'

'I-I never knew Edward Mackinnon had family.'

'Well, now you do. When Siobhan explained the connection, it made sense why Ken would pick you. His mother died before we married, but after I spoke with Siobhan, I pieced it together. That's why we came here after we married, to Dachaigh, to meet with his mother's only living relative – Siobhan Mackinnon, his aunt.'

It certainly explained how the man knew Aileen. Why hadn't he introduced himself when he'd stayed here?

Aileen rubbed her face, struggling to centre her thoughts.

Isla, who'd been watching the entire scene, patted

Aileen's back. 'You need sleep. At least a nap. An hour or two will help you focus.'

She spared one last look at her gran and her *aunt*. Goodness, what an odd twist of events! 'We need to get those boxes.'

'Later.'

'I must be dreaming. I must...' Aileen let Isla lead her to her chambers and this time when she dived into bed, she didn't stir for a solid three hours.

A SHRILL SIREN CRACKED HER EARDRUMS. AILEEN DIDN'T stir. It would ease up, it would stop. It had to stop.

Like an answer from up above, the siren ceased.

She sank deeper into the bed. Five more minutes and she'd force herself out of this warm bliss.

Brrrng!

What the blasted hell?

Aileen lifted one eyelid and stretched her hand. 'I'm up, I'm up.'

The siren didn't peter out.

Aileen let out a groan and dug her elbows into the mattress. Sunlight blinded her.

'Ah! Shit! It's noon. Why is it finally sunny today of all days?'

Brrrng! The siren... Her *phone* rang.

Not a bloody alarm!

She snatched up the handset and pressed it to her ear. 'Huh?'

'Get me out of here!' a voice hissed, and the line went dead.

CHAPTER SEVENTEEN

'Urgh!' Bile rose in his throat. Shards of glass — they had to be shards of glass — pierced his ribs. 'W— Ugh.'

He'd barely opened his eyes to the blue room — no, the white room with blue curtains — when something crashed.

Voices mumbled, then a brown-haired angel appeared in his vision. Had he got a fast ticket to heaven? The weight sitting on his head didn't think so.

The angel scowled, bringing into focus the streaks of tears on her cheeks and her red nose. Adorable.

'You think you can pull a stunt like that? Let me think you bloody died?'

The beautiful brunette sure talked funny, like it was his fault he was hurt. He'd fought with a bull and lost.

'Sh-Shut up,' he wanted to say. But his lips didn't move.

Something wet collided with his cheek. He felt that gentle splatter amidst all the pain.

'Oh, Callan!' A sob, not from him but from the angel, his girlfriend, tugged at something deep within. And then the familiar smell of lemon shampoo, a welcome scent of home amongst the sterile floor cleaner, soothed the ache.

A hand, his *banlaoch's* hand, smooth and cool, oh so wonderfully cool, settled on his forehead. 'He's burning up!'

'The doctor said his fever's going down. He's recovering and seems to have no memory loss.'

'He'd better not!' Aileen leaned over, until those fierce eyes met his, lips hovering above his... 'I would've kissed you, but you look like you grappled with a knife and lost. Not to mention the oxygen mask's in the way.' She moved, and the most incredible sensation stirred his dead muscles. A peck on his forehead. 'Oh, baby!' Her face dropped to the crook of his neck.

If he'd have been able to speak, he'd have reprimanded her that he was no child.

'Killer,' he groaned out. 'Car.' Callan had to take another breath. 'Chase.'

A finger caressed his head. 'I can't understand you. Later – we'll talk when you aren't hurting. The doctor says you need sleep to recuperate.'

He'd slept enough. Almost two days, the arson investigator, Detective MacNeill, had told him.

Aileen stroked his arm, the one not in a sling, and gave him a dazed smile. 'You're alive.' A laugh burbled through her tears. 'You're alive!'

His burning ribs and pounding head wouldn't keep him alive much longer. 'Urgh.' He lost consciousness.

HIS MIND WOKE UP, YET HIS BODY COULDN'T MOVE. THE insistent pain prickled like someone was poking him with needles.

'He's recovering. When they brought him in, they

could barely see his eyes – his face was as swollen as a boiled potato.'

An angelic chuckle drifted to his ears. 'Who found him, MacNeill?'

'I can't say, ma'am. The ER team said they thought he wouldn't make it. Covered in blood, he was. A boiled red potato. Jumping out a car like that's plain stupid, but…'

'Special circumstances. He might be bloody and beaten, but I'd rather him with a pulse than, well, what would have happened if he'd stayed put.'

Callan felt a pressure on his arm. 'He's alive. Oh, he's alive.' A sob. 'I'm sorry. I just…' Aileen cleared her throat. 'Please, tell me who found him. I must thank them.'

'I'll talk to the ER team.'

'Thank you for all that you've already done, MacNeill.'

A faint memory played in his mind. Detective Inspector MacNeill. What was he doing here?

Callan shoved at the blackness, willed his arm to move.

A gasp echoed through the haze. 'His fingers twitched!'

Bloody hell! If he couldn't instruct his arms to move, he could hardly catch a killer.

Callan fought again, tried again, only to be pulled back in until he tumbled into the void.

HE STIRRED, AND THIS TIME HIS EYELIDS FLUTTERED. He flinched once, tried to see through the fog, gave it another minute.

That weight on his head had eased up, but his torso burned like the pits of hell. 'W-Water.'

He sucked the water from the straw that appeared, relaxing when the cold liquid trickled down his throat. It was as if he'd spent the last week trekking through the desert.

Callan surveyed the dark room and saw Aileen rooted to a spot next to his bed. She placed the water somewhere to his right before placing a hand on his arm. 'The nurse'll be here soon. How are you feeling?'

'Urgh.'

The nurse came in. Poked and prodded him. Callan groaned. Was the pain bad? No. Would he like something to eat? His stomach protested, but he said no. Would he like soup? No. So please leave him bloody alone. His vitals were better. Good... Bye... The doctor would be here soon. Better. Hopefully with his discharge papers. Callan had work to do.

When the woman left him alone with Aileen, he forced out. 'Finally! MacNeill?'

She rolled her eyes. 'He apologised for not being able to share info on Macalister with us while he was here. Now I'm getting you that soup before your stomach eats itself. MacNeill should come by soon.' Aileen pressed his knuckles to her lips. 'You should thank him.'

'Why the bloody hell—?'

'He recognised you, you eejit! What were you thinking driving to Loch Heaven and back in the middle of the night? You should've told me.'

'Not when ye'd chewed my head off. Get me out of here!'

She pushed him back into the pillow instead. Callan moaned.

'Do something stupid like this again and I'll do much worse than chew your head off! Isn't it lucky a man on his way to work found you lying like a corpse in the middle of the road? If he hadn't seen you, he'd have driven over you... Or you could've died of hypothermia.' She swiped at her cheeks. 'Aren't you bloody lucky he got you here and then MacNeill comes in to meet with an arson victim and sees you all bloody and unconscious? And what do you do? You call me once and bark at me to come get you! Do you know how worried I've been?'

'I crawled up the hill after I jumped from the plunging car. Doesn't that count for anything? And MacNeill called ye – three times!'

'I was sleeping!'

'A woman worrying doesn't doze off.' Callan smirked, then grimaced when it hurt. 'Besides, didn't ye say my snoring puts ye to sleep?'

'Callan?' A laugh boomed out of her. 'You're incorrigible.'

He owned up to what was true. Finding the strength, what felt like the last ounce of it, he squeezed Aileen's hand. 'Thank you for coming.'

'And I'll never let you leave my side again, Mr Cameron. I swear on it.'

He believed her and knew he'd never leave her side, either.

Words floated to his ears, just a whisper. 'I love you.'

Callan's throat closed up. She loved *him*?

FROM WHAT THE VARIOUS PEOPLE TREADING IN AND OUT OF Callan's hospital room told her, Callan had jumped from the plunging car into the hedges.

The prickly gorse had ripped his shirt. But he'd managed to grab a small tree and halt his fall.

Jumping out of a moving car had left Callan with a couple of broken ribs, a fractured hand, and torn ligaments. His prosthetic leg had a dent on it and needed replacing.

His car had taken the worst hit. Aileen thanked the

powers, whoever they were, for it every second of the day. Even if Callan had taken the news worse than she'd imagined.

Shopping for a new car? Lord help him.

She watched him snoring now, pleased she'd got him back in one piece. She still hadn't met his family. Isla had dragged her away to grab a meal and a shower. The general consensus was that she reeked.

First impressions mattered, and after what she'd let slip just a few hours ago, she didn't want to meet her boyfriend's family in a state. They needed to know she could handle herself in stressful situations.

Now Callan's father, mother and sister had left, promising to come back later to make sure he ate. So Daniel had informed her.

She pushed away from the bed, unsure what to do. Should she have waited and spoken to his family? But Callan hadn't introduced them. Didn't he want her to meet them?

A blob of uneasiness settled in Aileen's throat. Maybe that's why he hadn't parroted those three words back to her.

Hell! She wasn't a blubbering idiot. Aileen knew her mind, and she didn't need Callan to say it back.

Aileen shook her head. The stress had robbed her of her senses.

The door opened to reveal Daniel, his plaid shirt crumpled and hair sticking in all directions. 'He awake yet?'

Aileen opened her mouth to reply when a husky moan tickled her ears.

'Aileen... What...'

Daniel traipsed to Callan's bedside. 'How're ye feeling?'

'Like I can sprint. Get me out of here.'

Aileen huffed. 'Don't be difficult. The doctor told you to rest.'

'I can rest at home.'

'They need to monitor you.'

'What am I? In primary school?'

Aileen rolled her eyes. He was, by the looks of it, fit enough to argue – or at least the rough parts of him were awake and thriving.

Knowing she wouldn't budge, he turned to Daniel. 'I have to solve this case.'

Daniel spread his hands, palms down. 'Calm down. Rory says ye're placed on compulsory sick leave. And ye've yet to heal.'

'That'll take weeks. And I know I saw something. I need to think! Get me out of here! Daniel.' His blue eyes, deep pools, bored into his best friend's. 'Come on, mate.'

Daniel ran a hand through his hair. He wasn't a man who said no, especially when the person asking was someone he loved.

Contemplative eyes met hers. Aileen shook her head. 'He needs rest, and I'm not letting him tax himself.'

'Hey! I can decide that.'

Daniel's shoulders drooped. 'Fine. We'll compromise. Ye said ye *think* ye saw something. I'll get ye a sketchbook and pencils. Sketch what ye saw.'

Sketch? If Aileen were to judge Callan's artistic ability based on his handwriting, his 'sketching' would involve stick figures.

'I can't.'

'Do ye want to help or not?'

Callan's eyes flickered to hers before settling on Daniel again. He raised his uninjured arm. 'I said I can't.'

Daniel hissed. 'Dammit! Ye're a stubborn rock. Can ye

not try? Someone tried to kill ye! What if you saw who it was in the car?'

'I can't sketch their face.'

'Don't sketch a face then – sketch the event, sketch what ye saw.' Daniel shook his head. 'Bloody eejit. Figure it out. I'm not letting ye out of here.'

Aileen stepped between the two men, noticing Callan's heartbeat escalating on the machines. 'That's enough. Callan just said he can't. And it's a matter of a night or two. Let's not get him agitated.'

Daniel sighed. 'Callan only draws the faces of people he dearly loves. I get that. But he can sketch a landscape, a scene.' He waved his hand. 'Forget it. Isla needs to head to the bakery and I've got to go get Carly from mum's. I'm off.'

Aileen's jaw slackened.

Callan only draws the faces of people he dearly loves.

At a snail's pace, she swivelled to Callan. He didn't meet her gaze. For the first time since they'd been in this room, he stared at his fingers instead of her.

Callan was an artist?

And he'd never told her?

Callan only draws the faces of people he dearly loves.

Oh shit! She had her answer now. He didn't need to speak – he'd shown it to her.

He could sketch and hadn't told her. He had a large family and had never introduced her.

She took a step towards the door. Did she even know this man? 'I-I need some coffee.'

'Aileen, I, er, I don't sketch anymore.'

'Is that what's in the notebook you carry around?'

Callan dropped his head onto the raised mattress behind him and winced.

Knowing this was getting them nowhere, Aileen

nodded. 'I should get going. Gran's here with Shaeline Macalister.'

'Shaeline's here?'

'She's my aunt.'

'Aunt? Your *aunt* sent you to jail?'

'Guess it's a day of unravelling secrets, huh?'

Callan gripped the bed sheet. 'It's not something I've done in a long time. Sketching or painting.'

'I don't expect—'

'And I saw nothing but those two cars. One was without the plates – Macalister's. And I don't paint things I don't love. Don't study faces I don't… love.' He mumbled out the last part.

Aileen cleared her throat. 'I heard that.'

'But I want to solve this case with ye. I want to solve it so that ye can stay here.'

She wanted to stay, too. But stay here with a man who guarded his secrets like they were national treasures?

Aileen clutched the door handle. 'I should get going…'

'And here ye said ye'd never leave my side.'

That got to her. Her feet stalled.

'Maybe ye can find some work for us to do here?'

Aileen groaned. 'Let me think.'

THEY DIDN'T RELEASE HIM THE NEXT DAY; SAID THEY wanted to study his vitals and ensure he had no internal bleeding.

That meant Callan had to suffer at least another day of salt-less hospital food.

If she wouldn't let him break out, Aileen had to hear him grumble.

'Ye could bring yer notes here.'

Aileen looked up from her laptop, her forehead creased, her fingers poised over the keyboard.

Irwing, based on what Isla had told them this morning, was still puzzling over the will. He'd made little headway in Callan's hit-and-run case.

Callan watched Aileen stretch out her neck muscles. 'I have to check on Gran, but yesterday I was going through one of the boxes Shaeline brought. And we need someone with a detailed eye to study its contents.'

He wished she'd loosen up. When Daniel had brought up his sketching, Callan hadn't known what to say. Friends could be a pain in the arse sometimes.

The nurse came in to refresh his bed, so he sat up. He chewed his lip to raw meat with pain in the process. And then the nurse, with a sadistic smile, suggested he sit in a wheelchair, so she could wheel him out to get fresh air.

Callan had done that at an enormous cost to his ego. Him in a wheelchair again?

As was his right after such an ordeal, he'd demanded a large steak burger and was denied.

Aileen, his nurse approved of.

When she entered lugging a large box, Callan eyed it like a child on Christmas morning. It might not be a present, but if it worked his mind, he'd tolerate the heaps of paper.

She didn't come over to inspect him as she usually did, still keeping her distance. Callan hated it.

'How're you feeling?'

'Hungry for real food.'

A flicker of a smile painted Aileen's face. 'Besides that, Callan.'

'A kiss?'

She smirked, eyes narrowing. 'What would your colleagues say?'

'Damn them to hell. Bloody good they did me.'

Aileen dropped something on the side chair and strolled over. Callan caught her hand and tugged. She bent to peck his lips.

How long could they do this? Would she leave?

Callan cleared his throat and focused on the box. 'What's that?'

'Shaeline brought along four boxes. That's all that she has of her former husband's case files.'

'The divorce really was amicable, then?'

'I haven't really questioned her yet. It's been a busy few days…'

'Why did ye get only one box?'

'It contains box files stacked with papers, Callan. I'm not a bodybuilder.'

If she trained like he'd instructed her to… He conveyed his frustration with narrowed eyes.

Aileen shrugged and opened the box. 'These files belong to 2004–05, as the label says.'

'That's when he closed up shop?'

A dirt-red file puffed out dust as she struggled to get it out of the box. 'At least he was meticulous.'

Callan jostled, trying to sit up, and moaned. 'Bloody hell!'

Lying unconscious for two days seemed to have melted his muscles as fiercely as ice cream in a desert. And with recovering ribs, ligament tears – partial, thank God – and a fracture to his hand, he had little mobility. And they'd need some time to fit him with a new prosthetic, too.

Aye, the killer had committed an expensive mistake.

Callan grunted while finding a comfortable spot. 'If ye'd wheel that table over, I can go through the file.'

The file landed on the table, upsetting more dust particles. Something tickled his nose and Callan sneezed. 'Ouch! Shite!'

'I should've recorded that!'

He shot her a glare and flipped the file. 'Amuse yerself now – ye won't be smiling when I get my limbs back!'

Aileen kissed him on the cheek, slid onto the bed beside him, careful not to bump into his torso, and tapped the first page. 'An enquiry into the effluent this factory lets out into a local river…'

'It could've got him killed – corporate homicide – but we should look for the French case first. Is there a reference to Beau Blanchet?'

Aileen peeked into the box and began flicking over every file. 'August 2004 – the Huxley divorce case; August to September 2004 – the Barrington inheritance case; September 2004…'

They continued all the way to August 2005.

'It's the last one. August 2005 – the Graham–Digby case.'

'What's it about?'

She placed the file on the table and they flicked through it, heads pressed together, eyes on the papers.

Macalister had printed off court transcripts, had some photocopies of newspaper reports, photographs, and police reports about damage to a property.

'It's a break-in gone wrong mixed with an ownership battle for this house.'

And it had nothing to do with Stirling, France or Loch Fuar.

'Are there any time gaps? Or untitled files?'

Aileen leaned down to check the box again and shook her head. 'Why do you think he'll have a file on Beau Blanchet? He didn't work on that case, did he?'

'There must be a connection. Why would he lead you

to that storage unit with that newspaper clipping otherwise? He has to be involved.'

'What if he killed the man? Or took part in his murder?'

'Then he needs to have that file somewhere – the planning of it, the documents. And if a client asked him to investigate Beau Blanchet...'

Aileen bit her lip. 'There is one person who'd know about that.'

'Yer aunt?'

CHAPTER EIGHTEEN

Shaeline eyed Callan. 'So you jumped out of a running car?'

'He can act heroic sometimes.' Siobhan smirked. 'Ye passed the test.'

'Did ye cut my brakes?'

'Ha! If it were up to me, I would cut *your* brakes, not yer car's. I'd have great-grandweans then. At this rate—'

'That's enough, Gran. We're here for work.'

Siobhan made a face at Aileen. 'Work on the personal things too. I'm not getting any younger.'

Callan tilted his head. 'If ye can get me walking, Siobhan…'

'Ye're creakier than me, young man!'

Shaeline snorted. 'It's a miracle he's alive. Count your blessings.'

Aileen struggled to reconcile the woman in front of her with the one she'd met a week ago. 'Thank you for bringing those files with you.'

'If I'd've known you're Siobhan's grandchild… Well, I'd sort of forgotten about our trip here after the honeymoon. I was floating on air back then. We had plans, dreams…'

'Ye came over, stayed here. Happy as a daisy.' Siobhan sighed. 'And so beautiful, too. Love is always so beautiful.'

'It doesn't last forever – at least it didn't for us.' Shaeline looked Aileen straight in the eye. 'We wanted children. I couldn't have any.'

It sent a chill shivering along her arms, a warning.

'We tried everything. But it didn't work out, and after a while, I was done with disappointing myself and him.'

Aileen licked her lips, buying time. How could she put this politely? 'Why? Why did you separate after decades of marriage? I'm sorry if it's too personal a question.'

Shaeline's eyes hardened. 'Ken might've had his faults. We're human but he never hurt anyone. For all the loss he suffered… He didn't deserve to be robbed of life. And if I can help in finding out who killed him…

'Ken kept me happy. I was the one who messed it up. Couldn't have a child. We had it all planned. I was to be a stay-at-home mum and he would have his private investigation firm. Even when I couldn't conceive, he asked me if I'd like to consider adoption. But I didn't have the energy in me then. That was in 2005. He gave up the business, I went back to work in another accounting firm and we never really reconciled as a family.'

Siobhan squeezed Shaeline's arm. 'It wasn't yer fault, dearie.'

Her aunt shrugged, rubbed her eyes.

'So ye grew apart?'

'Yes, Detective, we grew apart, and divorce was the only way out.'

But they'd continued to see each other, even for Christmas.

'Who filed for it?'

Shaeline stared at her bare fingers. 'Ken, actually. I took me a bit by surprise.'

'Ye said ye'd grown apart?'

'Well, I never assumed it was that bad and he... Well, Ken was always kind and considerate. He kept visiting after, asked me if I needed anything. Who does that?' Tears glistened in her eyes. She blinked several times until one streaked down her cheek. 'I'm sorry. Divorced or not, I spent more years of my life with that man than without. It hurts.'

Words stuck in Aileen's throat. She had felt that pain for a brief day. It had robbed her bare, and she'd only known Callan for a year.

Siobhan patted Shaeline's thigh, perhaps remembering the pain that she'd told Aileen always lingered. The unease of being cut in half.

Aileen eyed Callan, wondering if they'd ever be like this: old and grey, yet together. An image flickered in her mind's eye.

Too far ahead – her thoughts had taken her into a parallel universe. He hadn't even said those three words back to her. A wish was all it was ...

Shaeline swiped the last of her tears away and gave Aileen a shaky smile. 'Ken taught me to be more vigilant. One of the reasons I reacted the way I did to you being at my doorstep. I haven't lived alone for decades, so I'm a bit jumpy.'

'I'm sorry.'

'You catch the killer and we're square.' She turned to Callan. 'No offence, Detective, but I don't think the police are getting anywhere.'

Aileen intertwined her fingers. 'There's one case file I'm looking for: Beau Blanchet. It's a fraud case from France. Do you know about it?'

'We never discussed each other's assignments. But Ken did travel to France in, let me see... 2005? Yes, 2005! Right before he quit.'

'Is that why he shut his business?' Callan asked.

Shaeline frowned, staring at the ceiling as if she was travelling back to that time. 'I don't really remember why he shut the firm, Detective. It was doing well – believe me, I filed his taxes for him...'

'Didn't he say anything to you? Was he stressed out about something?'

'This was seventeen or so years ago. How would I remember?'

'Ah dearie, significant events like that ye don't forget.' Siobhan nudged her. 'Tell them.'

Her devastated eyes glazed over, and the confidence blooming on Shaeline's face evaporated. 'I lost a baby around then. A miscarriage. Ken had to travel to France the next month. He didn't want to go; I urged him to get away from me. I was the walking dead, and he had to get away to heal.'

Callan jabbed Aileen's foot. Of course she'd caught that too. Ken Macalister had indeed lost a child. A real child.

Aileen's heart cracked for the uncle she'd hardly known and for the aunt sitting in front of her. 'I'm so sorry, Shaeline. I didn't know.'

'It was a long time ago. We tried for a long time. And then... I was so happy, so hopeful... Well, that was the last time. I couldn't take any more and he didn't deserve more heartbreak.'

Callan leaned in, clutching the arms of his wheelchair. 'Ye think he quit the fieldwork and joined a security company because of that?'

Shaeline nodded.

Had Macalister kept that newspaper clipping as an admission of a crime he'd committed while grieving the loss of his unborn child? Or had he saved that article to remind him of the last case he ever solved – or didn't solve?

Shaeline huffed, clearing the memories with a shake of her head, and said, 'Ken seemed different after he returned. I was on medication for depression but... He kept checking the bolts on the door, made sure I had my phone with me and was checking in every hour with him. It was annoying, his paranoia. But I never asked why.'

Callan pulled out a copy of the will. 'I get now why he says he lost a child and a wife. How did he lose his dignity? What salvation is he talking about here?'

Shaeline proffered a hand for the will. She read it in silence, Siobhan peeking over her shoulder to get a look herself.

'And the part where he says "find the person who's robbed several families their fullest life". It's odd.'

'It definitely is. That's why I assumed this will was a hoax. But the more time passes, the more I think he was on to something.' Shaeline tapped her chin. 'What did you say about this French case?'

They told her everything they knew. Then asked if Ken had ever mentioned anything about that case, but Shaeline just reiterated she knew little of her ex-husband's career as a private investigator.

After speaking to murderers and ruffians, Aileen knew emotions and words were as easy to fake as phishing emails.

Was Shaeline here to lead them astray? Was she the one who'd hurt Callan?

Aileen leaned towards her boyfriend, like his shield in

battle. Shaeline would be a fool to pull anything with witnesses present. But...

Aileen drew the will from her aunt's hands and gave it to Callan. 'Want to join me in the kitchen?'

Before Callan could respond, she wheeled him out.

'It's damned inconvenient, you having the ability to drag me with ye like I'm some damned toy.'

Aileen made sure none of her family members had followed her in here. 'Do you think she might be lying?'

Callan dropped his shoulders and grimaced. 'Bloody ribs! She might be. I need to check her connection with you, even if Siobhan thinks it's real. She has motive.'

'First, she sends ye to jail, then she says she'll take ye to court, then one word from Siobhan, and she's here with the files. And she claims to not have any knowledge about the work her husband did.'

'And she lived with him.' Aileen pulled a few items out the fridge and started prepping them. 'I mean, I know what you're working on and we don't even share the same bed.'

Callan smirked, lifting just the left side of his lips. 'We do occasionally, and ye're nosy.'

'Shut up, Callan.'

'What are ye cooking?'

Aileen lost her annoyed façade and grinned. He was here, in her kitchen, alive. And she was cooking for him.

Satisfaction, like warmth after a day out in the snow, spread through her.

'It's hard to fake that kind of pain.'

'A human being is far more complicated than that, Aileen. I'll see if I can look into her, check if she has a criminal record. Until then—'

'We find Macalister's file on the French case.'

'Aye. And eat.'

Callan itched to get up and help Aileen haul the other boxes in. He gripped the arms of his wheelchair. The doctor had said his left leg should heal in a few weeks.

Bloody hell! At least he hadn't needed surgery...

'That's all of them.' Aileen dusted her hands off. 'Three heavy boxes of case files. Hope you're ready.'

'After being stuck in bed for days on end?' He leaned in and placed his fractured hand on the table. 'Could ye give me one file? You take the other.'

His injuries restricted his movements. The only thing keeping him from becoming an invalid was his brain. And he couldn't lose that to listlessness.

A file, similar to the one they'd read in the hospital, banged onto the table. 'That's the largest one.'

Callan flipped it up, careful to avoid flying dust particles. It was labelled '2002 – **PRIVATE**'.

Strange. He frowned, reading the first page.

A newspaper article about Olsen and Co, a company who'd illegally bought a piece of land from a farmer, stared back at him. The subsequent papers reported on farmers, agricultural land and dairy products.

Aileen slammed the file she'd been reading closed and added it to her finished pile.

Callan read on about coal mining and then stumbled across the financial accounts of a financing company.

He shrugged it off for later, found a map, and flicked his eyes over it. It told him nothing concrete... What was this file about?

'Private,' he muttered. 'It seems to be about anything and everything.'

Aileen glanced at him over the rim of the folder.

'There's another file in there titled the same. And they're both huge.'

'Did you find anything privacy related mentioned in the other files? All this file has are articles, maps and records on farming, finance or industry. I can't get my head around it.'

Callan flipped back over to the accounts. 'These accounts belong to a financial company apparently, and these newspaper articles talk about the illegal buying of farmland in fifteen countries.'

'Hold on.' Aileen placed her file aside. 'What did you say about those accounts? None of the other files have sets of financial statements in them.'

'This must be some fraud case he must've solved. Besides, why are we looking at 2002?'

'Because there's no mention of Beau Blanchet anywhere! And remember, even if they caught him in 2005, he'd been defrauding people for five years.' Aileen leaned over Callan's shoulder. 'Give that to me.'

She sat on the edge of another chair, tilted so he could read the file as well. 'A financial company, any sort of company, should have investments, Callan.' She flicked a few pages to a schedule titled 'Notes'.

'And interest income perhaps.' She ruffled the pages and settled on a page with the heading 'Balance Sheet'. Callan couldn't understand a word or number written on there, but Aileen's eyes told him something was very wrong.

She flipped to another page, tracking the figures with her finger. 'These accounts show a lot of money coming in as revenue. See the sales figure here in the profit and loss statement? But what sort of revenue? It isn't specified in the notes, which is mandatory. At least, it is now. There is no mention of interest calculated on financial instruments, either. And this money, in essence, is funnelled into the bank. A savings account.'

Callan raised an eyebrow. 'Saving is bad?'

'A financial company would invest the money, Callan! That's how they make money. Invest the money the investors give them to invest and earn a commission. Well, they may invest it into the market or lend it to earn interest. It's how banks and financial lenders operate.'

Aileen's full-forensic accountant mode had Callan biting his lip. God, she was brilliant!

'So what do ye think this is?'

'A Ponzi scheme, as clear as day.' Aileen plonked the file on the table and dug around in her satchel. 'Shit, where is the newspaper clipping?'

'Ha!' She slammed the folder on the table and scanned the newspaper article. 'Here it says £5 million was confiscated from Blanchet's house. He defrauded people for about £45 million but… they never found the rest. It's untraceable.'

'Er, how much does it show here?'

'This is just a snapshot of the year 2002. Let me see, we need accounts from 2004 to 2005.' She began flipping through the file again. 'Hold on, you check the other file.'

She dumped the file labelled 'PRIVATE 2' on his side of the table. Glad he could do something, he leafed through it.

Fifteen minutes in, his right knee was throbbing, but he'd struck gold. 'It was the 2005 financial statements ye wanted, right?'

Aileen pressed into his side and dragged her index finger down the columns. 'Aye, it's as the newspaper article says. But this amount…'

She flipped a few more pages. 'I need to study this.'

'What does it say?'

'I think this'll help us trace the missing money...'

CALLAN LEFT AILEEN TO IT AND CALLED ROBERT INSTEAD. The sod drove up to Dachaigh ten minutes later.

'Er, are ye sure ye should be working?'

A glare shut him up. He followed Callan's instructions, and half an hour later they'd pulled up in front of the police station.

Rory crossed his arms. 'They'll say I'm a slave driver. Ye look haggard.'

'Another minute in this chair and ye'll call me insane.'

'Ye'll need to clean that mess in yer office to fit a wheelchair in.' Rory smirked. 'Though there might still not be enough space for it.'

Trepidation tickled Callan's neck. 'Why?'

A minute later, he found out.

'Bloody hell!'

Irwing and his minions had taken over his office. Robert shuffled his feet. 'We all assumed ye'd need another week off.'

Callan snarled, his knuckles turning white. 'Open the bottom drawer in my office and get me the notebook and pencil in there, along with a table. Now! And set me up wherever there's a space.'

The only other unoccupied room was the cupboard-like one with the pantry and sundry items. The handles of his wheelchair scrapped the walls, but he fit in. Barely.

Robert placed a coffee next to the papers and left before Callan could snap another command. Eejit!

His notepad, the one containing his notes on the case, had met the same fate as his wallet and badge. Not to mention the phone Aileen had gladly replaced for him.

He also needed a car. And a tree with money.

Shite!

Callan shut his eyes and began thinking of the murder and the attack on him.

Ken Macalister came to Loch Fuar but rented a car in Loch Heaven. Did he drop in at the Downie household first to get a lay of the land? Is that why he went to Amy Downie to hire a rental?

A likely scenario.

He flirted with Amy by the looks of it, rented an unusual-looking car and stayed in Loch Fuar. Why not stay in Loch Heaven?

Callan scratched his chin.

Did he want to check in with his niece? But he never introduced himself. He knew he was about to die. So he knows someone would kill him. Amelia. He knew Amelia.

Would she have killed the man? As far as Callan knew, she had no alibi. He turned to the ancient computer and waited for it to whirl to life.

It took forever. He stabbed at the keyboard and a blue screen flashed. 'Crap!'

His forefinger throbbed with the constant movement. The official servers booted up, but it took forever for the computer to understand the keys he typed.

'Amelia Edwards' appeared in the search box and another eternity later...

'Not much here...' He clicked around, finding nothing of consequence. She had a driving under influence charge aged twenty-five and a parking ticket three years later.

Either Amelia's record had been cleaned or she'd been a law-abiding citizen since. Callan had his doubts about that, though.

He grabbed his new phone and stabbed at it with stubby fingers, then waited for Walsh to pick up.

'How are you?'

'About to go mental any second now. What do ye ken about Amelia Downie?'

'Tim's wife? Hospitable. You met her the other day? The woman who hosed—'

'Aye, aye, I ken who she is. Does she have a sheet? Visit the station often?'

'Hold on.' Someone spoke in the background, and the sound of movement drifted down the line. 'Sorry, I've been stuck in office all day. So, Amelia Downie, did you say? Not a peep, nope.'

Callan sighed. He had faith in Walsh and his assessments, but sometimes perps didn't ping a seasoned detective's radar either. And if she was in France and later in Stirling, she hadn't pinged Macalister's for sure.

'How do ye ken Tim?'

'He runs a garage, Cameron. We've had to go there for some questions regarding stolen vehicles, you know. But he's a decent man, and the family's tight.'

Not from what he'd seen that night. When people got that close, there were bound to be tensions. He needed to figure out how those tensions might impact the case.

'Amelia Edwards sound familiar to you?'

'Callan, I know Amelia Downie née Edwards is a law-abiding citizen. She couldn't have hurt you because, as you said, she— Ah, Christ. What have you found out?'

Some muttering and more movement sounded down the line. Walsh shouted incoherently, cursed, then came back on the line. 'Amelia Downie has a gun licence. Is that why you called me?'

'Gun licence? Who told ye—'

Robert ducked into the room, flicking a stray bead of sweat off his forehead. 'I found it out.'

'Sorry, Callan, I've got to go.' And the line went dead.

Callan glared at Robert. 'What the hell?'

Robert nodded. 'Ye said I shouldn't take things at face value. So I dug around some – well, first on Macalister, but nothing pinged, at least not for Irwing, and then I looked at the family. Ye ken they found bullets on scene?'

Those damned bullets.

Callan ran a hand through his hair. 'Amelia Downie might own a gun—'

'Irwing thinks the gun registered to her will be a perfect match with ballistics! She could be our killer!'

'Patience, Robert. As I tell Aileen, patience wins.' Just like he'd tried to be patient with his search. But it had led nowhere. If Amelia Downie had no former record, why would she murder a private detective she'd called in to solve a crime?

Johnny hadn't committed a crime, either.

Callan sat back in his chair and eyed his notepad.

Robert hitched a hip. 'What're ye doing?'

'Buzz off.'

'Ha! Irwing says I do well. Anyway, how's your leg and hand and… er… body?'

Callan eyed him out the corner of one eye. 'Strong enough to smack ye.'

He hadn't intend to kindle a smile on the eejit's face. 'I'm glad ye're back alive…'

'I'm glad to be alive and back too, Robert. But I need to ken who'd dare try to kill a police officer. If they'd succeeded…'

Robert opened his mouth to object, but Callan didn't let him speak.

'Someone cut the car's brakes. That's attempted murder. The killer is obviously cocksure they'd have got away with it, even with most of the police force breathing down their neck. That tells us something about confidence, eh?'

'Aye, also suggests it's not the first time they've got away with a crime.'

Callan smirked, lifting only the left side of his lips. 'Ye're getting a wee bit smarter. But I think the perp got away with one of the biggest crimes out there: defrauding people of their retirement fund. And now they've killed Macalister. A man who could've brought them down.'

'Ye think Macalister was killed because he'd solved that case?'

Callan couldn't say for certain. Macalister had known he would die, yet he hadn't brought his files here with him but left them with his former wife. Why would he do that?

Throughout this case, Macalister had played his hand from the grave, several steps ahead of them. And every time he'd kept his cards hidden.

To find the man's killer, they'd have to turn the cards and peek at them. But first, Callan had to see clearly.

He waved Robert off, picked up his notebook and pencil and dived into his memories – the moments right before the crash. That moment when the car had got so close, its headlights had smashed into Callan's bumper.

A moment when he'd looked into the driver's seat and seen... something.

CHAPTER NINETEEN

'I'll take ye for a camel if ye hunch like that!'

Aileen rubbed her eyes before checking her watch. 'Oh, I missed lunch! I'm so sorry. Are you—'

Siobhan waved her hands. 'I'm ninety years old! I can cook my own meals if I'm hungry. Or I can use ma phone to order them. You find the bampot who hurt the man ye love.'

Aileen managed a small smile, the word 'love' vibrating through her bloodstream like poison. 'I'm just…'

Her gran slid onto a bar stool and peered at the papers she'd scattered everywhere on the kitchen counter. 'Ah, I always thought ye'd become a stuffy lawyer, but this suits ye, doesn't it?'

'I've worked in accounting for so long. And it's easy really. The numbers talk. See here, Macalister has two sets of records. This one, the one in the second file, looks like a regular financial company's accounts. A regular P&L, balance sheet and cash flow. But delve into the details, it all falls through.'

She pushed a couple of sheets in front of her gran.

'Here, for example, this is the total cash invested by their investors. And these reports show a 15% rate of return. But where're the investments this financial company is supposed to invest in? Look closer and they've spread out the cash over a couple of banks receiving almost no real rate of return. The only way to repay an investor is to get new ones. And the extra cash, shown here as dividends, is paid to the shareholders... I'm boring you.'

'Well, I might've stolen jewellery, but I never messed with fraud for a reason.' Siobhan rubbed her palms together. 'It's just numbers for me, but you think these accounts are false?'

Aileen nodded. 'Two sets. The real one, and one for the tax authorities. They've shown operating losses, bad debts, you name it. But the company doesn't seem to actually have any assets if you look into it. They've rented out a place; there's no staff apart from Beau Blanchet and Mrs Blanchet. Even her name isn't on here! But that's not it. Blanchet's money, about ten million he earned as salary and dividend in five years, goes to his account and a total of nine million goes to his wife. Again, she's nameless...'

She flicked through the file. 'But his bank account has a nominee, a person who'll receive the money in the case of his demise. And guess who the nominee is?'

'The wife?'

'Yes! But the bank account, when the investigators got to it, had been cleaned out. It tallies, according to these reports I found online, with what the man had in his house and a property he purchased a while back.'

Siobhan tilted her head. 'But you think the wife cleaned him out?'

Aileen's eyes glittered. 'Oh, I think she'd been cleaning him out for a while. Those allowances he supposedly sent her were just the tip of the iceberg. Gifts in kind to his wife!

That's why the nineteen million is untraceable. It fits now! It fits! I must go get Callan— Oh! Your meal…'

Siobhan ushered her out the door. 'I'll put yer aunt to work. The therapy might do her some good.'

Aileen let her gran be. If the woman wanted something, she made sure she got it.

Her sedan flew over the stone bridge at a pace that would've made Callan proud. She screeched to a halt outside the police station and barged in, eyes wide and panting like she'd run all the way.

Crickets… The lights and heater hummed, but no one sat behind the reception desk or in the waiting room. There was just silence – the silence she'd been used to in this police station, not the sort of chaos Callan had been complaining about for the last few days.

'Hello?'

'Ah, Aileen.' Rory leaned against his office door. 'Er, are ye alright?'

A muttered curse sounded from the closet-like room she usually occupied. Something crashed, then there was another curse and Callan emerged, blinking at the lights, a piece of paper in his lap.

Rory bustled over to help him into the waiting room. Callan objected, but the narrow corridor had him conceding. 'Ye look like ye're on drugs.'

Aileen rolled her eyes. 'I think I cracked the French case. It's the wife!'

Rory dumped the coffee from the coffee pot into three mugs and handed them out. 'They arrested Amelia Downie.'

'Amelia was Blanchet's wife? Wasn't she married to Tim in 2005?'

Callan blew into his mug then took a sip. 'She has a gun licence. Walsh asked to see it, and she handed it over.

The calibre of the bullets matched the ones found at the crime scene.'

'That's it? Someone could've stolen it from her – or it could be someone else with the same gun, surely?'

'Aye, but not everyone also has a pale lavender two-seater with no number plates hidden in their garage.'

Air whooshed out of her lungs. She'd been duped again, hadn't she? Amelia had told her more about Ken Macalister than anyone. She'd known the most, and yet…

Shaeline Macalister knew him, too. And she'd been reluctant to say much at first…

Aileen turned to Callan. 'But you said cracking the French case would lead us to the killer.'

Callan set his empty mug aside and intertwined his fingers.

'Well?' she urged.

'Irwing found the killer, didn't he?'

He couldn't have. He just… Had she lost? Lost her chance to make her inn successful? Lost her chance at this life?

But it made sense. Amelia had been in France, in Stirling when Macalister quit, and she'd called him here. 'Why kill him in Loch Fuar? Why kill him like that?'

Rory shrugged. 'Irwing says she had access to the garage and its employees like Johnny, who finally admitted he was the one who removed the number plates and dumped them at the ELV yard.'

'She hasn't confessed. They're waiting for a lawyer,' Callan said. 'And Walsh said Irwing's taken over his office too. He's putting together more evidence to incriminate her. He doesn't want her to slip away.'

Aileen's stomach let out a growl. She massaged it, trying to figure out where she'd gone wrong. Why hadn't she seen beyond Amelia's friendly smile? Had she been so consumed by her jealousy of Amy, she'd overlooked it all?

Callan wheeled his chair over to her. 'Why don't we get something to eat at Barbara's?'

When he caressed her hand, something he'd never have done in front of Rory or anyone else before, Aileen wanted to cry. She'd lost. She hadn't brought salvation to Ken Macalister in the way he'd wanted. And she'd lost his money too. And with that, her life in Loch Fuar. Her friends, her inn, and her boyfriend.

Callan knew what this meant. She'd promised herself, told Russell from the bank she could come up with the money, pay off the debt. And stay.

Callan tugged her arm. 'Come on, I'm hungry.'

Aileen grabbed a hold of the handles on his chair. Rory helped them out before squeezing her shoulder. 'Take care of him.' And he slid away.

She could barely hold her tears at bay. Then Callan's calloused hand wrapped around hers in warmth and the dam cracked.

'I'm sorry,' she sobbed. 'I'm so sorry.'

'Darling, we'll find a way. Ye ken ye have friends here, a gran who loves ye.'

'And I let her down. The inn – they'll sell it to the highest bidder as soon as they boot me out in a week!'

'The town wants ye here. We'll find a way.'

She didn't believe a word he said. When a couple of people turned her way with curious glances, she swiped at her eyes, blew her nose without making much of a fuzz and wheeled her boyfriend to Barbara's Tea Room.

She'd kill for a cup of tea and a warm lunch.

The elderly yet elegant blonde didn't keep them waiting. Despite the long queue, Barbara waved Aileen straight in. 'There's always a seat for our town hero.'

She led them to a table in the back. The smell of roses and the clinking of porcelain cups sent a shiver of warmth through Aileen.

'Take a seat here; let me get ye the menus.' She squeezed Aileen's arm when she ambled by. 'Ye're a brave, sweet girl. Just like yer gran.'

A minute later, they were comfortable in their chairs, menus in hand.

'It's on the house,' Barbara insisted.

'Oh, but—'

'Uh-uh. It's my congratulations on surviving that accident that would put those adventure seekers on TV to shame.' She patted Callan's head. 'Ye scared yer mum worse than ye did when ye were suspended for fighting with that boy. What was his name? James?'

Callan blushed as she ambled away.

Aileen raised her eyebrows. 'Suspended?'

'Er, um, she's best friends with my mum. Hungry?'

She laughed then, fascinated by the man she called her boyfriend. And ravenous for this life she was living to continue.

Would it be a fantasy soon?

'Don't.' Callan caught her wrist and tapped the back of her hand with his thumb. 'Ye should've told me sooner; told yer friends who'd do anything for ye… But we *will* find a way, darling.'

Her smile dissolved into melancholy. 'I've thought about it, and there's no way. I won't get a job here, not in forensic accounting. Maybe I could become an accountant, but…'

'Ye'll get bored.'

Tears pricked her eyes as they often did these past few days. 'I was bored in my previous job. I caught anomalies, investigated frauds similar to Blanchet's. But I was still bored.' Turning her hand, she intertwined her fingers with Callan's.

The feel of his rough palms settled something inside her; gave her the courage to look into his eyes and confess, 'It's this place. The people, my friends and you. I've never had such people in my life. People who'd drive through the night to get me out of jail. Never, Callan. Y-Your family is so—'

'Smothering?'

'Loving. They love you so much.'

'Just like yer grandmother loves you.'

Aileen nodded. 'She does, very much. There's a reason she handed the inn to me and not to her sons. She thinks I'll do better than she could. Her sons would strip it bare and sell it off for a profit. They... they don't understand, but... That's what I'm doing, too. I'm letting Dachaigh down, letting Gran down.'

'And ye think Siobhan will stand by and watch ye suffer? For all I ken, she'd devise a heist and suddenly hand ye millions.'

A smile cracked Aileen's face, imagining her ninety-year-old gran wielding her stick and forcing bank officials to hand her money.

'She'd do anything to see ye happy, darling. So will Isla and I. And if it makes ye feel better, I think they're arresting the wrong woman too.'

'Don't say that. I don't need coddling.'

Callan tugged her arm and tried reaching over for a kiss, but the wheelchair had him further back than he wanted to be. 'Damn it!'

'I'm glad that *didn't* happen.'

Aileen blinked while Callan let out a curse. 'What the hell, Walsh?'

The detective, resembling a walking corpse, pulled up a

seat and sat. 'I always seem to find you in the most awkward situations. I'd be sorry to interrupt your little date, but since you pulled me out of bed at an awful hour only a few days ago, you owe me.'

Aileen bristled at the detective. No matter the cases they'd solved together, they always butted heads. 'You drove here?'

Walsh checked his watch. 'And I shall be staying. You have room?'

'Only if you sleep on the floor. And pay premium.'

'I stayed in London in my twenties.'

It had officially happened. Aileen would have to sleep on the couch. She'd given her room to her gran, persuaded two officers to share a room, and dumped Shaeline in another. Now Walsh wanted a bed? Talk about abundance after drought...

Callan pushed the floral teacup away and crossed his arms. 'Why are ye here?'

'I think – chuck that, I *know* – Amelia Downie is innocent.'

Aileen and Callan exchanged looks. 'What do we do about it?'

'Is there somewhere private we can talk?'

CALLAN WAS YEARNING TO SPEND SOME TIME WITH HIS girlfriend, catch up on that date he'd missed before this circus had changed his life.

He leaned against the car door as Aileen drove to Dachaigh.

Walsh eyed Callan over his shoulder. 'You'll need a car.'

'Trust you to state the obvious.'

Despite the bags under his eyes, Walsh chuckled. 'What are you to be so grumpy about me gatecrashing your date, thirteen?'

'Walsh.' Aileen shook her head. 'Don't start.'

'Aye, I need a car. Aileen bought me a damn phone. But I need a car, a new badge and new credit cards. And I need a new damn leg!'

Dachaigh loomed over the road that wound up the wee mound. Aileen eased into the car park, the vehicle jostling over a puddle before she pulled in to her usual spot.

Walsh cocked an eyebrow at Callan. 'Have you considered the perp might just be someone who was sick of your car? Wanting to get rid of that piece of—'

Aileen's elbow landed squarely in his ribs.

'That's not funny, Walsh.' But her eyes shone with mirth. Damn it!

'Ye liked that car!'

Aileen shrugged. 'It *was* old. At least now you can buy one with an inbuilt GPS, heated seats and a sound system.'

'Why don't I buy a mansion while I'm at it? Let me out!'

'Why don't you, Callan?' Aileen grinned and made sure Walsh had headed to the back to get Callan's wheelchair before pressing her lips to his. 'You're cute when you're grumpy.'

Callan didn't want to look cute. He ushered the other two inside.

A loud scream pierced the air, followed by a cackle from the living room. Callan rolled his eyes. Siobhan's horror nights had returned.

'Excuse my gran, she gets... excited about horror.'

Callan settled into the warmth of the kitchen, irritated with the small talk. 'Speak up, Walsh.'

Walsh extracted a folder from his briefcase. 'I'm not a

fan of horror, nor of implicating innocent people. I think Irwing's wrong for once in his life.'

'We need to prove it.' Callan scratched his chin. He'd given it a lot of thought, worked it from every angle. 'And I found nothing to help.'

'Amelia Downie has a healthy credit score, and the Downies live well within their means and have never broken the law, at least in the last decade and half. Why would she up and kill a man? Where's the motive?'

Aileen crossed her arms, a frown on her face. 'She knew Macalister, invited him to Loch Heaven, has his missing car in her garage and a gun that matches the bullets, but...'

The missing car, the same one involved in his accident. If she wasn't the killer, like Walsh believed, the killer had used the car to implicate her... No wonder they hadn't burned Macalister's rental.

'Owning the gun doesn't mean she pulled the trigger,' Walsh finished. It was exactly what Aileen had said earlier.

'Ye think someone took her gun to implicate her, then?'

'Exactly.'

Callan ran the scene in his mind. 'Macalister sat in the passenger seat, so somewhere along the way he got in the other car and abandoned his own. But if he'd cracked the fraud case and he knew who was after him, why would he get out of his car and into theirs?'

'He was prepared to die,' Aileen whispered with a tremble in her voice. 'He was prepared to die so the truth would come out. Don't you see?'

'So what, he tried killing two birds with one stone?' Walsh asked.

'Essentially. He stayed at Dachaigh because he *chose* me. He tested me, laid out the clues for me to find—'

Callan raised a hand to stop her. 'That's what he'd

been doing since the divorce? Laying out clues for ye to find? Arran, the newspaper clipping... But why didn't he ask his wife to hand those files over to ye?'

'I don't bloody know! Maybe to protect his wife and not make her an accessory. But he'd kept those files for me to find, those accounts.'

Callan folded his arms. 'I don't understand. Why now, after so many years? What changed in his life?'

Aileen's eyes glinted. She hustled over to the boxes, which had yet to leave the kitchen. She slammed down the two files labelled **PRIVATE** and **PRIVATE 2**. 'I read all the news articles and official police statements. They had the best forensic accountants search for that money, but they didn't have these accounts.' She held up the first file. 'They worked with an incomplete set, so they could never match them up.'

'Why didn't he share it with the police?' Walsh shook his head. 'You think someone threatened him?'

'Threatened his family maybe.' Callan cursed. 'Shaeline had suffered a miscarriage, hadn't she? She was in bad shape then... If the perp threatened his wife, Macalister would drop it all, even resign from his profession.'

Aileen nodded. 'Didn't Shaeline say he got paranoid about security after he returned?'

Walsh's forehead creased as the picture formed in his mind. 'So he left crumbs for you to find? All these years later, we can't get the fraudster. Statute of limitations. But on murder?'

A grin split her face. 'Follow the money and we'll find the killer and the fraudster.'

Callan waited for her to continue. When she didn't, he barked, 'And?'

'It's the wife. Beau Blanchet, according to Amelia, was

pea-brained. This entire Ponzi scheme had a mastermind behind the supposed mastermind.'

Walsh tilted his head. 'How?'

Aileen popped the file open. 'Bank accounts. The cash trail led the accountants investigating this case to the dead husband. But the wife had bank accounts where, in the event of her husband's death, she'd get the money. And she'd been transferring money to her account before that. Small amounts that wouldn't raise flags. So when the police got there, the bank accounts were already cleaned out.'

'And who is this wife?'

'Unnamed, unphotographed.'

Callan sat back without grimacing at the action. His body was on the mend. 'Keeping her unidentified isn't legal, is it?'

Aileen shrugged. 'Money under the table and anything's possible. And this was 2000, or almost 2000, and we didn't have the same security we do today. But I might have a way to get the information.'

'Ye'll need a warrant.'

'Hm, let's just say I might know someone who knows someone, and they owe me a favour.'

Callan raised an eyebrow. 'I didn't ken ye were of that sort.'

'I spent eight years investigating frauds. And I'm not holding back.'

Walsh nodded at Callan. 'Have you got anything better?'

Callan dug into his coat pocket and fished out a piece of paper. It crackled as he smoothed it on his lap. 'That's the last thing I remember before I went off the road.'

He saw that flash of light and then darkness every time he shut his eyes. He'd avoided sleep last night. Lord knew he didn't need more nightmares to colour his nights.

Aileen held the paper to better see the sketch. 'It has no face.'

He wheeled over to her and pointed to the car he'd sketched at an angle from the road. 'The other car tailgated me to knock me off the road at that curve. So when they got close enough, that's what I remember seeing.'

A bauble dangled under the mirror, a shape of a tree. A large hole gaped on the driver's side. 'What's that?'

'I couldn't remember that part. I just can't remember who was driving it or whether I saw anything.'

Walsh peered over Aileen's shoulder. 'It's a large black car with an anonymous driver. I don't see how that'll help us.'

'The sketch probably won't. But it's a start. And... Why does everything in this case come down to cars?'

Walsh leaned against the counter and crossed his arms. 'Coincidence?'

'If someone bumped their car with mine, won't it need repainting? Someone cut my brakes too, so whoever it was knew cars.'

'You think Tim framed his wife?' Walsh scowled. 'I just told you, the Downies are good people.'

And that tainted Walsh's judgement.

'"It's not always about the crime; fire can also point towards the criminal." Right, Aileen?'

She frowned. 'I said that about the handwritten ledgers I'd once found in a burning car.'

'Killing Macalister so close to the inn tells us the killer killed him right after he checked out of here. At first, I wondered why. Why not kill him somewhere private?'

Walsh huffed. 'What are you getting at?'

'We're missing something, missing some*one*. The killer

kept the car; that's very confident of them. But it's been an excellent tool so far to lure me in and to frame an innocent person, assuming Amelia is innocent. Let's run through the facts again. Three heads are better than one.'

Aileen dusted her hands off. 'I'll get my notes.'

'Call your contact for the wife's name, too. And get a board. I have something in mind.'

CHAPTER TWENTY

Callan imagined tying a bow to this case and shipping it off to a black hole. If not for Aileen, he'd have let the throbbing at the base of his neck win.

Not used to sitting all day, his muscles had cramped, shooting jolts of electricity through his body. He rubbed his knee, trying to dispel the pain.

'You should rest, Callan. The doctors said you need sleep.'

He'd sleep with Aileen tucked safely to his side, not battling alone to stay in Loch Fuar.

Callan let go of his knee, promising to rain vengeance on it later, and glanced at the once tiled wall, now covered with white sheets to create a pseudo murder board.

Walsh had taped papers together and drawn a straight line across them at a level Callan could reach.

Their stapled excuse of a board gave Callan some confidence. He eyed the line.

A red dot – a sticker Aileen had stuck atop the line – indicated Christmas.

'Macalister knew at Christmas this mission to Loch Fuar would be the end of his life.'

'Johnny told me he'd started visiting Pamela at around that time. They'd met at a Christmas party.' Walsh pointed a finger at the picture of Amelia tacked to the top. 'She didn't encourage him to do so. They've never spoken before.'

Callan couldn't wipe the embers of hostility he'd seen in Amelia's eyes while he'd been dripping water onto her kitchen floor from his memory.

'Amelia and her daughter don't seem to get along.' Callan waved to the picture of Amy. 'But I think Pamela idolises her aunt.'

Aileen stuck a green dot onto the timeline. 'That's the day Macalister arrived here. And the daughter told you he knew she was hanging around with Johnny within a day.'

Callan wrote below the timeline. 'Why did Macalister wait a week to tell Tim Downie about his daughter and her boyfriend?'

According to the daughter, Macalister hadn't broken the news to her parents but had warned her to be careful. Callan hadn't known the man. If he had to guess based on what he'd read, Macalister would've done a thorough search on Johnny. And that search had led him to believe Pamela wasn't in any danger.

So he'd bided his time.

Callan wheeled to the right and held his hand out for another sticker. 'Pamela says Macalister warned her the next day. But see our timeline, he didn't visit Schneider to change the will until after he'd spoken to her.'

'You think that's connected?' Aileen chewed on her lip. 'A change of life choices after speaking to the girl?'

Walsh stubbed his finger on the line to Callan's left. 'He

arrives at Loch Heaven, visits the Downies' and then rents a car?'

'Yes.' Aileen leafed through her notes. 'He rented that snazzy number at Amy's Rental and Taxi Services.'

Callan hated to point out the obvious – the rental place again.

'Why did he rent with them?'

Did Macalister want to check on the Downies'? Make sure his clients were legitimate?

Walsh harrumphed. 'His movements are as random as can be. He goes to a few museums, rents a fancy car that's easy to pick out in a crowd, visits a lawyer, solves a relatively simple case and dies.'

Callan caressed his jaw. 'And he stays with his niece but doesn't introduce himself. Perhaps to keep you safe from whoever was planning to kill him?'

'How could he be so sure he'd die?' Aileen crossed her arms. 'Did he threaten the wife?'

'Beau Blanchet's wife?' Walsh raised an eyebrow. 'You think Amelia was Blanchet's wife?'

'I might have to speak to Pamela. Find out what she and Macalister talked about. Perhaps she can give us a clue?'

'Okay.' Callan almost pushed out of the chair, then sat back when his right leg felt weird. No prosthetic. 'I'll come with.'

'Tim won't allow us near her. They've got his wife; he'll be guarding his child.'

A smirk touched his lips. 'I might ken a way to make it happen. Aileen, call Bonnie.'

. . .

CALLAN ROLLED OVER, CURSING WHEN THE PADDING OF cushions forced him to keep his left leg straight. Damned ligaments.

He had months to go before he would regain the full function of his legs. And until then, the prosthetist had cautioned him about fitting a new artificial limb.

He blinked sleep out of his eyes. The bedside clock lingered on 4 a.m. No wonder he'd woken up.

Aileen lay next to him, the gentle rise and fall of her back telling him she didn't care for the hour, though she'd be up and bustling soon enough.

Flashing smiles enough to split faces, some of the officers had checked out last night, leaving two empty rooms for Siobhan and Walsh to stay in.

Callan flexed his right thigh muscles, itching to move them. He'd never ceased exercising, not since he'd been fitted with a prosthetic and led to Old Brun's barn at nineteen.

With as much grace as a lump of slime, Callan leaned on his crutches. His left knee wobbled, fingers gripping the sticks until his knuckles turned white. A week out of it and his muscles had dissolved to mush.

He hobbled over to the adjoining room, sat his arse in the creaky chair, and froze. One noise and Aileen would jerk awake.

Early mornings, when the rest of the world was still burrowed into their beds, gave Callan a sense of solace. His habit of sneaking out with his art supplies had begun as a rebellion. Now it was a habit despite the hobby of his youth long forgotten.

He dug into the papers littering the desk and found the sketch he'd shown Aileen last night. Did forms of expression change? Had he bottled his art inside him when he should've let it out?

Last August, when he'd picked up the pencil and stroked it against the blank page, he'd surprised himself as much as his sister. Sketching his nephew had set him off again. After fifteen years…

In the silence, his mind travelled, swirling out of his body and diving into the past, right when the other car had shoved him off the road.

Callan shut the door to the present and entered the one deep in his memory. Having that recording camera in his head had helped him, always.

His gut blared, cautioning him. Aye, he'd seen something, something… What?

Rusty fingers, once deft, flew over the page. The car, the dark car, almost as tall as his, hefty, a truck?

No, not a truck, an SUV. A four-wheel drive to suit the frosty roads.

And the other car in front of him, wobbling, taunting, *unsure*. The SUV… It had blared down at him, eyes bright and wide, relentless, unapologetic, *sure*.

A bauble of a tree, glinting, almost real and then… eyes? Mouth? Face?

No, a big dark hole right behind him in the mirror. A mask?

Steering wheel. A dark naked steering wheel. And a pale hand, fingers clutching the wheel.

Delicate, white-knuckled fingers.

Fingers with an accessory. A gaudy ring.

He gasped and pushed himself up again, his breaths heavy, his eyes flittering over his surroundings. His hand caressed his racing heart. Water – he needed water.

Scrunching the paper in his hands, he wrestled with the crutches and hobbled out the door.

'Aileen.'

She'd awoken, a rosy hue on her cheeks, and those brown eyes sultry. Good God!

'Callan?'

Her raised eyebrows jolted him out of it. Too long, too long since they'd been alone, just them, his body whole and healthy.

Before he fought his way to her, she came to him and pressed a kiss to his chest. 'I saw the light in the study. You need to rest.'

'Stop fretting.'

Aileen led him to the stairs. 'Let's get breakfast. I have something to tell you. One step at a time.'

It took them too long to get to the kitchen. Walsh glanced up from his perch on the kitchen stool. 'Well, glad someone thought it was time to greet the day.'

'Shut up, Walsh.'

Aileen reached for the coffee pot and a mug. 'You made coffee?'

Walsh rubbed his eyes. 'I got a call from Tim. He was angry, sloshed. Irwing doesn't have enough to hold Amelia much longer.'

Callan picked up the folder Walsh had placed on the table. 'What's this?'

'Just came in from the station. The evidence gathered at Amelia's. Have a look at it. There's something about it that's awfully familiar, but I can't place it.'

Callan thanked Aileen for the coffee and waited for her to sit. 'I have something, too.' He set his crumpled sketch in the centre of the table.

Aileen held up the paper and spread it out at Callan's nod.

'I can't remember the face, but I recalled the steering wheel and the hand. It's awfully familiar, though I can't remember why.'

He unwrapped Walsh's folder, hoping to find some clue in the evidence collected at Amelia's.

Aileen's eyes narrowed in on the picture. She held it up to the faint light from the window. 'The ring, Callan. Was it gold?'

'I think so. Have you seen it before?'

'Yes, darling, I have, and its owner set off the green-eyed monster in me.'

Aileen pulled her laptop from her satchel. Her fingers flew over the keys before a smile settled on her face.

'See this.' She turned the screen towards Callan and Walsh. 'My contact came back with the papers Blanchet submitted to the bank. It's all hush-hush so you'll need a warrant but...' She pointed at the name. Blanchet's wife. 'Amy Downie.'

'Ah shite!' Callan faced the group. 'Shite! She took us all for a ride, didn't she?'

He stared at the photograph of the bag the police had collected from Macalister's rental. A leather bag with a luggage tag depicting *Water Lilies* by Monet. 'Walsh, I stumbled over this bag at the rental car shop. And what did Amy say?'

'She told you it was Tim's gym bag.'

Callan pointed at the photograph. 'And why would she lie about that?'

AMY DOWNIE HAD TOYED WITH HER BOYFRIEND'S LIFE. AND she'd pay for it.

One dilemma still stared Aileen in the face: who had been driving the other car? The bait to hook the detective?

An inexperienced driver? Someone inexperienced with

the Highlands? Their list of suspects belonged to this region.

Aileen dug her pencil into her cheek. Her eyes found another person of interest. 'Shaeline Macalister.'

Women conspiring to murder a man? Not the first she'd heard of it, but… Shaeline had an alibi. What would be her motive?

Aileen checked her phone again. She'd texted Bonnie last night asking her to get in touch with Pamela, her best friend, but there was no reply yet.

The girl would be over in a couple of hours. First, though, Aileen had breakfast to cook.

Pots sizzled, china clanked, and Aileen's feet scampered. She had four more mouths to feed, adding to nine police officers.

A tune hummed from her lips, belying the vigour of her pace and the angry hiss of the oil in the pan.

She worked in tandem to the smells and rhythms of the kitchen. The clock cooed the sixth hour.

Feet scampered above, doors clicked, and a brigade of officers followed the savoury tinge of bacon laced with bitter coffee to the kitchen.

Aileen worked her way through the dawn, feeding mouths and fuelling them to catch the real killer today.

When the van pulled out of the car park, she sank into a chair.

'A singing percolator, that's what you looked like.'

Aileen grinned at Callan. She'd badgered him back into the wheelchair, the crutches resting behind the reception desk. If he had to keep off his leg, he had to.

'Do you think Amy's in love with you?'

'Did she visit me in the hospital and sit by my side, bawling her eyes out?'

'I didn't bawl!' Aileen flushed, remembering the three

words she'd let slip. Truer words she'd never uttered. Unreciprocated words...

Callan wheeled over. 'Ye feed me like this, I'll need a bigger chair. Amy' – he enveloped her hand in his – 'doesn't need love. For her, everyone's a means to an end. She had a man over the night I caught Johnny. I think he drove the other car. Or maybe cut the brakes when Amelia hosed me down. But I remember now – many things, in fact.'

Aileen's gaze fell on the murder board, some loose sheets fluttering. She hadn't cared for Irwing's scowl that morning.

'Do you think Macalister knew it was her? Is that why he rented the car from there?'

'As a hello to spook her? Maybe. But...' Callan dug into his memory. 'When we checked the security cameras, Amy chatted him up for a good twenty minutes. Well, she gave the impression that she was flirting with him, but now I think their smiles hid the tone of their conversation.'

'Did you speak to Irwing?'

'I did,' Walsh said as he entered, beads of perspiration on his dark face. He wore shorts and a drip 'n' dry shirt, a stark contrast to his usually trench-coat-covered silhouette.

The man made a habit of working out, judging from the sculpted abs highlighted by the drenched shirt.

Callan glared at Aileen. 'A morning jog's supposed to be in the morning.'

Walsh made a show of checking his smartwatch. 'It's only half past seven.'

'Time to get to work. What did Irwing say?'

Aileen placed the cooling breakfast leftovers in the microwave and dumped bread in the toaster.

Walsh settled on the bar stool and thanked Aileen for the warm meal.

'I'll cook more if you need it.'

'I was only out half an hour; I won't have burned that much.'

'Slacker!'

The glare Walsh directed at Callan had Aileen tempering a smile. The police detective she'd run into at Isla's Bakery last year had preferred a life with no people. Now here he sat, bantering with a friend.

'What did Irwing say?' she urged.

Walsh swallowed. 'He's convinced it's Amelia and says I'm jaded.'

'We'll need more information to convince him.'

'Or to send over to Amelia's lawyers to get her out.' Walsh countered, clearly irritated with Irwing.

Callan waved a photocopy of the bank account details. 'Let's hand this to him. It's up to him to get a warrant.'

'Damn it, Callan! He won't listen. Says Macalister isn't connected to the French case at all. There's no evidence linking him to it.'

'What about the damn case files Aileen has?'

Walsh shook his head. 'Deaf ears.'

Callan hissed, slamming a hand on the table. 'What do they say about meeting yer heroes? What else do we ken about Amy Downie?'

They knew little except for her relationship with Tim's family, her business, and her style. And that she'd been in Europe fifteen years ago. But nothing concrete.

Aileen set her laptop on the counter and did what she should have done before. She opened the website for Companies House.

Amy had made a mistake in going after her boyfriend and Aileen would exploit it.

And exploit it she did – she took and took until they could call her a stalker. Companies House had it all.

Aileen's pen flew over the yellow paper, ink spelling out magical links.

Amy Downie had incorporated a company called Dainty Vêtements Limited in 2005. She'd registered it to an address in Stirling.

That business had made losses, despite the heavy investment of £7 million, to set up a high-street store and buy a factory, pay the workers. Aileen knew nonsense when she saw it. Primarily because the address of the shop pointed Aileen to a flat in Stirling – a flat in the outskirts of town.

Not an ideal office space for a high-street fashion shop, was it?

And the business had made no profit, and wasn't even a weed in the farmland that was the fashion industry. She couldn't find who Amy had employed, either.

The status of the company: dissolved.

Aileen clicked on the bio for the company's director, 'Amy Downie' and found her way to another company. Amy's Rental and Taxi Services Ltd.

This one also ran at a loss. Either the woman had a penchant for running unsuccessful businesses and lived off the dole or she had a trust fund stashed somewhere.

The dole wouldn't buy her fur coats (fake or not), days at a spa, and golden rings.

Aileen typed in 'Beau Blanchet' and came up empty.

She checked out 'Amelia Downie' and found her as a director in Tim's Car Care Ltd. Despite sharing the property, Tim hadn't partnered with his sister.

Her fingers poised over the keyboard. Who else? 'Amy Blanchet' she tried and drew blanks.

There had to be something more, more breadcrumbs.

A French website popped up on screen. Aileen typed, scrolled and dinged the jackpot.

Amy Downie had a business there – Downie Holdings Ltd. The company had been started in 2002 with a mere capital of a few thousand euros, but the address...

The address branded into her eyelids. She scurried over to the newspaper clippings and cried out. The company and Blanchet's residence had the same damned address.

THE SUN, FRAGILE IN THE SKY, LINGERED OVERHEAD. Aileen's sedan raced behind Walsh's.

Behind her trailed Irwing and his team.

Callan shuffled through the papers in the passenger's seat. 'Irwing found the marriage certificate in record time. And a warrant for the bank-account information will come through soon. Connections, eh?'

Irwing had taken some convincing, but even the man's thick head could read evidence. Once they knew who'd tried to run Callan off the road, finding information was like pulling open a curtain.

Amy Downie had lived with Beau Blanchet and married him in 2000. Then she'd duped him into a Ponzi scheme and let him take the fall. Did she murder him? Aileen couldn't know for sure.

According to Irwing, she had been with her niece all day during the day of Ken Macalister's murder. Pamela.

'Could you dial Bonnie for me?'

Callan cursed and tapped at her phone until the ringing boomed through the car's loudspeakers.

'I'm late, but I'm on my way!'

Aileen rolled her eyes. 'I want to speak with Pamela. I heard she's your friend?'

'Pam?' Bonnie panted down the line. 'Oh, of course, ye

ken her! She didn't come to school today. Her mother – didn't ye hear about her mother?'

'I did. One of the reasons I want to speak—'

'She isn't talking to anyone, not even me. Her boyfriend, he... They broke up. And her mother had her grounded since then. They found out about them.'

If Aileen had known, she'd have cautioned Callan as well.

'Pamela's at home?'

'Dunno, I DMed her.'

Callan raised an eyebrow.

'Direct message,' Aileen mouthed. 'If she calls you, give her my number. Tell her I want to ask her about Johnny and her mum.'

'Sure will.'

The line went dead.

'She's bound to be scared.' Callan flipped through the papers again. 'Ye ken, there's enough here to connect Amy to Beau Blanchet, but that case is way beyond the statute of limitations. I dinnae ken what the time lapse is in France.'

'Six years, I think, from the date of the fraud being committed.' But that didn't matter. Aileen's goal was finding justice for Callan and for herself. If she'd lost him... 'Let's stick to the plan. Amy didn't act alone, but she was the one who hurt you and killed my uncle.'

Walsh cut through the city centre, driving through a bustling neighbourhood to get to the garage. Machines buzzed, cars were hiked up on jacks, and the smell of engine oil and rubber reminded Aileen of the night she'd encountered Callan's mangled car.

She swallowed.

The banner 'Tim's Car Care' appeared as greasy as a

well-oiled door. The dirty blue matched the workers' overalls.

Tim, eyebrows creased and red beard frazzled, worked on a car, almost like he wanted to demolish that thing.

'Tim.'

The man snarled on seeing who it was. 'Is that what ye do, eh, Walsh? Turn on your friends.'

'Ken Macalister was murdered.'

'You and yer cronies think I don't know that? I know my wife and she wouldn't hurt anyone!'

What about your sister? The words sat at the tip of Aileen's tongue. She dammed them in. 'Is Johnny here?'

Irwing, at Aileen's firm request, was hiding in the van, away from Tim's eyes. They needed this man to sing – or let his employees do the singing.

With a grunt, Tim motioned towards the lad. 'If he's done something else, he's fired!'

'I'm surprised he isn't already,' Callan muttered under his breath.

The lanky lad lumbered towards him. His hair looked like it had been hacked at using a blunt knife, a bandana keeping the fringes out of his eyes. He thrust his black-grease-stained hands in his pockets.

'Yer boss not fire ye yet?'

Eyes scorched Callan. 'Ye survived.'

Callan snorted. 'Why, did ye want me dead?'

'The night the bobbies led me away, aye. But ye protected Pam when I'd lost it. I'm not like my old man. So nah, ye'll do.'

Callan jerked his head towards the cars. 'Big dark SUV, the day after ye got arrested – anyone bring it in?'

'Like my bud told ye last time, too many dark SUVs 'round here.'

'Ye cut my brakes the night ye broke in?'

'Ye think I had the bloody time?' His volume rose with his temper.

'Nah, I don't. Was yer buddy around?'

Walsh drew a sharp breath; Aileen's ears perked up.

Johnny shuffled his legs, not meeting Callan's gaze. 'Maybe.'

'Get him here.'

One look at Carl's gait and Callan swore. 'He's the guy Amy was waiting for that night.'

Walsh, hands in his trench coat pockets, spoke from the corner of his mouth. 'Think he'll rat her out?'

Callan wasted no time. 'My dusty-red SUV. I liked it. And you cut its brakes. Which left said SUV smashed against the rocks and me very close to going up in flames with it.'

Carl's cheeks drained of all colour. 'Dunno what you're talking about.'

Walsh took a step towards him and snarled. 'I can ask you in the police station.'

'I needed the money! I needed the money, and she gave it to me. She said it was just to scare you, but then I heard. They said you was dead!'

Callan smirked. 'Apparently I'm not.'

CHAPTER TWENTY-ONE

With Carl en route to the police station, Amy's name spouting out his mouth, they had another link between Amy and Macalister's killer.

'Damn it!' Callan tried to get comfortable in his seat, a checklist running through his mind. 'Pamela's still not called ye back.'

'Now that we're here, should we knock on her door? Her father won't beat you up, will he?'

Callan peered out of the car window and watched Tim swipe the sweat from his brow. 'We can ask him. He looks more beaten than someone who'd do the beating.'

Aileen asked; Tim agreed. If his daughter could help get his wife out of trouble, he'd try anything.

Callan sympathised.

'Amy dropped me off today, said she had to go to the mall. I'd appreciate it if ye could get me home too?'

An alarm blared in Callan's mind. Who would go shopping when her brother's family battled such an ordeal?

Callan glanced in the mirror, gaze skimming Tim's bald head. 'How's yer wife holding up?'

Tim's tone was something between desperation and frustration. 'She's scared – she hasn't done anything wrong. Someone's trying to frame her and we don't understand why.'

Aileen gripped the steering wheel tighter, pulling into their lane. Callan reached out to squeeze her thigh; felt her muscles tight as steel bars.

A police car lurked outside, the buzz of the radio floating through the doors Tim threw open. 'Amelia!'

In the time Aileen took to park, Tim had bounded over to his wife. Her hair was frizzy and her face appeared worn without her usual make-up.

'They couldn't keep me any longer. But, Tim, where's my baby? Where's Pam?'

Callan's heart thundered. Aileen leaned over to help him out. His hand stilled her and he peered over her shoulder. 'What do ye mean? Isn't yer daughter at home?'

Tim frowned, gazed at his wife, then peered inside the house. 'Her bike's still here. And she wasn't going to school today.'

The colour leeched from Tim's face. His wife yelled, 'Pamela! Where is she?'

Aileen's gaze flickered to their neighbouring house.

Amelia's eyes followed. 'Amy! That bitch.'

Anger washing her red, Amelia stalked over. 'Pamela, get out of there! I forbade you to go into that house, didn't I?'

Tim rushed after his wife.

Callan threw the car door open. 'Aileen! Get me out of here now.'

'Hold on – I'll get the chair.'

'Crutches!'

No matter what the doctor said, he hated sitting. And time was of the essence.

Aileen didn't complain.

The officer sitting in the police cruiser hurried over to Amy's doorstep. More people peeked out of their windows, watching Amelia thunder on Amy's door.

'Amy! Where is my girl? Amy!'

'Amelia!'

The woman didn't hear her husband.

'Amelia!'

Nor did she hear Aileen.

The adjacent door squeaked, and a woman with cloudy hair stuck her head out. 'She's gone. I was over complaining about all that slamming around in the middle of the night! Said she didn't care; she wasn't going to see my face after today. She took your girl too, in the morning. Said they were going far, far away.'

Oh hell!

Amelia glared at Tim. 'I told you to be careful about her! Told you to think twice before we let her into our lives again!'

Then she gestured at Aileen. 'Find her! Find my baby.' And she sagged into Tim's arms.

Callan's brain kicked into gear. The noise, the going far away... 'Tim, do ye have keys to Amy's place? Get in and tell me what's missing.'

Callan hobbled to Aileen's car, shaking his head as she approached him. 'I'm not creaky and grey! And I'll recover after we find the girl. Amy already has a head start on us. I'll call Walsh. Put a tracker on her if possible.'

Aileen helped him settle. 'Let's call Amy first.'

She hadn't picked up for Tim or Amelia. Amelia's threats of setting the police on her had fallen to the beep of voicemail.

'Try it out.'

Aileen's phone rang and rang again through the car speakers.

'Ah, I knew you'd call.'

Callan stopped fiddling with his phone, his ears perking up. Amy had answered.

'Is my blue-eyed babe with you?'

'Where are ye?'

'Oh, you sweet thing, how are those legs of yours?'

Callan's jaw hardened. His teeth ground against each other. 'Is Pamela with ye?'

Amy chuckled, a cackle that popped goosebumps on Aileen's arms and shot a shiver down Callan's back. 'No.'

'Where is she then?'

Aileen mouthed to Callan. 'Call Walsh – ask him to trace the call.'

Trace the call? Bloody hell! He punched in Walsh's number and waited. 'Where is Pamela, Amy?'

'About that. I wish I could stay and see those baby blues glistening as they crush the little twit. I dumped her where her blabbering mouth belonged!'

The phone went dead.

'Ah hell!' Callan smacked a fist on his thigh and cut off the call to Walsh. Crush... Dump... 'The ELV yard!'

The car's tyres skidded, chips of ice flying.

The sun was suspended a hair's breadth from the horizon, the curse of January. 'Will they still be working? What's the time?'

Callan wished he could drive. He wasn't as slow. *Damn it!* 'Aye, they shut at five. They'll be working on the last lot now.'

He'd dealt with a lot of criminals, but when it came to children... Hell, you needed to be a special kind of evil to hurt children.

Aileen took one hand off the steering wheel. 'Call the yard! She might be in one of the cars!'

Callan punched in the number and waited, but there was no answer, so he called the station. 'Robert! Get to the ELV yard. Check the cars. Pamela is in there somewhere.'

'What? Who?'

'Get there.' Callan cut the call.

Aileen floored the accelerator. With a seven-hour head start, were they too late to save Pamela?

Callan got hold of Bob's number. 'Bob! This is detective Cameron. Stop crushing the ELVs right now.'

'Eh? You lot don't tell me how to do my job.'

'Listen to me, you eejit. There's a girl there, a fifteen-year-old. We believe she's in one of the ELVs. Did someone dump a car today?'

'Aye, we've had a few, but they were all empty. Ye ken a fifteen-year-old can get out of a car?'

Not if she was gagged and bound. He heard the sirens in the background. 'Stop the crushing. Check the CCTV and help the officer who's approaching.'

Callan cut the call.

The road curled, twisted, hobbled over a few mounds and reached the crescendo of the hill.

He pointed to a corner. 'I went off here. The other person in Macalister's rental barely managed the bend.'

The curve twirled like the crooked finger of the witch who'd cursed it. Aileen gritted her teeth, eased off the accelerator and added some pressure on the brake.

The sun finally surrendered to the night and twilight, a splendour of red and purple, bruised the sky.

Callan's phone rang again. 'What?'

Robert spoke – quick spurts, incoherent shouts. 'We checked. There's no one.'

'No, check the latest pile…'

'We did.'

'The CCTV?'

Another shout rose in the background, dwarfed by the howl of the breeze. 'Rory checked it. Someone drove through the gates... There's no face. Car drove back out in ten minutes.'

'No face? What the hell?'

He cut the call. 'Someone drove a car in and left in ten minutes. No face.'

'Johnny?'

'They dinnae ken, damn it!'

Callan dialled, pressed his phone to his ear again and listened to the chaos in the background. 'Tim, did ye find anything?'

'Aye, everything's gone... Paintings, clothes... My daughter?'

Callan swallowed hollow promises. 'Tim, message me. Message me a list of what's missing. And check Pamela's room next. We need clues.'

'We're on it.'

Callan thanked him and cut the call, then he huffed and sat back. The tension had crept into his shoulders. It was about to be another long night.

Aileen raised an eyebrow, eyes trained on the straight road. Ten minutes and they'd be there. 'Message?'

Callan shrugged. 'I can barely understand what he's saying. Officers are all over his place and Amy's.'

Aileen swished the car to the left and slid into the road leading to the market square. They'd have to cross it to get to the ELV yard.

A cacophony of red and blue lights danced around the landscape as they approached, illuminating heaps of junk rising like waves in a tsunami.

Air, an inch away from freezing, smacked Callan's face

as he got out the car. His nose watered, and he shivered. Aileen bundled tighter into the coat.

Callan hobbled over to Rory and watched him direct the officers.

'Any sign of her?'

Rory sighed. 'It's dark and there are too many ELVs.'

'We'll join in.'

'Callan. Be careful with yer leg.'

He nodded at his boss and followed Aileen as she approached a police cruiser with its boot open, a flask of coffee promising a respite for his rapidly freezing internal organs.

'Can we borrow two torches, please?' Aileen asked.

The female officer eyed her and shrugged. 'It's a young girl. Appreciate the help.'

Rory directed them to the last row, somewhere in the blackness, an area even their torches couldn't illuminate.

'Wait up.' Callan adjusted his crutches, hissing as the cold metal bit into his skin.

'Callan, you need to stay off—'

'Later – coddle me all ye want later.' He pumped some steel into his voice, showing her that her arguments stood no chance.

Aileen flashed the torch around; Callan pointed the other way. 'Two lights, two pairs of eyes.'

Their double power proved unsuccessful when, after half an hour and their aisle almost done, they hadn't located any car with a passenger stuck inside.

'If it was Amy who drove Pamela here, she wouldn't have hidden her very well. She'd have been in a hurry to get away.'

Callan huffed. 'Perhaps we need to check the cars again. Particularly the boot. Let's double back after we're done with this last lot.'

Checking each car again would be a headache. Callan pointed to the beaten-up white family car. 'Amy would probably use an old make and model. Something with a key's easier to break open than something with an electrical lock.'

They began working on rest of the ELVs. The problem was that most of the cars were old.

'What about Amy Downie? Have they put up a whatsit on her?'

'A BOLO.' Be on the lookout for. 'Aye, but if she's got the money, a private yacht or plane will get her across the Channel. Finding her gets more difficult by the second. However, the weather's bad over the Channel so transport's been suspended for a couple of hours.'

Luck might just be on their side. But they couldn't freeze all of Amy's accounts because they didn't know which accounts were hers — not all of them at least.

'She's still got a seven-hour head start.'

She did.

Callan approached a navy SUV. As he reached over to peer inside, his eyes caught a red piece of cloth sticking out of the gap between the boot's door and the car's body. 'Ah shite!'

Aileen peered over and gasped. 'Is that a T-shirt?'

WHITE KNUCKLES GRIPPED CALLAN'S CRUTCHES.

Aileen shuffled her feet, hip bumping against his. Any second now, the breeze would numb her face. It had already frozen her fingers.

'What are they doing?' Given her height, Aileen could only see a sea of backs.

'They're trying to get the car open without hurting her.

She's not responding, and they don't want to jostle her if she's injured.'

Aileen's heart squeezed. She wound her arm through Callan's. 'It's cold, and she's been in there for hours.'

Callan didn't comment. He huddled into his jacket, eyes trained to the front. 'They've pried the front door open and pulled the lever for the boot. It looks like the one for lowering the back seats from inside was jammed.'

A pop announced the boot gaping its jaws.

Breath hitched, Aileen bit her lip.

Rustling drifted back to her – then a clank and a shout.

'Callan, what's happened?'

'They found her. Shit! She's gagged. Unconscious.'

Aileen shot up on her tiptoes and peered between the gaps in the crowd.

Paramedics rushed forward, a stretcher rattling behind them, as a police officer lifted a slip of a lass out of the car, so pale she shone in the darkness. She appeared so frail, she'd snap like a twig.

The paramedics tucked her on the stretcher, then one of them grabbed her wrist. Seconds ticked by. Was Pamela alive?

The breeze stilled; no one moved.

The paramedic shouted, 'I have a pulse!'

Shouts and sighs of relief rose in the cold air.

'Thank God!' Aileen sagged against Callan, seeking his comfort. 'Her every move makes me more determined to find her and get her behind bars.'

Callan rested his jaw on her head. 'Oh, we will. I've been thinking...'

. . .

Isla placed a warm scone with jam and cream alongside a cup of coffee each. 'That's all I've left. But I can keep the coffee coming.'

'Thank you, Isla.' Callan checked his phone. 'Just as I thought. Amy's wiped her place clean. No art on the walls, or in her attic. It's just a husk of a house with cheap furniture in it. None of her... Jeremy Hoos?'

Aileen snorted.

Isla shook her head. 'It's not Jeremy Hoo, but we caught your drift. Expensive shoes...'

Callan shrugged. 'Well, she'd have to take it all somewhere.'

'She could use a storage unit.'

'Of course, but she'll need to access it someday. I'll get Walsh on it, but I have a hunch. I have a hunch now that the noose is tightening, she'll want to cash in, disappear.'

Aileen grinned, an idea taking shape in her mind. A final trap... 'You should call our mutual acquaintance. He knows artefacts and collectibles better than clean nails and new sweaters.'

Callan woofed down his scone and called the man on loudspeaker.

'Charles Wyatt.'

'Mr Wyatt, this is DI Cameron. I'm looking for someone dropping a bunch of art, jewellery and clothes... All collectibles, maybe some antique. They'd want to cash in as soon as possible.'

Wyatt promised to call around, still grateful for Aileen's help in saving his money months ago.

Aileen sipped her second cup of coffee, content at her full belly. 'I feel alive again. And, well, it's hot to see you so savvy with technology.'

'Keep that thought in mind for later.'

A blush bloomed on her cheeks. 'Callan—'

His phone interrupted her.

Aileen answered. 'Mr Wyatt.'

'An agent in Loch Heaven. He's dropping a bunch of stuff as if it's on fire. It's contemporary, perhaps a decade old. Platinum and diamond, some gold, art frames covered in gold leaf, Renaissance canvases, clothes... Collectibles. The man favours the black market more than his dignity, though.'

'Just who we're looking for. Mr Wyatt, would you care for some excitement?'

The clock in the car read 5 a.m. They'd done more since the sun had dipped below the horizon than on most sunny days.

Aileen fidgeted, fighting the mouth-splitting yawns threatening to burst out of her. 'You think she'll be here?'

Callan nestled back against the headrest. 'A buyer willing to take it all off her?'

'*Almost* all. If Wyatt said he'd buy it all, she'd get suspicious.'

The police had parked their cars, unidentifiable SUVs with tinted windows, next to the two doors of the agent's office.

Amy had agreed to meet her buyer at half past five in the morning. She had to leave, she said, before the sun was up. Disappear was more like it.

Her haste informed the police of a few facts: the woman was still in the country and would wait for the money. Greed would end her.

Surrounded, Amy had no chance of escaping. They'd designed it so Sergeant Xin would accompany Wyatt, acting as his assistant.

Callan rubbed his thighs. They were warming up the

car now, planning to cut the engine off at around fifteen minutes past five.

At 5.15 a.m., Charles Wyatt arrived. His coat had a patch near his armpit. His hair stuck out like dried hay.

'Hell, she'll never believe he'll buy those things from her.'

Aileen chuckled. 'Looks can be deceiving. He has a reputation in the field.'

'Let's hope the black suit has the smarts to trap her.'

Aileen cut the engine, and they waited now, her foot tapping the floor. Seconds passed by slower than a bloody turtle…

'Stop it!'

'What?'

'Patience.' Callan gritted his teeth.

She stopped and when 5.24 turned to 5.25, she couldn't hold it in. 'Showtime!'

Callan rolled his eyes.

A shadow moved in her periphery.

'What is it?'

Aileen frowned, watching the shadow. But it had stilled again – perhaps she'd imagined it?

Callan's walkie-talkie crackled. 'She's here. Black taxi.'

Not a minute later, a taxi pulled up and a red stiletto emerged, followed by a cloud of blond hair. The woman had a white fur coat up to her chin, a little red dress peeking out from beneath it.

Between the hat shadowing her face and the upturned collar of her coat, they couldn't see her face. A purse dangled at her side.

The slam of the taxi's door echoed through the alley. Heels smacking the concrete, the woman sauntered into the gallery.

Silence shrouded its cloak over the misty morning again.

Irwing eased out of his car, gun cocked. Several police officers, fluorescent jackets shimmering in the dark, flooded the street.

Aileen glanced towards where she thought she'd seen movement just as the moon emerged from behind a cloud and realised there was a figure huddled on the pavement, huddled in a pile of blankets. She unlocked the car.

Callan placed a hand on her thigh. 'Stay here.'

She shook her head. 'You stay. Please.'

Before he could stop her, she hopped out and shut the door as quietly as she could, disappearing into the herd of police officers. She hoped her dark trousers and jacket would camouflage her. For once, January was on her side.

Aileen spun left, away from the police officers and the agent's office, and slunk into the shadows. Her hands were wrapped around a sleek cylindrical torch.

On tiptoes, she crossed the road and eyed her car, flanking the agent's office.

The car door swung open and Callan, cursing, fumbled out with his crutches.

He almost toppled. Aileen gritted her teeth. *Stubborn oaf!*

Righting himself before his nose kissed the pavement, Callan hobbled a few steps, then squinted at the huddled figure and limped off towards the office door.

Yellow street lights illuminated his chiselled jaw, spot-lighting his cheekbones and glossing his hair. He truly belonged on a calendar. Stubborn hunk.

His eyes studied the buildings, lights, roads, cars. A thrill zinged across her spine. He was searching for her.

It happened in a matter of seconds.

Callan fidgeted and froze. She'd been so lost in him, she hadn't seen the shadow move.

'One step and I shoot. Hands up!'

That voice – that voice sent shivers zipping down her back; unwelcome ones. Callan tucked his elbows in, peering over his shoulder. The silhouette shrugged off her blanket. 'Hands up I said!'

All police officers, including Irwing, gaped at the sound of Amy's voice, not drifting from the gallery but from behind Callan.

Crap! Focus, Aileen.

'You lot think you've got all the smarts.' Her chuckle belonged to the deepest pits of hell. 'A buyer, wanting to buy pretty much everything? Ha! I've been in this game long enough to know when I'm being played.'

A hand, belonging to a witch, ensnared Callan's shoulder. 'Now, let's behave so I don't finish off blue-eyed babe here.' Amy's breath rose in puffs.

The woman was enjoying herself at Callan's expense. Aileen slinked closer, dissolving further into the shadows.

Something metallic glinted at Callan's back – the barrel of a gun.

Aileen bit her lip, mind whirling. If she attacked Amy, Amy would shoot.

How to disarm a madwoman? Callan couldn't jump out of the way.

She had to distract her! How? Somehow!

'He comes with me until I'm safely on my plane. Until then, he's the sweetest insurance policy I have.'

Amy tugged, but Callan didn't budge. 'Did you murder Beau Blanchet?'

'Beau? I'll tell you our tale on the way. Dim as a shattered light, but a conscience filled like Santa's bag. He needed no encouragement to jump. But you, *babe*, you come with me. Now!'

Callan fought Amy's grip, but with the crutches, there was little he could do. 'Get yer hands off me!'

His eyes scanned the stunned faces. Trained officers of the law, all staring helplessly at him.

Aileen fisted her hands. What to do? The scent of Amy's perfume gagged Aileen. She swallowed, not daring to utter a single hiss.

She pressed against the wall, hand over her stomach. Something hard rubbed against her.

The torch!

Callan didn't relent. 'I'll come with ye, but I want to ken. What about Macalister? Why did ye kill him?'

Amy hauled him closer, her chest to his back. 'Coincidence?'

'Hardly,' he whispered.

'I'll tell you in the taxi. Move!'

She dragged him with her. The cabbie stared straight ahead, no emotions showing on his face.

'Macalister figured it out. And ye threatened him to drop the case.'

Amy halted, then shoved the barrel in so hard, Aileen itched to kick her arse. 'He loved his wife more than the money Blanchet stole. All I did was help him see the light.'

She shoved Callan into the taxi.

Aileen fisted her fingers.

Now or never.

She crouched, used the other car to inch her way towards the taxi.

Her hands held Callan's lifeline... One step and...

A shadow fell over Callan.

Hate was bitter on her tongue as she pressed her 'barrel' between Amy's shoulder blades. 'Feel that, Amy? You tried killing my boyfriend once and now you try again? You twitch, I fire. Drop the weapon.'

For that one beautiful moment, Amy froze. 'You wouldn't—'

Callan didn't wait to hear what she wouldn't do. He fell back onto the seat, used his leg and *wham!*

Aileen jumped out of the way when the gun went flying. Then she kicked it to a police officer and pounced. One punch on Amy's jaw and the woman tumbled to the ground. Ha! A punch had never felt so satisfying.

Irwing rushed over with several yellow-vested officers. Amy howled on the ground as Aileen pressed her knee into her stomach. 'Not laughing now, are we?'

A police officer strapped on the handcuffs. 'We've got it from here.'

The woman who'd stepped out of the taxi earlier had been gaping at the scene. Now she threw her hands up.

A police officer cuffed her, and another headed to the taxi. The cabbie's hands trembled as he stepped out. 'She hired us! We're just actors.'

Despite the chaos around her, Aileen found her idiot boyfriend. 'Using your leg, really? I had it under control.' She touched his cheek. 'Are you okay?'

Callan nodded. 'How did ye get a gun?'

Aileen grinned, holding up her sleek torch. 'Deception. I saw her huddled in the blankets, hiding in the shadows and knew this was the only way to get her. Sorry you went through that.'

'At least she didn't shoot.'

'I would've never let her, Callan. You must know that.'

Callan wrapped her icy hands in his warm ones. 'Come here.'

CHAPTER TWENTY-TWO

'You've waived your right to a lawyer?'

Amy Downie sneered. 'Have a sod with a stick up his arse tell *me* what to say? To hell with that!'

Callan leaned on his crutch. Given the circumstances, they had permitted Callan to observe the interview, and he'd be damned if he rode in on a wheelchair.

'Besides.' Amy spread her arms in the interview room. 'You've got nothing on me.'

Callan itched to wipe that smirk off her face. *Patience.* A little longer with Walsh and Irwing, and Amy wouldn't be smiling.

Irwing flipped a folder, dragged it across the table to her. 'Care to explain this?'

'The guy needs a new car.'

'And life. You killed Macalister and set his car on fire,' Irwing persisted.

'You can't prove shit.'

Walsh leaned in, eyes sharp. 'You sure? Because you've

become sloppy. That French job you pulled off without a hitch, but murder… Now that's a wee bit beyond you, eh?'

Amy reached up to flip her hair when her hand caught against the restraints chained to the table. 'I'll set my dogs on you once I'm out of here for cuffing me like a criminal.'

Irwing tilted his head. 'Aren't you a criminal, Ms Downie?'

She studied her nails like she'd grown bored with the conversation. 'Speak sense and I'll respond.'

Irwing reached over, plucked a picture of Callan's car off the pile on the table, and dangled it under her nose.

The sting still smarted. He'd only lost an inanimate object, but it reminded him of what else he'd almost lost that night. Poor judgement and he'd sped into a trap.

Dumping his dark thoughts in a pit, Callan focused on Irwing.

'Carl? You know Carl?' The detective stabbed a finger on the desk. 'The man you've been cajoling into doing your dirty work? And Johnny? They wasted no time before selling you out. Carl told us how you gave him money to cut DI Cameron's brakes.'

'You can't lie and cover up for a detective who can't drive. He wrecked his car and wants to pin it on me, for what? Insurance?'

Callan gritted his teeth. Was she for real?

Irwing waved off her comment. 'We have Carl's confession, along with evidence that proves someone tampered with the car's brakes.'

Amy shrugged. 'Not my problem. Carl's a man who visits your station more often than the loo. I can't believe you'd take his word over mine.'

'Money trails are easy to track. Your niece's word also counts. You forced her to drive a car. She's underage, as you know.'

'Humour doesn't suit you. I didn't force her to do anything. Did she drive a car, underage? Breaking laws, is she? Shows the world she's her mother's daughter. Amelia killed a man, didn't she?'

Walsh pressed his elbows into the table and curled his lip. 'No, Ms Downie. You achieved that all by yourself. You defrauded pensioners of funds, killed your husband, threatened a private investigator then killed him. Then you coerced a child to drive down a treacherous road, endangering her life, attempted to murder a detective, and kidnapped and dumped your niece, a child, in an ELV yard. Oh and I forgot, threatened a police detective again.'

Amy pursed her lips and stuck out a finger. 'Let's see… I didn't defraud anyone of anything. That was my ex-husband's doing. Such a vile man. I was wrong to marry him…' She sighed.

Another finger popped up. 'I don't threaten detectives, or coerce anyone to drive down any road. Nor did I endanger my niece or attempt to murder any detectives. I've never killed anyone in my life! And your suggestion that I might offends me.'

The third finger, her middle finger, she wagged under the detectives' noses. 'I didn't leave a child in an ELV yard. It's morally wrong, *and* I'd never visit such an undignified place.'

A loud silence filled the room. Irwing sat back and dropped his shoulders. 'You got me, Ms Downie.'

'Good. Let me out now.'

Walsh tutted, chuckling at Amy's incredulous expression. 'Every argument needs someone to corroborate it.'

Drawing the folder to himself, Walsh shuffled the papers and set one in front of her. 'Detective Cameron can identify you as the person who forced him off the road. So can Pamela Downie. And if you say she's just a child and the detective's too traumatised to know better, we'd like some clarifications on other matters.'

He set another paper on the table. 'You assaulted a police officer with a gun. Secondly,' he continued, despite Amy's reddening face, 'please explain how we found your DNA all over the driver's car seat on the two-seater Ken Macalister rented from you?'

'I own the damn car!'

'Oh, but, Ms Downie, the car has only Pamela Downie's prints and your DNA. Not Macalister's. Pamela was alibied by her teachers and friends in school the day of the murder, contrary to the alibi you provided us. Which leads us to believe Macalister's prints were wiped off. And Ken Macalister's bag, Detective Cameron and I, as you'll remember, saw in your place of business, so you were in possession of a murdered man's personal items. We also found this black SUV with broken headlights and a scrape on its bumper. It has only your prints and DNA on it. The paint matches DI Cameron's car.'

Amy's nostrils flared. The game was up. Forensics didn't lie. Her eyes flitted between the two detectives. 'He threatened me! Macalister threatened me. It was self-defence! He swaggers into my shop and smirks at me, says this time he won't stop. He'll tell the world the whole truth. So I had to look out for myself.' Tears leaked from her eyes – crocodile tears. 'A woman alone has to do everything to protect herself. My husband, my *self-centred* husband, defrauded all those people and killed himself...'

Irwing stabbed a finger on the folder. 'The day of Macalister's murder. What happened?'

'I messaged him to meet me by the lay-by near the inn. We'd talk like adults. He sat in my car and threatened me. Said *she'd* catch me... I had no idea what he meant. He sounded like a madman. And so I tasered him...'

'*Tasered* him?' Walsh butted in.

'With my taser.'

An illegal taser gun they'd found in her purse…

'Then you set Ken Macalister on fire?'

Amy swiped at her tears. 'What else was I supposed to do?'

The officers just stared at her for a second, incredulous.

'Did you intend to set fire to the inn?' Walsh asked for Callan's sake.

Her lips curled, and she snapped, 'If I'd known Ken meant that damned innkeeper would catch me, I'd have torched her place before I killed that old idiot! Damned pest.'

Callan's hands fisted. The madness in Amy Downie's eyes slammed into him. She could've killed Aileen too.

Amy banged her hands on the desk. 'Fine. I killed Ken Macalister. Tasered him, burned the damned car and left the bullets there to send that bitch Amelia to prison. And if the fire had blown over to the inn, I'd have been on an island by now, somewhere you idiots couldn't find me!'

Her fury rang through the banal interview room. 'But she had to stick her nose where it didn't belong. Killing that boyfriend of hers was the only way to keep her preoccupied.'

'Only he survived.'

'I don't deserve to be here!'

Irwing stood up, faced the one-way glass and nodded. 'Oh, Ms Downie, I think you do.'

EPILOGUE

Dear Aileen,
 I realise now I struggle with goodbyes. I messed it up with Shaeline, and with you. It hurt to never introduce myself. Yet I imagined what it would feel like to reconcile family, blood ties I lost so many years ago.

But this, this elusiveness, was a price I had to pay for being silent all these years. My silence hurt families. I did it to protect mine, a decision made by a man who'd lost a part of him, a child.

I knew it was her. She had the power to ruin my life. I never considered hiding would ruin the one good thing I cherished: my Shaeline. It tainted our life, the shame of not standing on the side of justice.

If I learned anything, dear niece, it's that it takes a second of bad luck to rob you of life. But a lifetime to build love. And love is life. Once you find it, hold on to it. Love is everywhere. You might worry about losing the inn, but you're surrounded by love, and it's strong enough to overpower any evil.

I lie to myself that with time I could have caught her – and saved my life too. But there was no way, and far too many ties. In the end, I had no energy. So I laid it out for you, a responsibility on your capable shoulders.

Amelia Downie's call to come to her assistance told me her sister-in-law was still at large, playing games.

And when Pamela Downie told me she was in love with Johnny, I put two and two together. He was stationed there to steal money by her aunt. A less pretentious scheme this time. Is it worse to steal from your family than poor pensioners? She never understood the difference. Pamela's words reassured me that her aunt would act again; that she would kill this time.

I had to do the legwork. And dear Arran, the sweet boy, was ready to play his part. Christmas was my one last lame attempt at goodbye to my dear wife and neighbours. But saying goodbye to you almost has me breaking my promise to myself.

Today, I have told the Downies I'll meet them, one last play at Amy, to rub it in, to warn her. But she's reached out to me now, demanding to meet me. This is the end.

But now that you're reading this, you've emerged victorious.

As promised, your reward, my life's earnings, will come to you, someone who deserves it, earned it. You've put another criminal away. A woman who stole so much from so many is off the streets.

Good work.

Stay well, my child. And remember, love is far stronger. Never fear it.

Yours even in death,
Ken Macalister

Aileen folded the letter. Her shoulders dropped. 'It would've been good if he'd said hi.'

'It would've tainted yer judgement and put ye in danger. He kept ye safe.'

Her smile tasted bittersweet. How could she mourn an uncle she barely knew?

'How's the leg?'

'I've got an appointment with the prosthetist tomorrow.'

And she had a follow-up meeting with Schneider. The money was hers, but things would take time to settle. She didn't mind. Schneider had transferred some money to her already. The sword hanging over her head had vanished. Dachaigh was safe.

'You'll be fine, Callan.'

He grinned. 'As long as you're here. Isla's hosting a party.'

'Don't remind me! She wants to host a ceilidh. Lord save us all.'

'Haven't been to one of those in a while. We can use the community hall. There's no room here.'

Aileen shook her head. 'I told her we'd get to it once you're back on your feet, so we can dance.'

A scowl appeared almost instantaneously. 'Hell no.'

Aileen tried to pout but knew it just made her look like an animated balloon. 'Please?'

'I don't dance.'

'Just like you don't sketch?'

'Aileen.'

She tilted her head. 'Callan. Your notepad is right there.'

Callan reached over and snapped it closed. 'I was thinking of holding a memorial service for Blaine. With each passing day... I'm not sure we'll ever find him. And I can't leave him hanging. I have to say goodbye in a ceremonial sense. Let him rest in peace.'

Aileen sat back. Her heart hurt for the eighteen-year-old, Callan's best friend, who'd been lost to the peatlands. 'Are you sketching him?' she whispered.

Callan nodded. 'As I remember him. I'll never forget…'

'You need closure. Real closure.'

'The environmental groups aren't happy. We may have to pull the search. So it's time to say goodbye.'

Aileen reached over and squeezed his hand. 'Whatever you need, Callan. I mean it. I'm always by your side.'

He grinned, all the tension easing away from his muscles. 'Oh, I found this shoved in a drawer when I was looking for a pencil by the way.' He held out a small book-shaped parcel to her.

Aileen's lips rounded in an O. 'Shit! It came the same day I found Macalister's wallet. I hope it's nothing from him. A clue or maybe the accounts…'

The recent stress and madness had driven it out of her mind.

She fumbled with the wrapping then grabbed the scissors. The strings fell away and the paper unfolded with a crackle.

Inside was a white rectangle. A canvas.

Aileen flipped it over in her hands and her breath caught.

A portrait; a woman with brown eyes and brown hair – *her* eyes and *her* hair – smiled at her. Her portrait.

And in the bottom-right corner was a signature – 'Callan Cameron'.

THE END?

Nope! Aileen and Callan will be back in *When Distilled From Rage*.

PLEASE WRITE A REVIEW

Thank you so much for reading this novel. Please write an honest review for this book. Your review helps me as an independent author reach new readers. If you've never written a review before, don't worry. It doesn't need to be a long literary essay, just a sentence or two is perfect. And if you have the time, leave one on Goodreads and/or Bookbub as well.

THANK YOU!

READ AN EXCLUSIVE NOVELLA

When a storm cuts off the tiny town of Loch Fuar from the rest of the world, a murderer strikes. And it's someone among them.

Download your free copy on www.shanafrost.com/exclusivenovella

AUTHOR'S NOTE

Dear Reader Friend,

Thank you so much for reading this book.

When I first started this series, I never imagined Aileen and Callan would grow on me like they have. I simply cannot be let them take a break from solving crimes. These five novels have taken me on a beautiful journey which taught me so much.

When Old Fires Ignite might have never been published if it weren't for the support I found in the book the *Artist's Way* by Julia Cameron. And I thank my mother for gifting me that book and saving me from a major writer's block.

I truly enjoyed this ride with Aileen and Callan and hope you enjoyed it too.

As always, I do the plotting and writing, but my excellent team makes my awkward draft ready for your eyes. And they deserve a huge thank you for their dedicated work.

Thank you Janae for your constant support and encouraging words, especially after you've suffer through my very-rough drafts:)

AUTHOR'S NOTE

Special thanks to my amazing copyeditor Laura Kincaid for her incredible eye for detail, and to my proofreader Charlotte Kane whose enthusiasm for Aileen and Callan always brings a smile to my face.

A huge thank you to Jean and Leonise, who've diligently been reading the Aileen and Callan Murder Mystery books as beta readers and helping me craft a better story every time.

And of course, the biggest love and gratitude for my incredible Reader Friends whose encouraging emails push me to persevere on the days when the going gets tough. (Yes, the countdown for release of the next book's begun...)

On that note, I must take your leave and get back to my writing cave. *When Distilled From Rage* won't write itself:)

See ye soon,
Shana

ABOUT THE AUTHOR

Are you looking to solve murders? Perfect, Shana loves plotting them.

As a debut writer, Shana Frost is in her secret den hatching murders and having a blast with Aileen and the gang. It's crazy in there...

When not in the den, Shana always has her nose buried between the pages of a fiction novel. After all, the tantalising aroma of a story is far more enticing, especially for a sensitive nose like hers.

Shana's powerful sense of smell has helped her sniff out murder mysteries and a wide variety of characters.

Occasionally, she finds herself wandering ancient hallways of a castle, or a museum trying to smell the tales these walls effuse.

The traveller Ibn Battuta wasn't wrong when he wrote, "Travelling - It leaves you speechless, then turns you into a storyteller"

Visit the website for more: https://shanafrost.com